"The sheer and compelling energy of Patricia Ann McNair's prose not only dazzles, but more so, draws the reader into the deep and complex emotional reaches of her irresistible, and compassionately rendered characters. *The Temple of Air* is both fierce, and unflinching in its affection for people, and place, and a wide range of tones—a kind of graceful caper by which this writer steals the reader's heart."
> — **Jack Driscoll, author of *Twenty Stories***

"*The Temple of Air* is a book of unusual pleasures, each story offers the readers a small roller coaster of anticipation, fear, surprise, recognition, satisfaction. This is a beautiful book, intense and original."
> — **Audrey Niffenegger, author of *The Time Traveler's Wife***

Praise for *The Temple of Air*

"Fiercely imagined, emotionally charged, Patricia Ann McNair's first collection celebrates the extraordinary lives in ways that will leave you breathless."
> — **A. Manette Ansay, author of *Good Things I Wish You***

"These narratives are fierce, fearless, brave, as stylistically pure as Raymond Carver, as hard-hitting as Mary Gaitskill, as lyrically impassioned as Stuart Dybek. Still, McNair is an original, even when her characters miss their good chances or hurt what they love, we feel compassion, we hear the pure note of human pathos. You won't be able to put these stories down."
> — **Anne-Marie Oomen, author of *As Long As I Know You: The Mom Book***

"The stories in *The Temple of Air* are steeped in a particular brand of hospitality and violence. They are definitively Midwestern, navigating deftly between the everyday and the disturbing, the prosaic and the poetic."

> — *NewCity*

"[McNair] reaches down deep into the cores of her characters, pulls out their secrets, the things that make them human, and presents them to you in this book…stunning debut collection."

> — *TheNervousBreakdown.com*

"The stories within *The Temple of Air* are indeed thought-provoking. But what the reader will truly discover are people whose tales will touch a heart, tear an eye, and warm a smile."

> — *Freeport Journal-Standard*

A Chicago Writers Association Book of the Year

Winner of the Devil's Kitchen Reading Award for Prose

A Society of Midland Authors Finalist in Adult Fiction

The Temple of Air

Also by Patricia Ann McNair

And These Are the Good Times (essays)

Responsible Adults (stories)

The Temple of Air

Patricia Ann McNair

Tortoise Books
Chicago

Dedicated to the memory of my mother, Sylvia McNair,
and the future with my husband, Philip Hartigan

Contents

"He watched their flight; bird after bird: a dark flash, a swerve, a flutter of wings. He tried to count them before all their darting quivering bodies passed: six, ten, eleven: and wondered were they odd or even in number. Twelve, thirteen: for two came wheeling down from the upper sky. They were flying high and low but ever round and round in straight and curving lines and ever flying from left to right, circling about a temple of air."

—James Joyce, from *A Portrait of the Artist as a Young Man*

Introduction

I first heard Patricia Ann McNair read at Martyrs on Lincoln. Or was it the Hopleaf? Or, perhaps it was...no matter. The point here is that McNair headlined many reading series, shared many stories, wholly imagined or otherwise. Memory, we'll all agree, is a slippery thing and these details are best debated at a later date. What's important here, what I vividly recall, is the feeling that shook me when, at this particular reading, McNair delivered her closing line. It's coming back to me: We're at a Columbia College Chicago Story Week event at Martyrs back in the salad days. Yes. That's it. McNair delivers her closing line to the standing-room-only crowd and everyone gasps. It's a punch to the gut, this ending line. We feel it viscerally—the rhythm, tone, emotion, word choice—it's all humming. We recognize craft, yes, but it's more than that: It's a physical tremor that moves through the audience, fleeting but nevertheless there, the one you get when an artist performs a piece with tenderness and abandon and power and you are living it so that, even when it ends, you sit there, waiting for the next word.

You know that feeling, right?

Regardless, McNair hits that line and a beat passes while we let the tremor pass and then the place erupts. Standing room only, remember, and even McNair seems a little overwhelmed at the response because she blinks at the uproar before thanking the crowd and exiting the stage.

That's my first memory of hearing McNair read. Maybe you were there? Maybe we were elbow to elbow waiting for the applause to end?

In lieu of a McNair live performance, you hold in your hands the next best thing or, in truth, the first best thing. For those of us who love the feel of a book in our hands, this is the very best thing.

That moment at Martyrs, of course, was not our first meeting. McNair and I taught for years in Columbia College Chicago's Fiction Writing Department back when there was such a thing. But I taught at night and she, generally, during the day. She was full-time faculty, I was an adjunct. I recall McNair, one of only a few full-time women in the department at the time, as someone who held her own in that male-dominated space. Maybe it was growing up with brothers? Not sure. But it wasn't an easy task. Certainly not then.

So, I didn't have much interaction with McNair but I do recall, one evening, riding on the Brown Line with her, on our way home after teaching. It was winter, both of us bundled beneath wool overcoats, scarves, hats. The train, as usual, smelled faintly of urine, or the stuff they use to mask the odor of urine which might actually smell worse than urine, and we talked about ourselves. Was that it? Or did I talk about myself? Yes. That's it. I'm not prone to divulging much about myself, or wasn't back then, but McNair asked questions. And I answered. And she listened. I'd always been slightly intimidated by McNair but, looking back at that moment, I now know that she was experiencing a huge life shift, one I won't mention here, and she at once seemed interested and profoundly sad. Before I got off the train at Belmont, she said, "I'm really glad we had a chance to talk, Chris. I really enjoyed it." And then she paused. "We've never really talked before."

I'm paraphrasing, of course.

Again, memory is a slippery thing.

In 2010, I founded a literary arts magazine called *Hypertext*. Since then, McNair's byline has appeared at least a dozen times in the magazine. Those pieces include short fiction and creative nonfiction. She's also been interviewed about her publications and conducted interviews of other writers.

James Baldwin wrote:

> *When you're writing, you're trying to find out something which you don't know. The whole language of writing for me is finding out what you don't want to know, what you don't want to find out. But something forces you to anyway.*

Looking back over her work in *Hypertext*, I'm reminded of McNair's range as a writer. Over the past thirteen years, in our magazine alone, her essays have tackled the horrors (multiple) of the former guy, silence, beauty, boredom, her teenage years, her father's death, her relationship with her mother and brother Roger the Dodger, among other topics. In her essay collection *And These Are the Good Times*, McNair's writing is marked by an honest vulnerability. She's writing into the discovery instead of writing to a predetermined end. Like Baldwin, she's on a quest, a personal journey, always a personal journey, stepping back to take in the landscape where those hard-to-pin-down universal truths reside.

Maybe that's why her essays and fiction are among the most visited pieces on the site.

She's also a sensitive and perceptive interviewer. When McNair's second short story collection, *Responsible Adults*, came out a few years ago, I wrote:

> *With startling honesty, precise observation, and a deep faith in the beauty of language, Patricia Ann McNair creates worlds where the so-called adults in the room abandon, lie, cheat, steal. They're familiar, these faults, you think as McNair traces the delicate cracks and gaping chasms of the human condition, her gaze unflinching, unnerving, watching as opposing forces collide, unleash catastrophe. Especially then. Who, she seems to ask, is left behind and why turn away? In this remarkable collection, McNair hits her writerly stride with a sureness that is nothing less than breathtaking.*

That collection came out during Covid. A lot has happened since then. This collection, the one you are holding, originally came out in 2011, making a debut in a world unaware of lockdowns, masks, or mass health misinformation and conspiracy theories. Yet the stories still resonate because of the universality of what takes McNair's attention. Her stories draw life from seemingly small and fleeting moments, moments other writers might miss, moments with the quiet power to make or break you—the joy of a baby giggling and squirming, a brother taking all of a parent's love, the feel of a man's hand on the small of your back, a lecherous old man's smirk, the realization that your wife and child no longer love you, the profound sadness of grief.

Those moments.

Rereading this edition of McNair's collection reminded me of all the things I loved about this book and admired about McNair's writing.

Aren't we lucky: It's here, again.

— Christine Maul Rice

Something Like Faith

And even as it happened, Nova could not believe it. "Jim," the wife said, Nova heard her. Like "Jim, pass the salt," or something. But he turned then from where he stood in the center of the gondola, just a little shift, a slight release of all that attention he was giving his tiny, tiny girl—*whee*ing her like that, in and out, in and out, his arms a hammock, one two three *whee.* Nova'd been watching, scrunched in there between the boys, on their own side of the ride. She hadn't wanted to go anyway, she was fucked up and scared of heights and it was a stupid shit carnival ride: "The Gondolier," big swinging cages, all that air. "Don't," someone must have said, but then the dad turned that slight, small shift, away from that last out swing toward those ridiculous, wide-spaced bars that are somehow supposed to keep everyone safe, but clearly can't when the dad turns his attention, just a bit away but enough so the little girl (a baby, really, all tiny and tickly, all screaming and squirming) tilts somehow and slips from Dad's arms, his hands. His fingers open up and his grip unfolds and gives way beneath the weight of her rolling off and apart from him and through the bars and over over over the side and down down down through the sky. And then it all runs together. The moments before and after become one absolutely single moment, a knot of time and activity that moves in a slow circle with the big carnival wheel. The dad goes down, just like that, sinks to his knees and his arms raise up, light as helium without the weight of his daughter to hold them, and it's like he's genuflecting. But no, Nova knows it's worthless, this gesture. She knows there's nothing out there past the clouds he's tilted his face up to. How the fuck can there be? How the fuck can there be a god to drop to your knees in front of in a world—in a moment—that lets you dump your little girl over the side of some dumb fucking carnival ride? But he's down there, low. Low like Nova's insides. A heaviness in her gut, a force greater than gravity keeps her pressed in on her side of the cage, pressed in tight between the bony shoulders of Michael, the broad ones of Sky, pressed against the back of their seat, against vinyl against metal. And the ride keeps turning, and maybe it's that centrifugal force, you know, like water in a swinging bucket, because Nova can't budge, she's held in solid and sure (and high, so very, very high) in the cage, in the air, in this tight, tight moment. Did it really happen? And for just a split of second, Nova thinks— no, hopes, almost prays (but of course she won't) that it didn't happen. It smells so good up here, after all. Like corndogs and cotton candy and freshly mowed lawns. Smells too good for anything bad. Smells safe, see? And they're high, after all, she and Michael and Sky; and they're kids. You know. Kids who are prone to imagining things. Only there's the wife, the mother, up in an instant and gaping, eyes and mouth wide, wide circles, lips moving. But no sound, no sound. And Nova can't help but marvel at how deeply silent the world is, all empty, safe-smelling air and sudden stillness. And the sky past the useless bars is so blue it hurts to look at it in the silence. But it's just that one silent instant before they hear as the baby bounces off of the other cages, off the solid, unforgiving spokes of the stupid ride—a big old Ferris wheel-type thing, too big for this small town, for the little carnival, for the dinky midway and especially too, too big for that tiny, tiny girl who makes (not with her mouth but with her body) the same exact sound after sound all the way down. A sound too horrific to be replicated, but a sound that splat and smacked its way into the souls of them all left behind on the still moving ride, a sound that played itself over and over in the dreams of Nova that night and, she would swear to it, each and every night forever after.

And then the screams come. From below at first, from those riders under them getting it finally, seeing that hurtling thing for what it is, not the doll that some of them must have thought, but a little girl at first, reaching and grabbing at the air and catching nothing except maybe some eyes here and there, some panicked eyes locked with hers. And then, mercifully, the little girl becomes just a body, dead and all, long (long, long seconds) before she hits the ground.

When Nova opens her own eyes—she hadn't known she'd closed them—she stares at her hands in her lap, the good one with all five nails polished deep purple and pointy, and the other one. And then she sees the mom drop to her knees beside the dad (arms still raised) and then onto her belly so she can stretch her hands out through the bottom of the bars, reach for what she can no longer have, and Nova feels her own hands clutch, feels her one strong fist and feels the other one, stunted from birth, its tiny pink thumb all by itself tightening and holding on. And when the mom knows what's true, knows that's the end of it, she writhes on the floor and howls and the dad does, too, and they're both down there, together, all they have left, and they braid into one another, one long rope of two bodies and a single, twining wail rising from them.

"Holy fuck." It's Sky who talks first. They are all squeezed in so tight together there, the three of them (brother, sister, friend) that Nova feels the words rumbling up from his body, feels the hollow breath of them on her shoulder. And she nods. And then the ride stops, a sudden, screeching jolt of movement halted. They rock forward and back in their seat and it's Michael, the friend, who finally acts. He's down there, too, on the floor between the seats at Nova's, at Sky's feet, all coos and rubbing and holding, and it's like he's left them, Nova and Sky, deserted them for these strangers. Like he has become one of the shattered family. And when he pulls these parents to him, he's much more than a kid, more than fourteen, he's like some grownup now or something, some large being, bigger than Nova has ever seen him, and the three of them rock there together, holding and crying and shushing and patting, and the mother reaches for the dad and Michael is there in the middle and he kisses them, one then the other, on their heads, on their arms. And they cling to him.

"Damn, Mike, what the fuck?" Sky says, and Nova wants to slug him. Not like she usually does, not like the way all sisters want to slug their brothers, but she wants to hit him in such a way as to really hurt him. She wants to make him ache throughout. She wants him to feel some pain, some deep, numbing pain. Like the one she feels filling her chest, pushing at her throat. But Sky's snickering now, and nudging her in the ribs with an elbow, whispering, "Copping a little feel there, you ask me." And it's too much for Nova. All way, way, way too much. So she slides as far from him as she can across the scarred vinyl of the bench (impossibly wide now with just Nova, small Nova, little for her thirteen years and big, thick, golden-haired Sky) and she turns and presses her forehead against the ice-cold bars and something lifts from the murkiness of her gut, from that low, heavy feeling that keeps her down, keeps her seated. Something rises up and through her and she gives into its rise, and she opens her mouth and lets it come. And first it's a sound, something deep and unrecognizable. Wild. And then it's something else. Something thicker. And she works to throw it up, this thickness. But even as she pukes and pukes and pukes, she can't get rid of it. And she knows that. Even as she continues to try to free herself, moaning and crying and purging. Nova knows that this is something that will always, always be there inside of her. Something raw and hot and overwhelming. Something like faith.

The story was built at the kitchen table. Nova tried to listen as Sky recreated the story for Edith, their mother, but it was as though she were underwater. His words, muffled by a rush in her ears, sounded round somehow, and empty as bubbles.

"They were going crazy, the mom and dad," he said. And he took a large bite from his tuna sandwich. How could he eat, Nova wondered. How could anyone, anywhere, ever keep anything down again?

Edith tsked, wrung her hands.

Sky talked through his mouthful. "I couldn't just watch it, you know. I had to do something."

Nova's head swam. She crossed her hands, the good one over the bad, on the table and rested a cheek on her knuckles. The tablecloth smelled of cooking smoke and mayonnaise. Her stomach roiled. Her mouth filled with saliva, the sting of bile. She wished she were still high.

"So what did you do?" Edith asked. Like it was the first time she heard the story. Sky was making his way through it for what, the third? fourth? time, the encores encouraged by their mother. She lived for this stuff, though, Edith did. This crisis and courage, death and transcendence. She nodded Sky on. And Nova couldn't help but notice, and not for the first time, how much mother and son resembled one another. And Nova, small and bleached near to invisible in the light of the big, golden-haired couple, looked like the outsider. Their mother fingered a small metal cross in the hollow above her heart.

The story had become Sky's own. He took the part of Michael, his friend, made himself a hero. He sat up tall in his seat, put his sandwich on the paper plate, wiped at his mouth with the back of his hand.

"Well," he said. He cleared his throat, gave a quick glance in Nova's direction. Her hair fell in platinum sheets before her face, made a curtain between herself and her family. She knew he couldn't see her eyes. "I didn't want to tell you this at first, Mom. Just in case you might get mad."

Edith leaned forward in her seat, her hands flat on the table, nailbitten fingertips reaching toward her son.

"Go on," she said.

"The mom was hysterical—as you can imagine. Crying. Screaming. So I—" Sky paused. Nova tried hard to hear through the rush in her ears. "I slapped her, Mommy."

Their mother fell back in her seat like she was pushed, like those people on the televangelist shows Edith always watched do when the preacher releases his grip on their foreheads. Nova stood up.

"Enough," she said—or thought she did, she couldn't be sure the word actually came out of the wetness that was her mouth. Sky went on talking.

"And then Sheriff Austin came. And the ambulance," he said. "And of course I rode with them." Sky's story faltered here since it was Michael who had actually gone off in the ambulance. It was Michael who had helped the weeping parents off the floor and back onto their seat on the other side of the wide-barred cage, Michael who held them in place as the ride made its full circle and they were finally allowed to stand on the pavement. Michael who clutched their hands and patted their backs as they fell to their knees next to the broken little body while Nova and Sky lost themselves in the crowd so when the sheriff got there they wouldn't be pointed out and wouldn't have to explain what happened or how it happened (like anyone could explain that) and why their eyes were red and their hair reeking. And they wouldn't be asked to empty their pockets: "Just a formality," Sheriff Austin would say, reeking himself but like booze, days old sweat. (Nova knew this. It wouldn't be the first time, nor the last.) And since they weren't around when the ambulance came and Michael left them, that was all of the story Sky knew for sure. He'd need some time to figure out his own ending, a better one than what he'd come up with so far.

"It was just so horrible after that. And sad," he looked at his mother again, and then at Nova, like he'd just noticed her standing there. He shook his head and made a slight wink in her direction. Nova flinched. "I just can't talk about it," Sky said.

"Enough," Nova said, for real this time. Mother and brother turned up to her, and Nova swooned, her whole body a wave. She gripped the edge of the table and looked down into the wide, blue-eyed, upturned faces of her family. "Enough," she said again when she felt herself steady, and she turned from the pair and left the house. The screen door banged against its jamb and Nova stepped under the porch light and into a sea of tiny flying things, and then she was running into the dark and away from her home, from the lies, from her brother calling "Wait! Wait!" Trapped by his own story in his own kitchen in the audience of his (and her) mother.

The blacktopped road back to town was spongy from the heat, even though an hour had passed since the sun set. Nova breathed in the summer night. She wanted the waterlogged feeling in her head to go away, she wanted to think of something other than what happened, other than Sky making the story even more horrible (could it possibly be?) to impress their mother. The thing was, though, Nova's mother believed this stuff. She believed most anything that had to do with heroes and faith, with saviors and those in need of salvation. But Nova couldn't stomach this kind of blind devotion, the unwillingness to question, the absolute submission. At least not anymore. Not since she'd been duped that one time, long ago, into letting God enter her life.

Sky and his dad (her dad) were newly back in town then. Up until that time, Nova had come to believe she didn't have a father. Her mother was cryptic and prayerful in her answer to Nova's questions ("the Lord works in mysterious ways,") so Nova couldn't help but imagine an immaculate conception of sorts. When, at ten years old, Nova found out that she actually did have a dad, a real, flesh-and-blood one, and she had a twelve-year-old brother, too, it was like remembering the words to a song whose tune had been playing over and over in her head so long she barely even noticed it anymore. The two of them, father and son, had come full of apologies and ripe with stories, and at the heart of each of those was the word of God. Nova supposed that's why her mother mother let them in, probably why she'd said yes when her father proposed. ("Finally," Edith whispered to Nova when they stood at the back of the storefront church on the day of the wedding.)

Sky could talk the word of God better than anyone; back then, he may even have believed it himself. He had the gift, their father said, a direct connection to the absolute truth. Pretty soon Sky started having Bible study meetings in their living room while their father held men's group at the storefront. Their home filled with kids from the elementary and middle schools, a few from the high school. Nova sat at the feet of her new big brother an listened to him tell stories of the places he'd been all over the Midwest. From Clinton to Mount Vernon, Milwaukee to Normal. He told of sick children on the road to recovery in God's light, of families pulled apart and brought back together. Here he'd always look down into Nova's eyes, and smile a smile that made her face burn.

"All you need to do is ask," Sky would say. "Ask God into your life. Ask him to protect you, to save you. He'll come, you'll see. The Father always comes when the children need him. When they are ready to receive him. Let your Father know that you are ready." And of course, Nova couldn't help but think of the return of her own father, there suddenly in her life just when she needed him, there to protect her from the unrelenting boredom of the small town, the dumb, undirected faith of her mother. Like some sort of hero he'd swept in and carried her off in his dusty pickup, the three of them, Nova, Sky, Father, and they'd driven the gravel roads of New Hope to the lake where he'd held her hands, both of them, and walked her out into the water and dunked her head and pronounced her newly born—now of the Father. And before then, Nova might have believed in God, but it was similar to riding a bicycle, her belief: something everyone did without thinking about it. Simple and unremarkable. But this child and Father reunion thing was something else. Something better. Like riding a bicycle without using your hands. Or feet, maybe. Like riding on air.

So she tried it. That night after the lake she laid still and silent in her twin bed, squeezed her eyes closed so tightly her forehead hurt. In her mind, and in her heart, too, she prayed. Not the usual stuff: *Now I lay me down to sleep; The Lord is my shepherd; Bless us, O Lord...* This time Nova spoke, she was pretty sure, directly to God. "Save me," she said. "I'm ready. I'm finally ready." She stretched herself long and taut and steadied herself as if preparing for a blow. She listened to her breath in the dark, she squinted into the darkness so hard it began to swirl. And then he came. She felt it. A bright whooshing sensation ran over her and through her, a wash of something cold and hot at the very same time. A feeling like panic and excitement, like joy and terror. She shuddered under the sweep of it. She nearly screamed. But she kept quiet and held tight to her sheets and rode it out under the blanket for the seconds (minutes?) it lasted. And when it passed, Nova's whole body tingled. And then she was asleep.

Later that night, something woke her. A noise, perhaps. The quiet bleat of a car horn, a door closing. And in that moment of blurred awareness, Nova felt a fat lump in her throat, a hollow pain in her chest. She thought it must be God still, working her over, having his way. But in the morning she was fevered and sore throughout, stricken with the flu. And at the breakfast table her mother was crying and Sky wouldn't look up from his cornflakes and Nova knew that the father was gone.

Headlights came around the bend in the road ahead of her. Nova stuck tight to the shoulder, as close to the weeds as she could get without stepping into the opening of the ditch. A white sedan slowed as it passed, a four-door family car, and Nova nodded when the old guy lifted a small finger in a wave and drove on. She wondered if maybe she were dreaming. It felt like it. Not the whole day, she knew what happened on the Gondolier was real, she could still hear the body-against-machine sound in her ears. But maybe this was a dream. This walking in the dark like she walked through water. It felt like it does in dreams, legs and arms moving in slow, slow motion. She lifted her hands up in front of her face and studied them in the light of the full moon. She wasn't dreaming. In her dreams she always had two perfectly formed hands.

She passed the occasional farm or trailer set back from the road. Some shone in the bright spot of an outdoor security light. Others, dark on the outside, had wide-open windows that flashed with the pulse of nighttime TV. Evidence of life. The night sounded around Nova, crickets and frogs in the ditch mixed it up with the far away plastic noise of laugh tracks and sirens.

The smell of skunk filled the air, and Nova breathed deeply. She loved the smell of skunk. Ahead in the road there was a dark lump with its unmistakable stripe glowing white in the moonlight. Nova looked both ways down the long, flat plane of road before she stepped onto the pavement and up to the body. Right over the thing like this, the smell was almost unpleasant. Too much of a good thing. But as she breathed in the sharp odor, Nova felt the rushing behind her eyes ease, felt her limbs pull out from the weight of whatever it was that had held her. She knelt on the road next to the body and pressed her tiny hand against a spot on its tail where there was more fur than open flesh and blood. After a minute, she lifted her hand to her face. There it was, the thick, sharp, wonderful smell on her small, pink palm, on her perfect, miniature thumb. Satisfied and clear-headed, Nova stood up and continued her walk into town.

"Mmmm, skunk." The words came from the rear of the Hi-Lo Grocery parking lot, and even before she saw him there in their usual spot, Nova knew it was Michael, the only other person she'd ever known to like the smell. She made her way across the parking lot and held out her hand so he could get a whiff. "Mm-mm," he breathed deeply.

Above them, the neon Hi-Lo sign made its quiet hum; its light bathed the lot in a watery blue. Nova sat down on the blacktop where Michael crouched low and tight against the wall. He didn't look good. His eyes were red and shiny, his face blotchy and streaked with grime. He sniffled, wiped his nose with the cuff of his flannel shirt. He was shaking.

"Cold, man, don't you think?"

Nova nodded even though it was at least eighty out still, and her neck and back were slick with sweat.

"How are you?" she asked. It wasn't what she meant to say, but it was all she could come up with.

Michael nodded. He lifted a bottle in a brown paper sack from between his knees, swallowed hard, then shook it in her direction. "Some?" Nova took the bottle and swigged. She had to fight down the wet burn of booze, had to give her throat and stomach and head time to get used to it, to recognize this feeling as something different, something better than the boiling that had filled her before. With the second swallow, she felt a knot in the back of her neck loosen.

"Where's Sky?" Michael asked. He wouldn't look at Nova; instead he stared at a dark spot of something on the back of his hand. Blood, maybe.

"Not sure. Home? Probably not, though. My mom must've let him loose by now."

"He in trouble?"

"You kidding? Sky? The golden boy?" Nova slugged on the bottle again. She passed it back to Michael who, instead of drinking, held the bottle, his fingers working its neck, wringing it. "Nah, Sky's not in trouble. He's never in trouble. You know how he is. Too slick for getting into trouble." She laughed a little. "Nah, Mom's just all over him cause of what happened." Nova paused, she wondered if she should tell Michael that Sky had taken his story away. He was always doing things like that, taking things from Michael—his silver lighter, his ten-speed, his leather jacket. Nova thought maybe that's why Sky let Michael, a skinny, loner of a kid a year behind in school, hang around. She leaned back against the bricks of the grocery store. Inside they had started the baking for the next day. The warm, full smell of fresh bread came out of the exhaust vent above their heads. "Skunk and bread," Nova said and inhaled with her whole body. "This must be heaven."

"Or hell," Michael said. He drank from the bottle again, swiped his nose, rubbed his palms over his eyes. "Fuck it, man." He looked her dead on, blue eyes gleaming. "Got any weed?"

"Matter of fact," Nova reached into the breast pocket of her T-shirt, pulled out a skinny little joint, the one she'd been saving for when they got off the carnival wheel that afternoon. The one she'd hoped would help her get her land legs back.

Michael struck a match against the wall, and they huddled around the glow of it. Nova sucked deeply and watched how Michael's eyes flecked gold with the match light. She held the smoke in, her chest full, her shoulders lifted, and passed the joint.

"Thanks," he said, and leaned his head back. Michael smoked towards the moon.

It went like that for a while. Drag and pass, drag and pass. Joint, bottle, joint, bottle. Nova waited. Something should be happening soon. She should feel fucked up. Michael should say something. Something, something, something. A car moved quietly down the street in front of the store. A dog barked a block away, another one answered. Nova stayed painfully sober.

"Want this?" Michael held the stub of roach out towards Nova. She shook her head so he popped it into his mouth and swallowed. "Lemme smell that hand," he said. His breath felt hot and damp on her shrunken palm. When he'd got enough of the skunk, Michael held her hand in his lap. For as far back as Nova could remember, no one else had ever held her hand quite like that. Like it was just a hand. Like it was meant to be held. She thought then, and wasn't entirely surprised by the thought, that maybe she loved Michael.

"Hey," she said.

"Hmmm?" He stroked his thumb up and down her tiny one. His face looked white and blue in the moonlight and neon. Luminescent, she thought. He blinked heavily.

"You're fucked up."

"Thank God."

Nova let that pass.

A couple strolled along the sidewalk at the front of the grocery store's parking lot. They each had a hand pushed into the back pocket of the other's jeans.

"Pretty late for a walk," Nova said. It was probably not yet midnight, but in the small town nothing was open past ten-thirty.

"Gawkers," Michael said. "Rubbernecks."

"What?"

"You know, like when you slow down on the road 'cause there's a cop there with his lights on. Like how we watch that war stuff on the news. Want to see the villains, the dead. In this case, the scene of the crime."

"What're you talking about?"

"Been going on all night. People going down to the midway on Main. Checking out where the kid fell.

The big wheel. Putting their hands on the yellow police tape.

"There's police tape?"

"Yup."

Nova let the TV-ness of the whole thing sink in. Yellow tape, gawkers—she looked at the dark spot on Michael's hand—blood.

"How'd you know what to do, Michael?" Nova asked.

"Whaddaya mean?"

"You know, up there." She lifted her chin as though she were pointing to the top of the wheel. "How'd you know how to do the right thing?"

"I didn't."

"I was there, Michael, remember? Yes, you did. You knew exactly what to do."

"Don't make me out a hero here, Nova." He looked at her, pushed a fine strand of her hair behind one of her ears. "I mean it." His lips drew into a tight line.

"Sky's the hero at home," she said. "He's telling my mom he did all those things you did. It's his story now."

"Good. Let him have it."

"But you should be proud, Michael—"

"Look!" Michael said and let go of Nova's hand. He pushed himself up from the ground, kicked the empty bottle across the lot. It shattered against a parking curb. "I didn't do anything, see? I didn't do anything!" He turned away from Nova and she saw his shoulders shake. She waited a second before she stood up next to him and put her good hand on the small of his back. She could feel the knobs of his spine. "Don't you get it?" He said, his voice wobbly and wet. "That's why I had to do what I did when I did. I didn't do anything earlier." Michael swabbed at his face with the back of his hand then hugged himself with both arms crossed over his chest. "I saw it coming, don't you understand? I saw it coming." He cried hard now, his whole body pummeled by the sobs. "I should have said something. I mean, what was I thinking? It made me sick to my stomach to watch it, the guy letting his little girl fly around the place like that. It was just waiting to happen. I should have said something. But I didn't. I was afraid, I guess. Tried to mind my own fucking business. Shit. I don't know. Maybe I was too embarrassed to say anything. I mean, who was I to tell a grownup what to do? Just a kid. A fucked-up fucking kid. So I just turned my head. I ignored it."

Nova didn't want to hear this. She'd watched the guy, too, swinging his little girl and all. Only to her, it looked nice how the baby laid there stretched out in the cradle of his arms. Innocent. Something she wanted to watch, to be part of. How could Michael see the same, exact thing and see something so entirely different?

"Damnit, how could I ignore it? I mean, I'm sure the guy must've thought he had a good grip there, but let's face it, if a kid wants to get loose from its father, how hard is that? I must have done it a million times when I was little. You must have done it." The more Michael talked the more Nova wanted to stop him, to yell at him to shut up, to close his goddamn mouth.

"Son of a bitch! Stupid, worthless, motherfucker!" He was yelling now, and he punched the wall once, twice. Then, almost too quiet to hear, "Damnit, why didn't I say something? I should have said something." He rested his forehead against the building and bent at the knees and slid down to the ground again. His head scraped and bumped over the bricks. He looked up at Nova. There was blood in his bangs, purple in the blue light, but he didn't seem to notice. "So I had to do what I did, because I didn't do what I should. Now do you get it? I'm no fucking hero, Nova. Sky wants to be one, fine. Me, I'm just trying to survive it."

Why did he have to tell her this? Couldn't he see he was spoiling everything? Why couldn't he just be a hero and be happy? Why couldn't he let her be happy? Why did he have to ruin it all?

"You need to go back there," she heard herself say.

"What? No fucking way."

"No really." And it was like things were spinning out of her mouth, advice and shit that she'd heard somewhere, on television or something, or maybe one of Sky's meetings. "Like when those people all got killed in that plane crash, remember?" She didn't have any particular plane crash in mind, there was a new one every year or so, but Michael nodded at her like he knew just what she was talking about. "Or that restaurant where all those people got killed when the roof fell in. Or those guys in the war." He nodded again. "Remember how all those people— the survivors—went back to those places where those terrible things happened? And when they went back there, then—" and here she reached both hands out to him to help him stand—"and only then, did those people really get past it." A load of crap, she knew. But something made her want to take Michael back to where the thing had happened. She wanted him to see the place again. She wanted him to feel it all again. She wanted him to pay for what he'd done to her by telling her his story.

At the foot of the ramp to the Gondolier, the couple they'd seen on the street hugged one another. The woman had her face buried in the shirtfront of the man; he stared over her head and into the center of the big wheel. On the ground all around the ride were small placements of flowers and stuffed animals. A three-foot cross made from tinfoil and cardboard leaned against the ticket booth. *$1.00*, a sign above the booth's window read. And another one misspelled in marker. *Plese Hold Onto You're Valubles.* The flowers had begun to bake in the hot night air, and the place was ripe with the rotting smell of garbage. Street lamps along Main Street threw uneven pools of light on the dark carnival attractions. Nova stopped Michael in the shadows of the ring toss tent.

"Wait," she said. "When they go." She could feel Michael shaking next to her; his teeth chattered. "You'll be fine," she said, and when she heard a certain edge in her voice, she reached for his hand, made herself raise his scraped knuckles to her lips. "You'll be fine," she said again softly against his fingers.

It seemed as though the couple had no intention of ever leaving their spot. Nova watched them pressed together, the gigantic, unmoving wheel behind them, and pushed against the flooded feeling that rose again inside her. "Why don't they go?" She whispered sharply and looked at Michael. His face streamed with tears, his chest heaved under his flannel shirt. Nova could hear the quiet hiccup of his sobs. Something softened in her, and she was just about to say that maybe they'd had enough for one day when the couple moved on and was replaced by a dark figure. A slow, stumbling man walked with an unsteady purpose to the spot that was wound round and round with yellow police tape. A spot Nova just then recognized as where the body—or most of it at least, wouldn't it have split apart on impact?—must have landed. The man went down on all fours and crawled beneath the plastic barriers. He rested a cheek on the ground and didn't move. It was like he was listening to the workings of the world.

"Fucking drunk," Nova said. "What nerve." She started out from under the shadows, but Michael held fast to her hand.

"No," he said.

She shook him off and headed for the man.

"Hey! Asshole!" Nova yelled.

The man looked up, and as she got closer, Nova began to make out his face, began to sense a familiarity.

"You," the man said, but it was like he was in a daze, the word came out soft as a prayer. He looked not at Nova, but over her shoulder, beyond her.

"Holy shit," she said when she put the man, the place, and the dead little girl together. She spun around and found Michael trotting towards her. "It's the guy," she said. "It's the father."

"Yes," Michael said and tried to grab Nova's arm. "Let's give him some privacy."

She shrugged out from Michael's reach and looked back at the man. "No," she said. And then again, "No."

And then, without premeditation, Nova felt herself launch into a full-out charge. Michael moved behind her, but she was way ahead of him. She broke through the police tape and felt herself land on the man, felt him fall back with the weight of her, felt his skin under her fists as she pounded on his face, on his neck. And again, it was as if she were dreaming, only this was like that dream she had where she would be beating someone, her mother maybe, or Sky, or someone else, and no matter how hard she hit, she couldn't make them feel it. The man's face came into focus beneath her hands. His eyes flashed surprise, but behind that was something else. Something muddy and impenetrable.

Hands circled her ankles, and Nova knew that Michael had caught up. She tried to kick him away, but he held fast. The funny thing was, the man lay still while she hit him for what felt like forever. When Michael had a good enough grip to pull her down the length of the man's body, it was as though he slowly came to. He blinked and blinked, and with a jerky momentum, the man tried to catch Nova's fists. He latched onto the bad hand, the smelly one, and when he held it in front of his face, Nova saw all that she hated to see. First his lips pulled back and he bared his teeth against the odor of the skunk, and then she saw him flinch when he recognized that he held only part of a hand. And, worst of all, his eyes widened with that look that Nova long ago (about the time of her father's departure) decided was pity. He opened up his mouth as though he were going to say something, and in that moment, Nova planned to break his fucking teeth in if he dared to tell her he was sorry.

"Goddamnit, Nova!" Michael had her by the waist now and swung her up and over his shoulder. She hated being such a little girl. "Leave the guy alone."

Nova slugged at Michael's back, flailed her legs as hard as she could against his chest.

"Put me down, you dickhead! Put me the fuck down!" She was screaming now, the words scraped her throat, rattled her chest. Michael bobbled under her. "Shh, shh," he was saying a loud spray of sound. "Let me go!" She could see from where she hung over Michael's back the man stand up and brush himself off, she saw him move in their direction. Her head rushed with heat and blood and her body seethed.

"Stay away from me!" she yelled at the father. "I'll kill you, you motherfucker!" It was a wonder Michael could hang onto her. "I'll kill you, you motherfucker. I'll kill you! Motherfucker! Fucker! Motherfucker!"

And then she felt Michael fold beneath her and felt herself pushed from him. When she scrambled to her knees, Nova recognized Sky's broad shoulders and golden curls. She saw the pulling back of his arm, the release and swing repeated again and again. Michael's face rolled side to side, more bloodied with each punch from Sky. Nova crawled toward them. Michael looked at Nova through swollen eyes, his lips moved, his mouth opened. "Gaaahhh," he said. Crimson muck spilled over his teeth. "Gaahhh." It was like he was speaking right to her; Nova strained to hear. "Gaahh..." or maybe it was "God." Or maybe: "Good."

"He hurt you?" Sky asked. His voice was calm. He kept his eyes on Michael's face. A white smudge of mayonnaise marked his cheek and Nova felt a stinging desire to wipe it away, to hold her brother's head in her hands. Her protector, her hero, the only one she had. But Nova couldn't make herself move and Sky continued to beat his friend, his hands, raw and blood-covered, traveling from the head to the chest and back up to the face. He had Michael's arms pinned under his knees even though Michael wasn't struggling. "You okay, Novie?" Sky asked in that calm voice. Nova nodded. It was like Michael was letting this happen to himself, like he wasn't even trying to stop it. And Sky kept at it with a controlled rhythm: beat, beat, beat. Nova believed her brother was doing this for her, she had to. This had nothing to do with Michael, what he'd done, what Sky had not. This, Nova told herself, was about Sky and Nova. Of course it was.

Michael's head lolled back and forth, each blow the sound of meat slammed against meat. He spit blood and something else, broken tooth maybe, then coughed and gurgled. Nova wasn't able to look away from her brother's heroics, even as she heard the man come up behind them.

"Holy Mother of God," the man said. "That's enough now, don't you think? You should stop now." Even still, the man stayed back, watched the beating alongside Nova. "Stop it now, son. You're killing him, son."

"Yes," Nova said and looked away from the hero and up at the man. She saw under his eye a small patch the size of the nail on her miniature thumb. She smiled up at the father. "Yes," she said again, her chest thick and aching with pride. "He is."

Just Like That

Officially it was senior prom, but Arnie said it was more like a regular party when you think about it, but a going-away party with a bunch of kids we didn't like that much all dressed up and crying and hugging—and why would he want any part of that? Not like any of us were going all that far away: mostly we were just heading down the road to Highland Community College for a couple of years, and okay, some were going into the army, and maybe Vietnam, who knew for certain. But still.

Arnie was the only one who was really going far—a full scholarship to something-I-T out East, a place that was tailor-made for a guy like him. You know, brilliant. Not that nerdy kind of brilliant, physics and algorithms—although he was great at that, too—but a different kind of genius. The kind that could sort through all the crap and find the threads, the connections, the way everything could— if you looked at it just right and put in some kind of order—make sense somehow.

Still, it was prom night, the only one either of us would ever get a chance to go to, and I did sort of want to go. Don't ask me why. Maybe because it was a rite of passage, you know, something to mark a specific time in our lives. Or it could have been because I was one of those kids who was going away. I guess I'm sort of smart as well, because I got a scholarship, too, only across the river to a state university. No big deal, but my first time anywhere at all really, besides here. Here, New Hope, which is a small town you probably never even heard of before. Or maybe you did, after that night, the night of prom. Still, even if you've heard of it, it's the kind of place that's not too hard to forget. Which, when I think about it, was another reason I thought it might be fun to go to prom. A way of remembering.

So I talked Arnie into it, like I can talk him into a lot of things. Like skitching. You know, when you grab the back of a car, the bumper, and it's icy out, and you hold on and the car pulls away, slow at first, but if it's your friends driving and they know you're doing it, they'll go pretty fast pretty quick, and next thing you know they're pulling doughnuts in the parking lot of Jack's new Super Hi-Lo, and you're swirling on the ice, holding on for dear life and feeling your heart right up there near your ears. It's great. Really. But Arnie, brilliant as he is, could see all the things that could go wrong with a situation like this—which is exactly why it's so fun—and it took some convincing for him to try it. He did though, maybe because I said he didn't have to, I'd go off with Derek Jerabek and do it, and Derek and Arnie had this feud so old and deep that I don't know if they knew what was behind it anymore. Anyway, the next night Arnie's right there with me at Jack's Super, waiting his turn to grab a bumper, and he's wearing his Converses, the best kind of skitching shoe, all slick and thin in the sole. And when it's his turn, Arnie won't let go, he's riding that bumper like a cowboy on a bull, hanging on and hollering. And it's Derek behind the wheel and he's pulling one-eighties and three-sixties and figure eights. But Arnie holds on. And finally Derek has to stop so someone else can have a turn to get on board. And Arnie's face is frozen in this loopy grin, and I have to help him peel his hands off the bumper, one finger at a time, and his sneakers have worn clear through in places, and he's hyped, I mean hyped like I've never seen him before and he wants to go again, right away, but his fingers aren't straightening up and his fingertips are blue, so I talk him into coming home with me for a little while to warm up, which he does but only when I promise we'll go right back out. We get to my house and I'm sort of worried, his hands are so cold and not just his shoes, but his socks have holes, too, and I blow on his hands and rub his feet, and he's talking that talk guys do when they're excited, you know: "That was so fucking cool! Did you see that? Did you see me on Derek like that? Shit!" And I want him to shut up because, like I say, I'm worried, he's so cold, so when he tries to pull away from me I decide to switch gears and get his attention, and so I pull his hand toward me and slide it up under my sweater and onto my warm belly—and it's so cold, his hand, but I hold it there and try not to let my teeth chatter. And Arnie shuts up, just like that, silent as a block of ice, and looks at me, and I put his other hand under my sweater too, and then slide it under my belt, down where it's really warm, and we lay back on my bed and I get him under the covers and we're both shivering but we just stare at one another a while until his hands get warm and his breath goes heavy.

It's not like this is the first time we did anything like that. I mean, we grew up right next door to one another, so we used to play *You show me yours, I'll show you mine* when we were kids. And when we got to junior high, we were best friends, and one time I had this crush on this guy Sky Spalding. He was in our grade, but a little older than the rest of us, a new kid who got held back because he and they were moving all the time. I still remember how he had these great greeny-blue eyes. And once he asked me to sit back in the stacks with him in the library and he was back there with Derek, and we were all just sitting there and talking when all of a sudden this guy Sky says he knows that I like him and would it be okay if we Frenched. Well, I could feel my stomach knot up, I was so excited, my first time French kissing anyone, and here it was Sky with the green-blue eyes. So I nodded, feeling a bit shy, too, maybe because Derek was there. And so Sky leans over and puts his lips against mine and sticks his tongue out and it feels sort of stiff and tastes like—I'll never forget this—salami, and he just holds it there and wiggles his head around, and I've got my eyes closed and am waiting for it to feel like something special, and I hear Derek over there snort or something, and I open my eyes, and even though Sky is kissing me, he's giving Derek this sidelong glance. And then Sky pulls his head back and wipes his hand over his mouth and he says, "You're good," and even though I don't know how this could possibly be, I mean I just opened my mouth and let his tongue in, I'm feeling a bit proud about that. And then he puts his hand on my neck and down the front of my blouse and inside my bra and squeezes my tit in his hand, once, twice, and Derek is there still, wide-eyed and open-mouthed, and I feel sick in my stomach for so many reasons I can't even begin to sort them out. I want to pull Sky's hand right back out of there, but that seems like the wrong thing to do for some reason, like after I already was there for the kiss and all, could I really back off now? And Sky's hand is rough and sort of sweaty, and pretty soon he pulls it out himself and I'm just sitting there not knowing exactly what to do or say, but smiling a little like it's all okay, no big deal, but I feel my face is burning, and my scalp is starting to prickle. And when Sky and Derek swap a glance at one another, lift their eyebrows, I excuse myself, say I have to go somewhere or something, and I walk away as casually as I can, and I can feel their goddamned eyes on the back of my jeans, and I go to the girls' room and lean over the sink and look at my face which I suspect has changed, but it's the same, really, only I think a little sad looking. And later, at home while I'm babysitting the twins and Arnie comes over I want to tell him about it, because I feel like I should tell someone. I'm sort of excited even though I'm still feeling a little something else I haven't yet figured out.

But Arnie already knows, that's the way it is in a town like this, nothing is a secret for very long, especially when it comes to boys, and he looks sort of mad standing there in the door, and so I tell him my side—he already knew about the crush on Sky—and here's the funny thing. When I tell him, I start to cry, who knows why that is, but I do a little, and Arnie's holding me like he has once or twice before, like when my folks got divorced, like when my dad died, and then I'm really crying. Arnie asks what can he do, and I think about that, and I figure out that I want him to kiss me, to touch my boob, because I know that with him it will be different, nice, caring—friendly, I guess—and so he does, only he's a little nervous at first, his hand is shaking, but he's warm and his tongue is wet and soft and his hand is smooth and we stay there like that for a long while, the two of us on my couch, the twins napping in the next room, and he just leaves his hand on my breast like that, and when his tongue slips in and out of my mouth, I taste it with my own tongue and it's sweet, milky, and we both get a little fogged up, and I'm not crying anymore, but more like floating. And after a few minutes of this, he stops, pulls away, and looks at me. His glasses are steamed. He says, "Better?" and his voice is rough. And I nod and rearrange my top, my bra. And Arnie says, "Good," and he gets up and goes to the kitchen and gets us a Pepsi which we pass back and forth, not saying anything else.

And every once in a while since then, we would come together like this, fiddle around a little. It wasn't about sex, I don't think. I guess we loved one another, when you think about it, but in a friendly way, in a way that has to do with knowing each other better than we knew anybody else on the planet. So it wasn't about lust, but it wasn't exactly about love either. It was more about something else. Like what I was saying about Arnie's brilliance, about connections and making sense of the big picture. That's it, I think.

So of course it made sense that we should go to prom together. And we were in my back yard taking turns behind the lawnmower and talking about the dance. Well, I was talking about it, trying to make my point to Arnie, who just nodded and looked away over the back fence and squeezed my dog King's chewed-up rubber ball in his hand. And the twins, Jimmy and Jerry, who were seven, were ahead of us supposedly picking up twigs and toys and sticks and things, but mostly just picking up King's dog doo with plastic bags on their hands like mittens, and they'd pretend to throw it at each other before dropping it into the bag they carried.

"Tell me again why you think we should go," Arnie said, and the mower roared between us, and the twins screamed and laughed and ran in circles, and the cicadas made that electric noise they make when it gets hot. It was just May, but eighty out, and it sounded like summer already.

"Come on, Arnie," I said and pounded on the mower's handle. "What's the big deal? It's just a few hours out of your life, and besides, it might be fun."

Arnie snorted in that superior way of his that he reserved for teachers who had a hard time keeping up with his answers to their questions. I watched the muscle in his forearm tense and release as he squeezed the ball, watched the little blue vein over his wrist pop up.

"Okay, think of it this way," I said as we turned back toward the house, making another line in the grass. "It's a favor to me. You might not feel like this, but I think that if I don't go, I'll regret it somehow. Maybe not right away, but you know, years from now, when I'm old, and I'm thinking back over things."

Arnie hated it when I talked like this, about growing old, which I do a lot for some reason. He called himself a "fatalist," like it was something he should be proud of like his having a high IQ was. He always thought an end—some end, who knows?—was near. I thought we'd both grow remarkably old, break records like those people who ate yogurt in Siberia. Maybe live forever.

"If it sucks," I said, and Arnie said, "Which it will," and I went on like I hadn't heard him, "we can change the night and leave. If we don't go, we can't change things. We just won't have gone. Period." And I was pleased with myself, because I knew Arnie got what I meant, and it was almost one of those brilliant things he might say.

We were closing in on the last few swipes across the lawn, and the twins were rolling around with King now, whose tongue was hanging out and dripping in the heat. Mom and Mrs. Lawlor, Arnie's mom, were on the patio drinking sun tea and listening to the radio. They both were frowning, and Mrs. Lawlor shook her head. When I got closer, I could hear enough of what was being said to know it had to do with the war. Arnie was still near the back fence, staring out across the field. I saw him nod his head a little, like he was talking to himself like he sometimes does, and then I saw him hurl King's ball as hard as he could towards—well, it was all flat, vacant fields back there. Under the right conditions, that ball could roll for miles.

So we went to prom. And I thought Arnie's mom might burst when we left, the way she looked so proud and was snapping all these pictures and talking about how she couldn't wait until Arnie's dad came home later that week from his work trip so she could show him and tell him all about it. And my mom—who pretty much thought Arnie was the only male worth anything ever since Dad left us when I was eight and then came back for a bit when I was ten, which is when the twins were born, and then left again and a couple years later ran off the road one night after leaving Supples Tavern—Mom was even smiling. And we were dressed up, Arnie and me, nothing too fancy, but Arnie wore a navy blue coat and tie, the one he wore for debate team, and I had on a long purple velveteen skirt and a lavender blouse that in the right light you could see through to my white camisole. Which was the style. We took a pass on corsages, because it wasn't really a date, but still, we both were excited (I was at least) and even though the weather had gone insane, rain and more rain, and lightning, thunder, and wind, I knew as we ran out to Arnie's VW that this was going to be some night. And back at the house, the moms were in the window, and the twins were there, too, and they were all waving. We pulled away from the curb and the wind battered against the car and the branches of the trees all bent low like they, too, were waving us on our way.

•

It was pretty in the gym, streamers and balloons, everybody all dressed up, and especially the lights, which were covered up with colored film. And the smell of perfume and hairspray and flowers nearly hid the smell of wet sneakers. And the music was good. I was glad that they had decided against the band, Derek Jerabek's older brother's one, the Hendrix Connection—you can guess what they played—since his brother had been sent over to Vietnam and they still didn't have a lead guitar. Instead they hired a disc jockey and he played records we all heard every day, the sort of thing we all would dance to in the privacy of our own homes.

Arnie and I loved to dance; we danced all the time at my house. We got right on the dance floor with everyone else, all of our long dresses sweeping over the floor, the boys undoing their ties, hands, arms, legs everywhere. And we all kept moving like we had something to prove, like if we stopped, something might catch up to us. And we danced until we were drenched and the disc jockey put on something slow. Someone turned down the lights even more, and everyone pulled together, pushed their bodies tight against each other, two by two, and pretty much just stood in the middle of the floor, shifting foot to foot, not really moving. There was a lot of kissing going on out there, and every now and again you could see one or another of the girls pulling her head back and looking up, her face all powdery and glowing in the light, in a haze, it looked like. I kept waiting for Mr. Harvey, the principal, or Pastor James who always chaperoned, or one of the teachers to step in, but they didn't. And from where Arnie and I stood on the side, drinking pink punch in silver paper cups, I watched all the making out and body pressing and felt something stir in me. I tried to look past it all, though, and there were the teachers and Pastor James and Mr. Harvey, in a huddle, talking and appearing, I don't know, worried.

And then the lights went out. Just like that. And then there was a big crash, a heavy thunderclap that was so loud and close it shook the punch in my cup. And through the gym's high narrow windows, we could see the lightning flash over and over. The panes rattled. A couple of the girls, the more dramatic ones, screamed.

"Young people," Mr. Harvey yelled over the crowd, "Young people!" He always called us that. The rest of the teachers called us kids. "Listen," he yelled, and then there were a couple of flashlights shining on him; Pastor James had one, and Miss Daniels, the librarian, had another. Mr. Harvey put a hand up to shade his eyes. "We have a bit of a problem here," he said.

"Duh," someone yelled. It sounded like Derek. It probably was. No one laughed.

"Seriously," Mr. Harvey went on. "We have been informed that a funnel cloud has just touched down in Shelby. We are under a tornado warning."

Things went quietly wild then. Everyone talking and spinning around, some of the girls started crying and the boys, trying to be brave, talked in steady voices and held their dates' hands.

Mr. Harvey spoke again. "I'm sorry to say this, but prom is now officially cancelled." And people made noise like they were disappointed, like they had

Just Like That

forgotten that just a minute ago someone had told them that a tornado was on the way. "Young people, please. If I might have your attention."

Arnie put his arm over my shoulders then. "You're shaking," he said. I tucked tight into him.

"We will now proceed, in an orderly fashion, to the basement." We'd had enough tornado drills to know better, we lived in what people called a tornado alley, and most of us had seen the funnel clouds each summer over the flat fields, but still, when Mr. Harvey said the word "basement," kids piled into the doorway of the gym, ran down the hall, and crashed together into the stairwell. The generator had kicked in, two spotlights lit the way. Mr. Harvey and the other adults chased after the kids. "People! Kids! People!" they yelled. Arnie held me tightly, which helped my first instinct—to jump into the crush of kids—ease up some, and we walked quickly after the crowd. Mr. Harvey turned toward us. "Come along, you two," he said, but then he saw it was Arnie, brilliant Arnie, and me, who he knew by name only because I was never any trouble, really, or anything special for that matter, and he just nodded and trotted toward the stairwell where everyone else was pushing and yelling.

Just when we were about to get to the stairs, Arnie stopped me. He looked into my face. "You okay?" he asked. And you know, I really was. We could hear the noise below us in the basement, and we could hear the wind making its chugging sound outside. "Some special night, huh?" Arnie said. And he was smiling, and it was that loopy smile, like his skitching smile. And I don't know why, but I stood on my toes and pushed my breasts against his chest and put my arms around his neck and kissed him, tongue and all. And his arms went around my waist and he pulled me closer, and I could feel his hard on, right through his pants, through the velvet of my skirt. And I rubbed a little against it, felt it move over my belly, and the rain hit the window like handfuls of pebbles. Arnie let go of my waist and took my hand and pulled me into the boys' locker room. He led me along one wall and into the shower room. "Here," he said, his voice hollow and echoey. "Sit down." He put his jacket on the floor and I sat down. And then Arnie was beside me, and we sat still and quiet, listening to the battering of things outside, to the wind, to the thunder, imagining what made what sound—was that a lamppost? A car? The rooftop? And I started to shake again. Arnie wrapped his arms around me.

"We could die," he said, matter-of-factly. And of course, I'd been thinking exactly that, so I just nodded. "My poor mom," he said. I imagined Arnie's mom in their house in the dark by herself, nervous and flighty like she gets, her hands butterflies she can't keep still. And then I hoped she was at my house with my mom, who in a case like this, an emergency situation, would know just what to do, would take them all down to the cellar, the twins, King, Mrs. Lawlor, and they'd be down on the linoleum floor, leaning against the dryer, the washing machine, and Mom would get their minds off things, singing something, James Taylor, maybe, or old Beatles.

"My poor mom," Arnie said again. And then, "I got my notice."

And try as I might, I couldn't figure out what he was talking about. I didn't want to sound stupid, though, in these maybe last few minutes of our life, so I didn't say anything.

"A few weeks ago. I thought I'd get a student deferment," he went on. "But they've changed the rules."

And then, even though it was hot in the shower room, I started to get cold. I knew what Arnie was telling me. Notice. Of the draft.

"I go for my physical next week," he said.

Arnie and I hardly ever talked about the war, but I knew that he had very specific ideas about it, like he had about a lot of things. Whenever someone we knew—like Derek's brother—enlisted or got drafted, Arnie would go into this mood that was part sad, part angry. And I knew when he got like that, quiet and steaming, it was best not to talk to him. At all. So that night we just sat there saying nothing, sat and listened to the tornado hit the town.

And then Arnie stretched out on the floor, and I kept sitting there listening past the wind for what I don't know. But what I heard after a while came from up close. And it was Arnie, crying, which was very unlike him. The only time I heard him cry before was after Sky and Derek got me in the stacks and later, after Arnie and I kissed and everything and he went to the kitchen for the Pepsi, I heard him in there, crying like this, soft and really, really sad.

I lay down next to him, put my head on his chest. Shushed him. But that didn't help at all, the opposite in fact. Because the crying really started, and his body shook, and I held on, my arms tight around his waist and his crying ran through me, and I couldn't help it, I started to cry too. But I knew I was crying not just about Arnie, about Arnie going away, to war maybe, but about everything, everything that had ever happened before in my life that had hurt me: the way Dad came into my room that first night when he said he had to leave, the way he didn't tell me the next time he left, the way Mom's face crumpled into itself when she told me about his crash, the way the twins came home with Mom from the hospital and Dad was already gone, months gone, and the goddamned twins with their bald heads and red, flabby faces looked exactly like Dad did in the mornings when he was hung over. I cried about Derek and Sky feeling me up in the library, I cried about Mom going quiet for those months after the twins were born, staying in her bedroom, leaving me and Mrs. Lawlor to take care of the babies, of the house. I cried about not knowing what was going on outside while we were there in the shower room, I cried about not knowing what we'd find when we went outside, about what might be lost. I cried about not knowing—let's face it—anything at all.

We pressed together, Arnie and I, and the kissing started again, and we kept at it, good and long. Then I took off Arnie's glasses, unbuttoned his shirt, lifted his tie over his head. I pulled my own blouse out of the waistband of the purple skirt, and pulled it up over my head. But here's the thing. There we were, on our way to naked, and all the rest that goes with that, but instead of going forward, you know, going all the way, this is where we stopped. And I think maybe if we'd been two other people, like

Derek and one of the other girls, we might have—probably would have—kept going. But let's face it, we were just Arnie and me. So instead he wrapped me up in his arms, pulled my head under his chin. And we stayed like that on the floor. And at first we started to tell little stories, you know, "remember when" and all. But then we stopped even that, stopped talking and just lay there, while the town took on the storm, while the world outside reeled.

There had been no siren, no sound at all that warned us about the coming of the tornado. What there was later, though, was a ringing of all the church bells in town to let everyone know it was over. In my sleep I heard them in my dreams, loud and low, but I can't remember what I dreamed. Arnie stirred under me, and we pulled apart and rearranged our clothes. We heard the drumming of feet in the hallway, everyone else running up from the basement, running toward whatever was going on out there.

Months later, after the town had cleaned up the mess left behind, cleared the trees out of the streets, hauled away the overturned cars, put up new roofs, rebuilt Jack's Super, Mrs. Lawlor turned up on our doorstep and fell into a heap before Mom could even get her to say what the army had told her. I was home from college for spring break, working parttime at Jack's. I stood in the doorway, and in the pale, white spring light, I watched Mom go to Arnie's mother, watched her sink to the concrete and circle her arms around her friend, watched her hold her. And my knees gave a bit under the weight of it all, but I reached for the doorknob and held on as best I could and for some reason I thought about that ball Arnie threw over the fence that day when we were mowing the lawn. And I wondered where exactly it ended up once it stopped rolling.

"We didn't die," I had said to Arnie on prom night before we left the shower room. Arnie just looked at me, his lips turning up at the corners, but it wasn't a smile. Not really. Still, he nodded, I remember, and bent down to kiss me, his aim off, and he brushed my jaw with his lips.

"After you," Arnie said when we got to the locker-room door. And I stepped around him into the empty hallway. We walked hand-in-hand toward the wide exit doors, and I pushed hard on the heavy silver bar that released the latch.

"After you," I said. And Arnie ran his hands over his jacket like he was smoothing it. He straightened the knot in his tie.

I stood by and held the door for him, and my best friend walked right past me, just like that, leading the way out and into the wet, wrecked night.

The Joke

"So you don't mind a little dirty joke, huh?"

I shook my head. What'd he think I was, some kid? Fifteen and out there way after dark—on my own I could've been. So when the old guy with the tiny scrubbed hands, small as a boy's only veiny and bluish, offered me a lift, I thought, *sure, a place to sit for a while.* "Nice ride," I said. Big polished four-door with the seats wrapped in plastic that smelled like adhesive tape, like a family car.

He tapped his nails, white moon slivers, on the steering wheel, switched off the engine and began to speak real low, his head tilted toward mine. I had to lean in to hear him, had to strain to listen as he spoke just above a whisper about a stream of things like women getting their clothes ripped off by accident, and men accidentally putting their cocks where they didn't belong, and hookers and blowjobs and butt fucks. I sort of laughed now and then. I wasn't getting it, but I acted like I did. You know. And by the time I got that it wasn't a joke, it was just dirty, it was too late because I was already there, already said I didn't mind, I would listen. And I didn't know how to stop listening, how to get him to shut up for chrissakes, shut up, shut the fuck up, and the smell of that car, that plastic, that awful thick glue smell made my

stomach churn and my eyes smart, and I couldn't
turn away when he reached down and pulled his
zipper, pulled his dick out, the small wrinkled gray
thing that he yanked on until it bloated up too big
and purple for his little boy hands, clublike and
purple, larger than it should have been he was such
a little guy—I could take him, he was so little—and
when he whispered he wanted me to touch it, what
else could I do? I was already there, already said I
didn't mind, already laughed, damnit—so he took one
of my hands and put it around the thick pole which
was sticky and felt squirmy and loose, and he
groaned and said Show me your tits, and I figured
what the hell. We'd come this far, not like I could say
No, I don't want to do this, because I'd already started
doing it and what could I do to stop this from moving
forward now, stop it and make it go back? And
besides, it was better to use my hands to lift my shirt
than to touch him, thank God I'd worn a bra, that
was all he'd get to see. But when I pulled up the tank
top it was like I was peeling my own skin, it hurt
damnit, it hurt for no reason I could figure out. So I
yanked it up fast like you strip off a Band-Aid, and
with the shirt in front of my face at least I didn't have
to see him, to see it for a while. And behind the shirt
I felt my eyes burn and fill, felt the tears roll down my
face, but no sound, not from me. And then I asked
him not to touch me, whispered it quiet like a prayer,
but it didn't matter what I said, he didn't care, didn't
want to touch me because he was touching himself
and moaning and coming into his own dry hands and
I pulled down my shirt just in time to see the thing
jerk and squirt and I reached behind myself for the

door handle and nearly fell out of the car but caught my footing in time to back away, step away from the car which he started and took off in, wheels spitting gravel, leaving me at the side of the road. Crying and—that son of a bitch—alone all over again.

Running

The race was Hoof's idea. Sunday morning, all hungover after another Saturday night at the Inn with Annie and Jim and they're both, Jess and Hoof— moaning about needing to run.

"Why don't we ever run together," Jess asks for maybe the hundredth time since they'd moved out to the country. In the city they'd run along the lakefront, stop at a stand on the beach, share a soda or a big bottle of water. Then they'd walk back to the apartment, hand in hand, fingers sticky from the sweat that runs down your arms in Chicago summer humidity.

"You run too slow," Hoof says.

"I can keep up," Jess says. "Especially if you run more than your usual mile."

"I like my mile. Short and quick," he says.

It's a point of contention between them, and they both know they're not talking about the running. It's a long-haul thing; Hoof's not a long-haul sort of guy. They'd reached a time in their lives when they're supposed to be settled, more or less, but since they'd been together these past eight years, Hoof's had three jobs, gone back to and then quit graduate school, moved in with Jess then broke up with her, and then married her, got that substantial inheritance from his father and decided to build them a nice big house in the country where they could do whatever they wanted. Not work, he meant. Retire early, kind of. Jess, write like she always wanted, and Hoof, well, whatever took his attention: computers, woodworking, gardening, collecting things. The one great room of the cabin (it never got bigger than two rooms) was filled with his projects. First it was just the coffee table, then the desk that was supposed to be Jess's, the chairs, and on this morning they had to push a dozen catalogues and a bushel of tomatoes out of the way in order to set their coffee cups down on the dining table.

They haven't made love in months.

"Come on, Hoof," Jess says.

His real name is Alfred. Alfred Huffner. But Alfred is a nerd's name, a boy with too-thick glasses and a pocket protector, a studious, plodding achiever in the fifth grade. Chess club, maybe. In high school they called him Huffer, because of the dope, he says. Because of the asthma, says his mother. But now it's Hoof. Hoof is better. He is yellow-haired and tan, broad-shouldered, a brilliant smile and a look in his sleepy brown eyes that makes it hard for Jess to not want to forgive him for not finishing things: the dishes, an argument, the cabin.

"Come on," she says again. "Let's do it my way for once."

She's whining, which she knows Hoof hates. It's what his mother used to do to wheedle him into things—take her grocery shopping, mow the lawn, call his dad for more cash. Still, whining works with Hoof.

"All right, damnit," he says. "We'll run together."

He's holding his head like it hurts. It should. They were at the Inn until closing. Annie, Jim, Hoof, and Jess, and sometime along the line Jim suggested shots of tequila, but Annie and Jess kept on with their rum-and-Diet Dr. Peppers. Hoof got to the drunk place he gets nearly every Saturday these days, where his eyes start to slip around, find a spot and slide off, and Jim got quiet like he does while Annie starts to pick on him. It's like he's got it coming, the way he takes it from her ("Jim you're drunk," "Jim, you're embarrassing me," "Jim, just look at you,") and sometimes Jess has to excuse herself from the smoky bar made tight by Annie's sniping and step out into the wide-open emptiness of midnight Main Street to keep from screaming.

She wonders what it's like to live with someone who is at you all the time. The sound of disapproval must be deafening. In Jess's and Hoof's house, it's mostly quiet which, when you think about it, has a deafening quality of its own. Hoof hardly talks anymore; his quiet fills the two rooms. Except when he has an attack. The noise then is gruesome, his breath raggedy and gurgling, like what drowning must sound like. He never had an attack in the city, at least not that Jess witnessed, so the first time she heard him gasping like that she ran to his side, tried to help. She didn't know what to do—pat his back, call 911—so she circled the couch, closing in on him like his body seemed to be doing, watched while he sucked on his inhaler and batted her hands away. His mouth opened and opened, and his eyes went wild and wet and filled with something. It wasn't fear, although Jess was scared as shit. His eyes pushed at her, like if she couldn't help, then she should get out of his way. Like her being there, seeing this, wasn't at all what he needed, it could only make things worse. Jess finally understood and left him to fend for himself. And now whenever it happens, she waits it out in the small bedroom, listens to the fight he puts up, ignores the claustrophobia blanketing her, the effect of no breath, of no escape.

This morning, neither of them is in running condition, so they take their time, move slowly through coffee and water and vitamins and cool showers and changing into running clothes. When Jess's ready, she leaves the confines of the cabin to find Hoof on the broad steps of the porch, still holding his head.

"Ready," she says.

"I'm not sure," he says.

"Aw, Hoof, come on. You said."

"All right," he says, a sharp whisper with an edge to it, and Jess considers backing down, giving him a break, but then he comes up with the idea.

"Let's race," he says. And he's smiling a hard smile, and his sleepy eyes are marbles now and he's pushing her again. She can tell.

"Sure," she says, and shrugs like it's no big deal. "Let's race."

Only he'd slaughter her in a race, and she knows this is also his idea. He'll give in to the running together in order to prove how even though he's got asthma, she still can't keep up, how he would have to ratchet his workout way, way down in order to do it Jess's way. She runs slowly but she runs long, too. Five miles, six sometimes. Anyone can run fast for a mile, she things, but she's pretty sure that she wouldn't be able to keep up with Hoof for even that.

"You'll have to run farther, though," Jess says.

And together they figure out a course to follow, a path of seven-plus miles that seems to make it fair: longer than Jess would run, so she'll have to slow way down, much longer than Hoof does, so he can stop and go, run it in sprints.

"What's at stake?" She asks.

"Good question," Hoof says, and his smile is hard again.

And they're ready to run.

The hangover takes some time getting beyond, but Jess works her way through it as her legs find their rhythm and she watches the familiar pass of dirt and gravel under her feet. She breathes in the warm, expansive, green-smelling air, breathes out the tight headache from last night's binge. This is the thing she likes best about their move, this daily run. The world seems somehow bigger out here, opening in all directions. The way the land slopes and swells, the way part of the path edges a stream, part of it curves around the little lake (an Indian name meaning Water Lingers) and the bigger one (Water Lingers Still), and she even likes the straight shot of highway, a strip of gray that just goes, and goes, and goes. And this is what Jess wants to share with Hoof, the reason why she longs for them to run together. She'd show him things; they'd talk about things. "See the blue house there?" she'd say. "It looks like sky in the trees. And look, the trailer with the sign out front: *Clothes, $1 a bag.* Is that buying or selling?" Some days Jess wants it to be buying. Some days it would be better to sell. She'd show Hoof the crosses on opposite sides of the road, always freshly white with painted red numbers, *1971, 1967,* and plastic wreathes. They'd make up stories about all the country people. Like they use to do in the city. Since they moved out here, Jess's figured out that it isn't the writing she wants, it's the stories. In the city, each day they'd come home from work and talk about things. The job, the people they met, the oddballs on the El.

Jess passes the newer subdivision where Annie and Jim live, six styles of house in four different colors, coordinated street signs and mailboxes all built behind a curving stone gate. SuburbLand, she calls it. Anywhere, USA.

Ahead is where she'd turn if this were her usual run, where the logging road circles back to the cabin Hoof built. But the race path they decided on goes on another half-mile down to the country road. When she'd hit the highway, Hoof was already a dot way out front, but he's long gone now, running hard and uneven. Jess imagines his body working to make more room for more air, shifting side to side like it does when he gets a momentum going. The one time they'd canoed on Water Lingers, he'd wanted to pick up the pace in a way the quiet little lake couldn't afford, and Jess held onto the boat's sides as Hoof paddled right side, left side, leaning and leaning until the rig capsized and they went over and came up spluttering. Paddles, canoe, picnic basket, and beer cans bogging on the shattered surface around them. And she nearly drowned from the laughing and Hoof, who'd said he was good at this sort of thing, looked pissed.

Just off the country road is a small trail that leads down to the big lake's side. Jess nearly misses it, but then it's there, overgrown and golden in the first days of fall. And the lake is there, too, the trail opening up on its vastness, the cool of the water filling the air. And there, too, is Hoof, on his knees and throwing up, one hand in the water. Jess stops on the trail, yards away and behind tall grasses, unsure what to do next. She can see it's not an attack but the hangover, and Hoof sits back on his heels and wipes his mouth. She's close enough to hear the noise of his sickness and the aching sound of his moaning.

When his father died, Hoof told Jess about it over the phone. "I hardly knew him," he said, and she believed him when he said it didn't really matter. But later that night, on the balcony of their apartment in the city, they looked out over the lights to the black void that was Lake Michigan, and Hoof told her about the time his father asked to see him. Hoof was just out of college then, about to start his first job, and his dad invited him to dinner. Hoof spent three and a half hours on a train that took him out of the city and past cornfields to the town his father had settled in after the divorce. "He had a gift for me," Hoof said. At the station, Hoof's father met him in an old sedan and took him to a Denny's. "A Denny's," Hoof said and laughed, popped open another beer and leaned back in his chair, looked up the ladder of lit and unlit windows of the high-rise across the street. Hoof kept waiting for his dad to say something about the present, about Hoof's graduation, but all the old man talked about was a bridge. "We could see it from the restaurant," Hoof told Jess. "It was this green thing, like the metal had turned. No big deal, just your average bridge. 'I made that bridge,' Dad said after a while, 'I built it.'" And he was smiling. Proud. And like I said, it was just your average bridge. 'Yeah?' I said. He kept looking at me, like he wanted to say something else. Nodding. 'Yeah?' I said again. And then our food came. And we ate mostly in silence, passing the ketchup and Tabasco back and forth. Salt and pepper. We dressed our burgers exactly the same. And every once in a while I'd catch Dad looking out at the bridge and sometimes I thought I could see him watching me, but then I'd look up, and there he was staring at the bridge. That damn bridge. After that we had some ice cream because it came with the meal, and then Dad took me back to the station where I'd get the train back to the city and before he got back in his car he shook my hand and handed me a fat envelope and I put it in my pocket and it wasn't until I was halfway home that I thought to even look inside. No note or anything. Five thousand bucks, though. In hundreds. But no note."

And when Hoof got to the end of the story, maybe the last one he ever told Jess, she thought he might be crying. He wouldn't look at her. His voice was rough but his eyes, she could see in the nightlight of the city, were dry. Jess moved her chair closer to his, but he stood up and cleared his throat and went inside to the bathroom. She stayed where she was and listened. On the balcony, though, the only noise came from planes high overhead and some drunks below, rolling bottles on the sidewalk and laughing. And then Hoof went straight to bed without even saying good night, and the next day, and maybe the next, too, he didn't talk to Jess at all.

He's still on his knees lakeside and Jess doesn't want him to get mean like he does when she sees him like this, weak, so she backs down the trail as quietly as possible and turns to run. She moves blindly at first, trying to outrun the closing-in feeling, to put as much land between Hoof and herself as possible. And she's not entirely surprised when sometime later she looks up and around and realizes she has absolutely no idea where she is. The trees look taller here, and the trail gives way to prairie grasses and grasshoppers. She could turn around, but she doesn't want to go backwards this time. Jess wants to move on, even if she doesn't know exactly what that means. She skips over the weeds and insects and nothing looks familiar and after two years in the two rooms of the cabin with silent Hoof, she can't help but feel good about this. When was the last time she was lost? Her legs feel light on the uneven land, and her headache is gone. Jess runs and runs and runs. There's nothing to stop her.

When they first got out to the country, Jess wanted Hoof to read her stories. She wanted him to talk about them with her. But when she finished something, he'd just nod and set it aside. "Good," he'd say if she asked. Or, "Fine." It wasn't enough. Jess didn't care if he liked them, really, that wasn't what it was about. She just wanted something to start them off, to get things going again like coming home to each other from work did back in the city. So Jess started to write stories about other men. She made them all up, they both knew that, but she gave them to him one after another and watched him read silently, watched that pulse move just under his temple like he was chewing on something hard. The stories weren't any good, even Jess knew that, but something must have been working in them because by the time he finished, Hoof looked nothing but angry. And the next one she gave him would be worse than the last, the woman more Jess, the man less Hoof, and she kept hoping he'd say something maybe, even tell her to stop. But he didn't. And after a while when she gave them to him he'd just put the pages down and pick up a catalogue or a book or his beer. "Hoof," she'd say. "I'll get to it," he'd say. Only he didn't. Hoof stopped reading them and so there was no good reason for Jess to write them.

She's out there in the fields and woods she doesn't know for a long time, and after a bit Jess stops thinking about all the things she thought she knew for certain (the day of the week, the bratwurst Hoof will cook on the grill, the twelve-pack of beer Annie and Jim will bring to dinner, the way Annie will glower at Jim who will look at her like he didn't mean it, whatever he's done this time, the way Hoof won't look at Jess no matter what she says unless he feels he's being challenged, the way the evening will slip into night and they will all drink too much and when she climbs into bed, Hoof will put his back to Jess) and think about what she has yet to find out. How she can find her way back to the cabin. How she can keep on running if she wants. How the land opens up beyond that next stand of trees. How Hoof will or won't cry when she tells him she's leaving.

It's funny how you see some things so clearly in certain moments of your life. The land did open just past that stand of trees like Jess thought it would. And the sun was bright there, yellow and so harsh it made her eyes sting. But just past that is where SuburbLand was built, and then the sight of what she knew made Jess feel bad and good at the same time. She walked down the close and planned streets of the subdivision, and up to Jim and Annie's door. She looked through the little diamond of glass and saw the two of them watching TV on the couch, Jim's head in Annie's lap, Annie's hand in Jim's hair. And instead of knocking, Jess turned around and ran back home along the familiar path.

There at the cabin sat Hoof on the porch, his shirt off, his chest gleaming and wet, the waistband of his shorts dark with sweat. He held out a jug of water, and pulled Jess onto his lap. They sat there and no matter what, she couldn't bring herself to say anything, but then Hoof did. He told her about this deer he came across in the woods.

"Near the lake," he said. "It was little and still had its spots. I almost didn't see her. She was down in the brush."

Jess nodded him on, felt the damp silk of his hair against her cheek.

"I was wishing you were there to see it; I couldn't believe it was letting me get so close. I kept expecting her to jump up, run away. I thought, goddamn! This is really something, me and her. Only..."

And Jess waited, like she'd learned to wait over these last years, for Hoof to either finish or just give up.

"Only when I got right over her, she was dead. It didn't matter how close I got, she was already gone. A hole the size of a quarter under her ear. Her eyes were open, big and bright. Only there were flies. Lots and lots of flies."

He took a long swallow of water. Cool condensation dripped onto Jess's thigh.

"Kids, probably. Kids," Hoof said. "Where were you?" He said, "I didn't know where you were."

"Me either, Jess said. She thought of Hoof on his knees next to the lake, moaning. "Lost, I guess," she said.

They went into the cabin that Hoof built and they showered together and made love before Jim and Annie pulled into the gravel drive.

"You win," Jess told Hoof while they were still on the bed. He nodded. "What do you want?" Jess asked.

"What do you want?" Hoof asked.

He held her gaze like he could, his eyes wide enough to let Jess in. And she thought of what she'd meant to say, what she had decided on the trail.

"A new house," Jess said finally.

Hoof nodded.

"Sure," he said. "I'll build it."

Before Jess could reply, Hoof shifted beside her, gathered her up and tucked himself around her. And under the familiar weight of his muscled arm Jess imagined how it must be for him when the air doesn't come. Even though you can't really see it, you know it's there, right there, all around you. Somehow, you just need to get it. And so you open your mouth and try over and over, but still you just can't do it. It's like this: no matter what you do, no matter how hard you try, you just can't get what you need.

When is a Door Not a Door?

I just supposed it would be a little kid. You know, *baby*sitting? So you can imagine my surprise when the mom opened the door and there was this, well, *young lady* in the shadows behind her.

"Good morning," said Mrs. Emory. She was my mom's boss. My mom got me the job—said it would do me good, said I needed structure. Want to know what I think? This structure thing was more for her than it was for me. Something she needed because of Danny (my brother) and all. Anyway. "Emily," Mrs. Emory said, and crooked her arm around the waist of her daughter to pull her forward. "This is Christy. Christy, Emily."

Emily Emory? Poor kid.

Emily looked me up and down, her wide almond-shaped eyes waggling in her round, flat face. I gave a little wave. "Hi," I said.

"Hi," Emily said. She was at least two inches taller than me (I'm littler than most my age) and probably outweighed me, too.

"Hi," I said again, standing like a dope on the front step, shifting from one foot to the other.

"Hi," Emily said. Her mom smiled at her like she'd just done something wonderful.

I laughed and said "Hi," again, but Emily repeated it solemn as shit and I immediately felt a little sorry I'd started this.

"Well," Mrs. Emory said, and moved to the side enough for me to come in finally. She held her hand out in a sweeping motion, hostess style, and Emily did the same. Only I don't think Emily was joking, and it kind of gave me the creeps.

The living room was like something I'd seen on television, *The Avengers* maybe, or *Love, American Style*. Brass and glass everything. Big, soft leather couches, the color of caramel, and butterscotch shag carpet about two inches long. These people had a bundle. Mrs. Emory dressed like a boss. She wore a skirt and a blouse that I'm pretty positive was silk. It was one of those multi-colored things, something meant to look cool and young, but mostly just looked expensive. She wore her hair short and no-nonsense, all streaked up and sprayed in place. She was old, I couldn't help but notice. Lines stretched across her forehead and in rays around her mouth, and her eyes had a sort of milkiness to them that reminded me of my grandmother. Not that she was that old. But still, Mrs. Emory was pushing sixty, I'd bet, and that made me wonder about Emily.

"How old are you?" I asked Emily as we sat down across from one another in the leather couches. Emily looked at her mom. Mrs. Emory nodded.

"Twelve."

I tried to keep the surprise off my face. This kid was big for twelve. Tall and, well, *developed*. She had these big boobs that were beginning to hang down toward her stomach, and judging from the way her blouse sort of flattened over them. They were not yet holstered by any sort of bra—training or otherwise. And boy, could she have used one.

"How old are you, Christy?" Mrs. Emory asked. Nice as pie, but still I sensed she might have been as freaked as I was at how much bigger Emily was then me, and I can't say why for sure, but that irked me.

"Fifteen," I said and sat up straight. I pushed my chest out some. I had a pretty good set of boobs myself. "Going on sixteen. I'll be a junior."

Mrs. Emory gave me one of those fakey kindergarten teacher grins. "So your mother says." She was still standing in the middle of the room, and I sort of wished she'd either sit down or I hadn't, but there wasn't much I could do about that.

"What grade are you in, Emily?" I asked.

Mrs. Emory put a hand on her daughter's shoulder. Emily looked up at her and then back at me, her wide eyes blinking. "Oh, Emily's not in a grade, exactly. She's at a special school." And the way Mrs. Emory said it, low and whispery, it was like she was revealing some huge secret. And then I began to get what was going on with her, like all of a sudden it got through to me. Emily was—what was the word my mom said about these kinds of kids?—*slow*.

"That's nice, huh?" I said, and my voice got louder, I could tell, and that was stupid because Emily was just slow, not deaf. Still, it was like I couldn't help it. My words just kept on going that way, loud and disconnected. "Special school?" I looked at Emily, she stared back flatly. "Do... you...like...it?" I said, like an asshole. Emily just shrugged. Mrs. Emory's smile stretched a little tight across her teeth.

"Well," she said and patted Emily on the shoulder. "I suppose I should be heading out." But she just stood there, making no move to head out whatsoever. "You girls will get along fine, I'm sure." She kept up the tight smile, but her eyes looked worried. I nodded up and down emphatically.

"We'll be fine. You bet." And I stood up and took a step to where Emily sat all hunched up on the opposite couch. She leaned back with her whole body to look up at me. I put my hand out in her direction, but she just pushed back against the cushions and moved her eyes side to side from me to her mom. I worked to keep my voice normal, not too loud, not too slow. Normal. "Emily? Whaddaya think, huh? We'll be fine?" Emily shrugged and laced her fingers in that way they teach you in school and then turned her hands over to show the flat plane of her palms.

"People?" she asked, and looked up at her mom who I'm pretty sure by now was rethinking this whole babysitting bit. And I'll tell you, that made me sort of steamed. Not like I couldn't handle some twelve-year-old kid. Some twelve-year-old slow kid, for chrissakes.

I sat down on the couch next to Emily, scooted over as close as she would allow me to. Close enough that I could smell her, something like cooked carrots and baby powder and sweaty armpits. "Here," I said and made my hands into the church, fingers tucked down between the knuckles. Emily repeated my moves. Mrs. Emory did it, too. "Here's the church," I said, and then made a point with my index fingers.

Mom and daughter did the same. "Here's the steeple," I said and then turned my hands over slowly. "Open the doors and see all the—"

"People!" Emily said in a booming voice. Mrs. Emory dropped her own church and clapped for us both.

"Yes!" She said and smiled for real this time. "Good job, Emily. Good job, Christy." And you ask me, she was going a little overboard here, you know, gushing. "Oh, yes! You two will get along just great!"

Then she took me on a tour of the house while Emily played the hands game over and over and over again, her voice sing-songy with the rhymes.

"Thanks so much for taking some time off from your summer vacation," Mrs. Emory said as she yanked open the double-wide refrigerator to reveal shelves of Pepsis and Hawaiian Punch and shiny red apples and Tupperware fitted into perfect little stacks with pink, blue, and green covers. "I really, really appreciate it. I wasn't sure what I'd do without a sitter, especially since her last one...." And Mrs. Emory's face went dark in a flash, and sort of mean, really, too, but then just as quick it cleared and she put on what I guessed was one of her boss smiles, you know, shiny and sincere-looking and all. Then she said, "Well, you know what they say—when one door closes...." I nodded, but I had no idea what she was talking about. Mrs. Emory reached for a small plastic square, a sandwich holder, I think, and an apple. She turned to look at me, and I couldn't help but notice under her perfect hair that one of her eyebrows was just a smidgen shorter than the other. "Anyway, thanks again, Christy, really. I mean it.

Sincerely." I nodded and waved it off like it was no big deal, but you know, it kind of was.

We went back into the living room where Emily was still playing church-steeple-people, and Mrs. Emory gave the big girl a kiss on the top of her head. "See you later, sweetie pie, okay?" Emily gave her mother a blank look and shrugged before she turned her attention back to her hands.

At the door Mrs. Emory said, "Thanks again, Christy, dear." I hate it when someone you don't even know calls you dear. Unless it's a cute guy or something. We shook hands and I started to push the door close between us when Mrs. Emory grabbed my hand in hers again. "And Christy? Dear?"

I made myself smile. "Yes? Ma'am?"

"I'm sorry about your brother," she said and held onto me. I looked at the mat beneath her feet. *Emory* swirled in silver cursive over a background of royal blue and a yellow so bright it made my eyes smart. I blinked and nodded, not willing to look up. "I mean," she said, and then stopped. "Well, anyway. I'm sorry."

"Yeah," I said and shook off her grip.

Man, why'd she have to go and say that?

I'm not sure how the news came, but I picture the words in little dark lines on the slip of a telegram. Something like "We regret to inform you" and "missing in action" I'm thinking. All I know for sure is that when I got home from school that day two weeks ago, the last day of classes, Mom's car was already in the driveway. It scared me, her car there like it never was before five, and I ran all the way from the corner to the front door. There Mom was waiting for me, just standing in the foyer, arms at her sides. And when I came in, she tilted my head back and looked into my eyes. "Cee," she whispered—it's what she calls me when it's just us—and then she got this really weird face, like her features were melting. It was so, I don't know, *extreme,* that at first I thought she must be making some sort of joke. But just as I was about to smile a little, to push her hands away from my face, she slid all the way down my body, folded up and into herself until she came to rest in a pool at my feet. When I got past the whole freakiness of the thing, I knelt down there next to her, and we hugged each other and even though I had no idea what was up (okay, I had an idea, you couldn't know anyone over there in that stupid war and not carry around these ideas) I started to cry and Mom was crying and we both hugged and cried and that's when she told me. And we just stayed there, down on the cold tile of the foyer, tangled up together and crying.

And since then, we hardly ever talked about it.

Emily had a roomful of toys, little kids' things, mostly, but very expensive shit. I'd watch her in there, surrounded by all those huge stuffed animals and a pastel painted dollhouse big enough to sit inside and Raggedy Anns and Andys with their own wooden rockers and a whole shelf of Barbies and some electronic gizmos that made farm sounds or flashed lights or rolled around the room with the touch of a button—and she'd just sit there on her bed with its perfect pink gingham spread and fluffy pillows and she'd play church-steeple-people. I mean, where's the sense in that? It sort of got to me, only I'm not entirely sure why. I mean, I was mad, see, but I wasn't sure if I was mad about the toys or about her not playing with them or what exactly. I plopped down on the bed next to her and put my feet up on her headboard. She slid a little closer to the footboard.

"Emily," I said. I pulled a piece of Bazooka from my pocket, crumpled up the wrapper and the joke without even reading it. They were all the same. Emily fiddled with her fingers, but kept quiet and watched me while I chewed. "You know what, Emily?" I said. She shrugged. "I'm bored."

"Want to see my panties?" Emily said. I about choked.

"Excuse me?"

"Want to see my panties?" She had one of those low, precise voices, you know, hitting the t's and p's hard. Emily stood up and started to yank on the sides of her yellow cotton trousers and I could see a red line where the elastic waistband had dug into her pudgy white belly and I sat up quick and put my hands on hers.

"No, Emily."

She let go of her pants and let her arms hang loose. Her thin little eyebrows pulled all down and scrunched. "No?" She said.

"No," I said. "No. Thanks, though," I added. To be polite. "Hey, you know what let's do?" I said after maybe a million years of silence in that toy-stuffed room. "Let's go to the park. Okay? Would you like that, Emily?"

She shrugged.

•

Emily walked slowly past the houses that were big but pretty much the same, stopping to look at everything: a smooshed worm on the sidewalk; the Mexicans mowing the lawns; an old guy with a wild ring of white hair around his spotted old head coming down his driveway toward his mailbox (he paused midway and stared back at Emily like they were playing lookaway or whatever you call it, until I took her hand and gently tugged her along); a tiny egg lying in the grass, blue and perfect except for one end that was cracked open. I couldn't blame her on that one, it was pretty cool, and we picked it up and looked into its hollow insides and then she asked could she keep it and I said sure. But when she cradled it in her hand I couldn't help but remember that time when Danny and I found a whole nest, eggs and all, under the big maple in our front yard. And Danny—being the kind of person he is, better than most—got this idea. And I stood there waiting for him to climb up the ladder and place the nest back in the tree, and I handed the eggs up one after another, gentle as can be, and the next day we found the nest on the ground again only then the eggs were all broken and empty and Danny said "Shit" for the first time and we laughed at the word even though it was really sad about the eggs.

Emily was stopped again, kicking at something I couldn't see on the sidewalk.

"Come on, damnit," and I pulled her hand and felt the weight of her body resist me before she followed. But I kept on walking. I wasn't about to look at her round, stupid, hurt eyes.

When is a Door Not a Door?

The houses around the park were the same colors (brown, mustard, beige) as the other ones in the subdivision, but were huge, big enough to hold millions of people each. And it was one of those perfect days, all sun but not too much heat, and dry. Still, with all those big houses and all that sun, the park itself was empty. I figured it must have been that everyone around here was on vacation, or maybe the kids were at camp (like all of my so-called friends were) or already grown or something. Anyway, it kind of gave me the creeps. To top that off, Emily was sulking and didn't want to go on any of the rides or anything, even though they were some of the coolest I've seen, all done in wood and rope so they sort of blended in with the park itself. There was this set of swings like nothing I'd ever been on, old tires and rope ladders and a huge rope web stretched millions of feet between a couple of big, fat, wooden stumps like a giant hammock. I was hoping maybe Emily would like to crawl around on that one, because I sort of wanted to, but she didn't. She just sat on a bench whispering "open the doors" over and over and stared hard into the blue egg, mashing it up against her eye enough so that it started to crack a little more around its opening. I suppose I could have played on the park stuff by myself, but I was fifteen, after all, and it would be more than a little babyish. I just sat there with her, looking around and preparing myself for more boredom. I opened another piece of Bazooka, but before I could toss the comic, Emily reached for it.

"Read," she said.

"Sure." Something to do at least. "'Hey, Joe!'" I read, and Emily had her big head tipped down over the little square of drawings and I could smell the shadowy stink of her dirty hair. I went on, really working it for some reason, making voices and stuff. "'When is a door not a door?'...'I don't know, when is a door not a door?'...'When it's ajar.'" I handed the comic over to Emily who studied the pictures for a whole minute, and then looked at me and opened her mouth and laughed one big "HA!" Then she said, "More."

So I pulled out another piece, only this time I handed the gum to her. She held it up to her nose and took a couple of big whiffs before she shoved it into her mouth, chewed once, twice, with her mouth open, then swallowed the stuff down. "Read," she said.

"'Did you hear the Mexican weather report?'" I read from the first panel. The bright sound of ice cream bells came from around the corner. I looked across the park for the familiar white truck.

"Read," Emily said again.

"Chili today and hot tamale," I recited without looking and handed the comic over to her. She studied it the same as before and then "HA!" She folded it into a tiny square and stuffed it into her fist with the other one and the egg that was more broken shell now than anything. "More," she said.

"All right," I said, "but this is my last piece. Why don't you chew it for a while this time," I suggested. But of course, Emily swallowed the gum down again, and to tell you the truth, I couldn't really blame her. I've done the same myself millions of times. The ice cream truck circled the park slowly.

"Whaddaya say, Emily? Ice cream?"

She looked at me and then at her watch, which was not real, see, but a toy one with a picture of

Barbie's face and painted-on hands that pointed to the twelve and six. She shrugged.

"Yeah, it's early, I know," not quite eleven, but I was hungry and in charge. "Tell you what, let's have ice cream now, and then we'll go back to your house and have peanut butter sandwiches for dessert. All right?"

That damn shrug.

I left Emily on the bench and went to wave the truck down.

"What'll it be, Smiley?"

He was the cutest guy I had ever seen in my whole entire life. Sandy gold hair, sort of long, and these freaky eyes. Greenish, but blue, too. He wore this bright white T-shirt and these tight white jeans, and he stood behind the wide serving window with his hands reached up high and holding onto something, his whole body stretched long. Man, the sight of him made my mouth water. Really.

"Uh," I said, and stared at the thousands of pictures on the side of the truck like I hadn't seen them a million times and like I wasn't going to order the same thing I always did. "Hmm," I said.

"That your mom?" the guy asked. And I turned around startled for a second, like maybe Mom had snuck up on me like she'd done more than once when I've had guys over and we're down in the rec room messing around, like how I caught her that time looking in my drawers—good thing I'd shoved the rubbers down into the toe of one of my old rubber boots. But the guy was looking at Emily. And from the back, you could tell why he might've thought that, her being so womanly and sitting all hunched over like she does and wearing these yellow cotton trousers and white blouse like a mom would.

"Nah," I said, and then, don't ask me why, "she's my sister."

"Your sister?" And his eyes sort of lit up. "Older sister?" He was probably twenty, I figured, old as Danny the last time I saw him, but the way I figured it, not too old for me, so his acting that way, all interested in my older sister, sort of pissed me off.

"No," I said. "Younger."

"Younger?" He let out a low whistle, his teeth glinting just a bit between his lips. "Man," he said, "she's big."

"She's slow," I said. Like maybe that would explain it. "Okay, I know what I want."

The ice cream guy leaned way over into the cooler to get my order, and I got a good eyeful of his butt, nice and round and hard.

"Seventy cents," he said when he was upright again.

I fished three quarters out from my back pocket. "Keep the change," I said, kidding, only he nodded and winked at me.

"Thanks, Smiley." Pretty funny how he kept calling me that. The thing is, I'm really not much of a smiler, as you might imagine. Still, I put on a big one for him when he passed the ice cream to me. "Here you go. One for Smiley, and one for Smiley's sister."

"Emily," I called back to the bench. Emily got up slowly and, holding her fistful of comics and eggshell out in front of her, walked over to us. If she had been my real sister, I think maybe I'd be embarrassed about this time, you know, feeling like the ice cream guy might wonder if whatever was wrong with Emily could be wrong with me, too. But since she wasn't my sister, and I didn't really feel embarrassed or anything, I watched for his reaction. I could see his eyes widen as she came at us, all that loose boob flesh just rolling under Emily's blouse. I tossed my hair a little and arched my back to push up my own chest and decided that tomorrow Smiley was going without a bra.

"Hi, Emily," the guy said when she got close. "I'm Sky." Great name. Perfect.

Emily dropped her chin down and stared at the ground. "She's a little shy, Sky," I said, and "She's scared of boys."

Emily began eating the ice cream bar, taking big bites out of first one side, then the other. She stood a yard or so from us, holding one of the comics open and she mouthed different words between bites. "Hot tamale, when is a door, it's ajar, knock knock."

"She can read, it looks like," Sky said, and then he glanced at his watch and climbed back into the driver's seat. "Gotta go," he said, and ran his hand back through all of that golden hair of his.

"Sure," I said.

"See you, Emily," Sky called over my head. He shifted into go gear. The truck lurched a bit. "See you—hey," he said just as he started to pull away, "what's your name, Smiley?"

"Christy," I said. And then, easy as pie, "Christy Emory." And I sort of even liked the way it sounded.

•

Back at the house we had peanut butter sandwiches like I had promised, and we ate them on the leather couches. Emily hadn't liked the idea at first. "Uh uh, no eating," she'd said even as she trotted after me into the caramel and butterscotch room. "Uh huh," I'd said and laid the plates and napkins out like a picnic, popped open two sweating bottles of Pepsi. The leather squeaked under our butts, and whenever I moved Emily laughed "HA!" and said, "Excuse you!" To tell the truth, it was kind of funny at first, but it got old pretty quick. When we finished, Emily stood up and brushed her hands together and said "Nap time," which seemed like an excellent idea, and before I could even get up and clear away our things, she was down the hall and in her room and closing the door behind herself.

I wandered around the house opening closets and drawers, rummaging through Mrs. Emory's thousands of silk scarves, through her nightgowns which were for the most part flannel and not at all sexy. Mr. Emory was a mystery to me. I'd never seen him, never even heard Mom talk about him. Not like she would or anything (she didn't even talk about her own husband—ex—the guy who was my father that I only knew by Christmas and birthday cards that came postmarked from Alaska) but still. So I searched around for the signs of Mr. Emory, and in the back of the closet of what I figured for his study (heavy wooden paneling, fat leather-bound books, the hugest desk I'd ever seen) I found a little safe that had been left open (what's the point?) and there were dozens of those little folders of coins, round circles cut into the pages where you could stuff a dime, nickel, half-dollar or whatever above the gold-lettered name and date label. There were coins from as far back as before the turn of the century. I flipped through until I found the year I was born, 1956, but that page was empty. Matter of fact, the coins were all from before 1950 (when Danny was born) and I'd be lying if I said that didn't tick me off. Like whatever happened after that wasn't important enough to hold onto.

I sat there inside the closet in front of that stupid safe with the little book open on my lap, steaming. I wanted to do something, to make a statement, only I wasn't sure what that should be. I could've stolen some of the coins, shit, I could've stolen the whole lot of them. The only thing is, I may be a liar (and more than a few other not so great things) but one thing I never have been is a thief. So instead I searched my pockets for whatever coins I had, scanned them for the dates. There was one from 1959, but other than that they were all from the sixties. Shit. Still, I flipped back through the pages to the year Danny was born and put the shiniest quarter I had in that slot. In my year I put a nickel. And I thought about putting one in this year, 1971, to mark the news about my brother, but I decided against it. For some reason that seemed better left untouched.

At dinner that night Mom asked me how my day was. Only when I answered her, told her about Emily and her slow self and her wanting to show me her underpants and all the big bucks things the Emorys had, well, I could tell she wasn't really listening. We were having macaroni and cheese, one of the dishes I can really make well (just follow the box and add a bunch of parmesan) and Mom hadn't even bothered to put any on her plate. Instead she had a glass full of bourbon and a cigarette, and the whole time I talked, she sort of nodded and all, like she was paying attention, but her eyes were fixed on the six-inch Sony with the sound down, where the goddamn evening news had the bad taste to be showing film from the war like it was appropriate dinner entertainment. And even though it was in black and white, it still looked horrible, sickening, bloody and evil, and it was nearly enough to make a girl lose her appetite and I couldn't figure out why Mom would want to see that, but she did. She moved her face forward, pulled the little TV box by its handle even closer, nearly pressed her nose up against it. She squinted.

"Christy, look!" She said and sat back just an inch, moved her big head out of the way. She poked a finger up against the screen, and its cigarette-stained tip looked yellow and fake next to the stark black-and-white flat reality of some passed-out bloody guy on a stretcher, one leg shy. "Is it him?" Mom asked, her voice tight and squeaky. The soldier was big and dark-haired; we are all small and light. "Oh God, oh God. I can't bear to look. Cee? Cee?" But she was looking the whole time, her eyes glued on the moving picture of someone else's son. "Cee? Cee?"

And it killed me to say it, but I did. "No, Mom, it's not him."

The bloody black-and-white picture switched to a close-up of a big, greasy plate of fried chicken, and Mom poured herself another three fingers and sat up straight and wiped her face with both hands. When she looked at me, it was like she could barely stand the sight of me. Like she hated me. "You don't know," she said so low it was hard to even hear. "It could've been him." And she might as well have spit razor blades at me, it felt just exactly like that. She lit a new cigarette off the one that was still burning. She ground the old one hard into her empty plate. "You don't know." She stared out through the sheer yellow kitchen curtains toward the driveway.

I stood up, my entire insides pushing against my skin, hard and thick like the knot you get in your throat that means you're going to cry.

"You gonna have any of this?" I asked, looking down into the pot of rubbery orange noodles.

And when she didn't even bother to look at me, much less answer even a "hell no" or anything, I dumped the whole mess into the roar of the garbage disposal.

My mom was always doing things like that, trying to see things that weren't there. Me, on the other hand, I'd try to *not* see the things that really *were* there. Like the time a couple weeks later when Sky and me are rolling around in the rope web at the park, making out like crazy (we'd tried talking the first few days, I can't even remember about what, but finally figured out we were better at this) and Emily comes back from a trip to the public john, shuffling over to us with her pants, undies and all, down around her ankles. Sky stops short, pulls his tongue out of my ear and gives a low whistle. When I see what he's looking at—Emily half-naked and flawless and so unexpectedly beautiful it makes my gut ache—at first I bury my head in his chest and try to wish the picture away, but from this angle I can see the bulge under his zipper and can hear his breath speed up and I know it's not going away. So I swing down off the web and tell him not to look while I pull Emily back together, cover up her smooth, white legs, her round, sloped hips, her silky, golden triangle. "Here, let me help," I say, and Emily tries to explain: "I got stuck." But I don't really care what happened, I just want to not see how perfect she is anymore.

And later that day I doze off in Mr. Emory's study during naptime, and I dream a little about Danny, I think, and then I wake up and Emily is above me, shaking me. And her fingers are like claws in my shoulder, her face looms over mine, her eyes shining and hard as marbles. I come to pretty fast, but not fast enough I guess, because she begins to pull me off the couch, and there's nothing I can do to stop that, her being so much bigger and stronger than me.

"Emily, man, cool it," I say and try to right myself, try to shake loose of her grip, try to sit up before I land on the floor. But she has me. And the wind's knocked out of me as I hit ground, and I lay there for a second, trying to breathe, and then she kneels on my chest—which doesn't help the breathing one bit—and starts to shake me some more, her whole face hard and mean and tight and I can't help but think how she looks like her mother. She says something quiet, like she's trying the word out, but I think I hear it anyway: "Slut." My head begins to bounce on the floor, and I know that if she wants to, she can really, really hurt me. My mind goes into overdrive and I pull a wrestling move Danny taught me, and then I'm on top of her and before I can even think about it, I'm slapping her, once, twice, across the face. And her mean, tight look just slides away, and it's blank-faced, slow Emily down there now, only her eyes fill up, and she looks at me with such flat calmness—even as the tears run over and down the sides of her cheeks and fill her ears—that I swear I feel my heart just crack wide open, and I stand up and walk over to the window and look out onto the perfect rows of Mrs. Emory's flower garden. Only I can't see the plants, all I can see is Emily's face. Emily's round, flat, drenched face. Shit.

And then a few days later I'm outside the Emorys' house, on my way home but I'd brought my backpack and forgotten it in the living room, so I turn back to the front door and reach to push the bell. But before I do, I raise up on my toes and look inside the little diamond-shaped window and can see into the caramel and butterscotch room, and there's my backpack on the couch and there's Emily and her mother. But Emily's sort of slumped over, shoulders forward, and Mrs. Emory is trying to lift her daughter's chin, but Emily keeps dropping it down, tucking it into her chest. And I remember how the week before I'd tied this handmade choker around Emily's thick neck, how when we stood next to each other and looked at our reflection in the mirror I couldn't help but see that she was nearly a head taller than me. It was like a picture out of one of her kiddy books: the small, smart human person next to the big, dumb, not-quite-human giant. And even as I'd thought that, I'd hated myself for it. But now I see Mrs. Emory use one hand to push against Emily's forehead, and the other to swipe the string of beads off the girl's neck. Beads fly everywhere, catching the light before they fall, and Mrs. Emory is screaming, I can tell by her face, and I can hear some of it, "...slut...dirty...not my..." and Emily gives her that same flat, calm look she gave me that time in her father's study, and I can't see this for sure, but I'd bet she's crying. I wish then that I was a better person. Because a better person would go back in there. A better person would do something. Danny would do something. And then Mrs. Emory says something else and Emily pulls down her trousers and that's when I have to leave, I have to get out of there even though there's nowhere for me to go but home.

And since I don't have my keys, I'm going to have to ring the bell, and I don't want to because every time the doorbell rings in our house lately, we both freeze, me and Mom, afraid of what's out there, of all those things we don't yet know. So I pace the front walk for a bit, hoping Mom will see me out here and will open the door, will be glad I didn't ring, will be glad it's me this time. But pretty soon I figured I've walked a hundred miles up and down in front of our house, so I go over to the kitchen window and look in. And there's Mom in her usual place at the kitchen table behind a full, smoking ashtray and a glass of booze, only her head is down and she is sobbing so hard her shoulders lift and lower and her whole body shakes. I look around to see if maybe there's another one of those yellow pieces of telegram paper only there's nothing but her and the smokes and the whiskey and that damned Sony TV. My gut feels empty and my head feels full, and I don't know why but it's like I'm looking through these super strength glasses or something. Every line is straight, every angle sharp, every color vivid as hell. And I can see everything, more than just my mom, my house, my kitchen. Everything. Like: there's Emily, sent to her room where she sits and plays church-steeple-people a few times, then takes stock of her little inventory of Bazooka comics, eggshell, ice cream sticks, and a couple beads she pinched from the floor when her mother turned her back. There's Mr. Emory (even though I don't know what he looks like) in his study, smoking a pipe and flipping a corduroy slipper on the end of his big toe, leafing through his books of coins, humphing over the shiny newer quarter and nickel. There's my dad (even though I only sort of know what he looks like) in plaid flannel and work boots, chopping down a huge tree all by himself under what I figure to be the goddamn Aurora Borealis. And there's Sky, restocking the freezers and counting out his bank, slipping a couple of bucks into the tight pocket of his white jeans like I've seen him do before when he didn't know I was watching. And finally there's Danny, far, far away and face down in a nest of weeds and sticks. And I can see—even though it will be months and months before we find this out— I can see sure as shit that Danny is dead.

Now this is stupid, but when the doorbell rang and I looked through the window and I saw the back of that head with that sandy hair, for a second, just a second, I believed in my soul it was Danny. I flung open the door. Sky stood on the stoop, his hair streaming with rain.

"How'd you find me?" I said when I could.

Sky pointed down to the silver letters on the welcome mat. "Your name," he said. And by the time he added, "The only Emory in the book," I remembered that he thought I was Emily's sister, that he now thought I lived here in this big house. I knew better than to let him come in, but that didn't keep me from stepping aside so he could. The electricity was out from the storm, the foyer was dark. Sky gave one of his low whistles when he saw the plush living room, candles everywhere. He winked at me. "Beautiful *and* rich, babe," he said. "Anything else you're keeping from me?" I thought about everything Sky didn't know about me, which was just that—everything. I thought about how I never told him anything and how, too, he never bothered to ask.

Emily slinked around at the end of the hallway, keeping close to the wall.

"It's just Sky," I said. "You know, Sky?" He waved and Emily turned her face away, pressed her nose up against the wall like kids sometimes do when they're shy all of a sudden. "Get us a towel?" I asked her, and she skittered past toward the bathroom, the back of her head to us.

"I figured I wasn't gonna sell a lot of ice cream in this weather," Sky said.

It had been raining all morning, no thunder or anything, just the heavy downpour. Emily had been nervous all morning, too. And scared, I could tell, she wasn't willing to let me out of her sight. The three of us sat in the living room, Sky on the big leather chair I figured was reserved for Mr. Emory, since I'd never seen Emily or her mom sit there and since Emily kept giving him some sort of evil eye—or at least the best she could come up with. We sucked on Pepsis in the candle glow. None of us said anything for a long time.

"Ask Emily what's the Mexican weather report," I said, finally, when the quiet got to be too much.

"Emily," Sky said, playing it up like it really was important to him, "what's the Mexican weather report?"

"Chili today and hot tamale," she said, like she knew the words by heart but they were some foreign language and she had no idea what they meant.

Sky laughed, a big, loud, phony laugh, and Emily slid deeper into her place on the couch, wrapped her arms around herself. Rain splattered against the windows.

"Maybe it's time for a nap, Emily," I said. She nodded a little like she does when I tell her something she wants to believe—like it's okay to have ice cream before lunch—only she's not sure I've got the proper authority. I took her arm and walked her down the hall and got her laid out on her fluffy pink bed with her comics and eggshell and ice cream sticks and beads all within reach on the pillow next to her, and went back to Sky in the living room.

Only Sky's not there. I get a little nervous, but only for a second, because his truck's still out front so I know he's not really missing.

When I find him, it's in Mr. Emory's study and he's got the silver candle holder down on the floor with a single candle and the way he's sitting there all cross-legged and his hair spilling over his sweet, sweet face, well my breath stops up short in my chest and I have to stand in the doorway for just a bit, hold onto the doorknob until the rubber in my legs solids itself up enough for me to walk normal, to pull the door almost closed and then to ease down on the rug next to him, to let him pull me in, kiss me, unbutton my blouse, and so on. And when we're down there on old Mr. Emory's rug, you know, just where I suppose I'd been longing to be all summer and I'm thinking this is it, this is it—and of course it is because we're both pretty much naked and we're kissing and all and it feels just like it's supposed to, skin on skin. It's raining hard now, the windows rattling and there's thunder now, too, only far, far away. And I think "flood" for some reason, just like that, the word, I mean, and then Sky turns me over, and it's like I'm floating the way he moves me, easy as that. And as I'm turning—my face away from his, him kissing my neck, my back—I'm thinking, yes, yes, right, right. But then I notice how the closet door is open and behind that, the safe, and I can't help but hope that Sky doesn't see it, but it's like he's oblivious, and then he jams into me and it hurts. Then I'm thinking this *isn't* right, this *isn't* what I wanted—but it is, you know, him inside of me and all, filling up what's empty. Still, I scootch up on all fours, pull away a little, and then it's like he's getting his balance, getting grounded, because he pushes my shoulders down onto the floor and I'm down there like that, ass high and my shoulders, my chest, my neck and everything are raw, rug burned, and it's like rubbing up against sandpaper, and it hurts, every bit of it, front and back, it all hurts. My nose starts to run, and I fumble around to wipe it with the back of my hand and I'm crying a little, too. Still, I pretend like I'm digging it, wanting it to be over more than anything. Sky is back there pounding and pulling on me and when I hear Emily it's sort of muffled at first, and I suppose that maybe I thought she was still down there in her room, doing church-steeple-people or maybe reading her comics, but then it gets louder and then loud enough over all of our body slapping and Sky grunting that I know even before I turn around but can't quite see from there, even before I lift up and look down and through the mess of our bodies, through my legs, then his, I know that Emily is there at the door. And she is, of course, eyes wide and mouth moving, but then she's gone, and the front door opens and slams and even though the thunder has stopped, it's pouring out there so what else can I do but go myself. I pull away from Sky and his face is priceless, skin like milk and blue-green eyes dark as stones and beautiful. He looks surprised.

"Emily," I mumble and roll away and pull into my clothes and he's all the while still there on his knees and naked.

"What the fuck," he says. He's mad now, and not like I blame him, but still. And I can see him eyeballing the safe there in the closet, but I can't be bothered with that. I know what's going to happen, but it's like a force set into motion that can't be stopped. "Go ahead," I want to say, but whatever I say can't possibly make any difference.

•

I know where to go to find Emily. I run to the park, the big houses a beige wet blur around me, my bare feet smacking the sidewalk, smooshing worms all the way. "Emily," I say, but I don't yell it. The rain is letting up now, and if I'd look, there might even be a patch of blue in the dark. But that's not what I'm looking for.

When I find Emily she's soaked through and tangled up in the big web, legs and hands sticking through the openings, face mashed against the ropes. When she sees me, her eyes get bright and it's like she's already forgotten what just happened.

"Emily," I say. She smiles a little, only her lips are pressed almost shut because of how tangled she is.

"Got stuck," she says through her clenched mouth.

"Yeah," I say. My chest aches, from the running I'd like to think, but I know that's not it.

I pull this way and that and an arm comes loose, then a leg.

"Helping me," Emily says.

I nod, but of course I'm lying. See, even as I start to unwind the crisscross of netting, I know that I can't help her. Not really. And the more I tug, the more she gets free and then she's laughing. It's a real laugh this time, a big old belly laugh, low and full. So there's Emily in the air, caught up in the web, and here's me on the ground with my toes in the mud and she's laughing and—what do you think?—I'm laughing, too. I'm laughing so hard my eyes are streaming, my whole damn body is shaking. It's funny, don't you think? Goddamn hilarious how

When is a Door Not a Door?

Emily, sweet, slow, laughing Emily thinks *I* can help *her.* But me—small, smart, human person—I know the truth. And the truth is—now it kills me to tell you this—the truth is, I'm absolutely no help at all.

As Far as I Get

One of those Tuesday evenings when the air through the car window feels like something worth remembering, like the memory will be even better than the now. And here's me coming back from a little fishing on the river. Day off. Night, too. Summertime. I'm thinking New Hope can do without me for a few hours, and I needed to be alone for a while. Only that's part of my problem, being alone. Ellie's been gone three weeks. My Faith, too.

   Nothing much biting, though, so I'm on my way home and my creel's empty, my stomach, my gas tank. Pull into the Stop & Go, and I'm filling up and there's a car in the lot I know. Edith's. And there in the passenger seat is her daughter, Nova. Still light out, the days are so damn long now, and inside the store is brighter still. Through the shop window I can see Edith in the aisles, at the counter. She puts down a box of cereal, a can of something. I can see Mrs. Martinez who's always there and polite as can be at the till. She's dusting or something, like she does. *Got time to lean, got time to clean,* she said to me one time when I said *Why're you always working so hard?* Small talk. Edith slides her hand down the racks beneath where the register is. I can see this now, because I'm looking. I'm watching. Nova is, too, it looks like from where I am. Edith rests her hand for a minute on the Lifesavers. Puts her hand in her pocket. On the candy bars. Pocket. Mrs. Martinez is ringing her up and Edith's smiling. And anyone who knows Edith at all knows she doesn't smile much. Not since Nova's dad left some years ago, not since her boy Sky did a few years after.

Am I a cop now? My day off. Am I a neighbor? Am I a friend? Am I just a guy? Filling my tank? Minding my business? Edith steps toward the door and Mrs. Martinez turns to watch her go, hands on her hips. She looks through the window at me, shakes her head and raises her eyebrows. It's like she's asking me something.

"Edith," I call as she walks outside. I slide the nozzle back into its holster. Click the pump off. It's like she's in a cloud or something, a soft place, because when she looks up she only just sees me, the cruiser. I use it as my own car, just in case. To save money, truthfully, but yeah, sure, just in case. Edith blinks like she's coming out of a dream. Her face goes soft to sharp, happy to something else. Like it's morning too soon. Like the dream was too good.

"Hey, Sheriff," she calls back. She's tossed the bag with the can, the cereal, through the driver's side window. Edith's hand's on the door handle, she's pulling it up. I start to move toward her. Nova is watching us now. Her mom. Me. Mom. Me. "Good to see you," Edith says. And I hear that tight thing in her voice I know is guilt. I hear it all the time. Drunk drivers. Domestics. Check kiters. Kids with grass in their pockets, spray paint on their fingers. Boys with bloody noses who say they weren't fighting, just fooling around. "In a hurry," Edith says. "Dinner-time," she says.

"Wait up," I say. It's just a couple steps over the parking lot to her. But Nova's window's rolled down too, and I'm thinking that maybe she doesn't need to hear us. Maybe she already knows. Like Mrs. Martinez knows, I can tell from the way she watches us through the storefront window, the way she looks kind of sad. But Nova? Maybe she doesn't need to know I know.

I wave Edith over. And I am Sheriff, right? Not just my job, but what everybody calls me; it went from "He's the sheriff" to "He's Sheriff." Seems like I've been Sheriff longer than I was ever Steve. Despite her old lady name, Edith, she's young, sort of. Even though she's a mother. Even though she had a husband. Something in her, about her, always looks girlish. Like my Faith when she used to dress up in Ellie's clothes. Edith scans the parking lot, but it's just us there. She walks to where I'm standing by the pumps still.

"Summer, finally," she says, that small-town small talk. Ellie would always say that when they start to talk about the weather, it is time for us to go. Say goodbye. Barbeques. Birthday parties. To me, though, when the talk turned small, it usually meant there was something not being said. It meant I had to listen harder.

"Yes," I say. "School's out now, right? You two getting a little mother-daughter time? You and Nova?" And what kind of name is Nova anyways? Nova and Sky, Edith called those kids. Her own name so heavy, maybe, so down to earth. I'm smiling at

Nova turned around in the front seat, watching, watching.

Edith knows what I'm saying even though I'm not saying it yet. Reminding her. You're the mother, I'm saying. You are the goddamn adult. She gets it, she does. She's nodding. We don't say anything at all for a while, but Edith doesn't look away. Like I say, she gets it.

"You be careful," I say. My day off, after all. What am I going to do? Put her in the cruiser? Take her to holding? "Nova," I say, and tilt my head toward the girl.

I was the one who picked Faith's name. Ellie laughed at me. "Faith? Why not Hope? Like this goddamn town?" She wasn't from here, Ellie. We met in community college over near the river. I wasn't Sheriff then. Just Steve. Steve and Ellie, and then: "Because she gives me faith," I said to Ellie when we made our lists of names. Just one on mine. And when that little girl was born, Ellie couldn't argue. That's what Faith looks like.

Edith keeps nodding and she's frowning so hard her young skin looks old, cracking. I'm thinking she might cry. "Yes, Sheriff," she says finally. "You're right. Thank you." She stands still with her hands in her pockets, fists around the goods, probably. But she's not going to move until I do. So I do. "Good," I say. And I nod, too, and head toward the shop to pay for my gas, get a bag of chips, a sandwich from the cold shelf. When I pass the car, Nova's still watching me, her face a mask. The one teenagers wear. The one I've seen on her before when I'm asking what happened that night her brother nearly killed his best friend in a fight. The one she pretty much wears all the time since her dad disappeared, since Sky took off.

The one, I swear to God, I've seen Faith, my ten-year-old Faith, practice in a mirror.

"Nova," I say through the window. Like hello. Mask. I open the door to the shop. Behind me I hear Edith get into the car. Mrs. Martinez is there at the till, looking at me like she wants something. "My day off," I say and shrug. I hear Edith's engine start. I put some money on the counter for my gas, my chips, my sandwich. I put down some more for what I know Edith still has in her pockets.

Outside I watch her pull out of the lot. She goes real slow.

Careful now.

Back at the courthouse I'm checking in on things instead of going right home. There's nothing to check on, really. But still.

Before I'd gone out to the river that morning, I saw Pastor James at the diner when I stopped for coffee, toast. Was a time when Ellie made me big breakfasts, bacon, eggs, jelly, orange juice. "Need your strength," she used to say, "all that sheriffing. The Sheriff of No Hope." I used to laugh at that, the way she twisted the town name: New Hope, No Hope. But then Faith got to calling it that, too, and well, I'd be lying if I said it didn't sting a little. I grew up here. I wanted my daughter to grow up here. Ellie never said it outright, but she hated my job. She hated the town. The people full of religion and little else, the lack of curiosity, the boredom. The kids with nothing to do but cause trouble.

Her breakfasts, though, that was love, I've got to believe. But that was a while ago. These days when I wake up and she's not in bed next to me, I keep hoping maybe she's in the kitchen. Cooking. Listening to the radio. Humming along. Sometimes I think I can hear her. But now every morning at the diner I take my coffee black, my toast dry. Kind of like a penance.

"Steve. Friend," James said. Even though we were never that. Acquaintances, I'd say. More like. But this morning maybe he could see something I was trying not to show. He sat on the stool beside me at the counter, twisted the newspaper in his hands into a tube, told me about that Men's Group meeting in the evening. "Join us," he said.

"We'll see," I said. Thinking, no, not my thing. "Thanks," I said.

But after fishing I find myself at my desk. Puttering. Shuffling papers. Not wanting to go home. Big house. Empty. I'm leaning toward Supples Tavern, I can feel that. The great thirst that hits me now and again, especially since I've been alone. But not just since. The great thirst was another reason Ellie and Faith left. I was never a mean drinker, but a sad one. And the sad hung on sometimes for days. Ellie'd stood it long as she could.

"It's not good for Faith," she said, packing her things, our daughter's. School'd just let out for summer. This packing wasn't a surprise. Nor the leaving. She'd been saying it for a while.

And it's three weeks later and here's me trying not to go home and I'm trying not to go to Supples. I step out on the stoop of the courthouse and watch the parking lot empty. Clerks, the judge, clerical staff, going home to their families, dinner on the table. Smell the charcoal starting up here and there, hear the cicadas. A few cars moving up Hill Street and turning on to Market. Couples, parents and kids, going into the Inn for ribs and salad bar, the diner for a BLT, maybe Supples for a cold one and some chili.

Lately I'd been noticing through the window at the Inn, in a booth at the diner, over at the Sub Shack on the highway, an old guy by himself. Not the same old guy, but one guy same as the others. Sitting and staring over his sub, his plate full of ribs, his BLT, at some spot in front of him. Chewing slow. Making this out-of-the-house thing last. God, seeing this guy, each of these guys, was like a knife in my gut. Their loneliness came off them like stink. And sometimes I'd stop by, say hello. *Tom, how's it going? Earl, how're things?* And when they looked at me, breaking their stare away from the nothing, I could see the relief wash up in their eyes. But it was like they'd forgotten how to be with people. They'd been alone too long. Wife died. Kids gone. Nothing but this sandwich to get them out of the house. They'd make something like a smile and answer with one word. Maybe two. And it was so damn hard to hold things up on my side alone, I'd move on quick. Feeling sorry for them. Feeling sorry for me. What's that saying? There but for the grace...

So when I see James get into his old wreck of a car in front of the door to his apartment over the Inn, I make my mind up. He's heading to the meeting. And it feels like maybe this Men's Group is the only thing can keep me out of Supples this night. Maybe if things go good, keep me out other nights, too.

I get in the cruiser and follow him.

The meeting starts as I expect. James up front, welcoming us all. Me especially. New guy. That's embarrassing. Never one much for being called attention to. There's a prayer then, and not being religious, I don't bow my head. Don't close my eyes. And I'm not the only one. Some do. Believers, I suppose. But a handful look around, fidget, wait that part out. "Amen," we all say though, when it comes to that.

We sit down, eight, ten of us. The Church of New Hope is just a couple rooms, and Men's Group meets in the Sunday School room. Guess it wouldn't be right to use the main hall, the place for prayer and preaching. So here's us grown men sitting at little desks and there's ghosts on the whiteboard from last Sunday, I'm thinking. Shadows of words, wiped away but not clean. "Do unto others," "All God's creatures," that kind of thing. James reads some passage from the Bible. I don't know what exactly, not knowing the Bible much. Something about work. About working for God. About working with your heart. It makes sense to me. The heart part more than the God part. And this old guy next to me—one of those I usually see alone with his sandwich over at the Sub Shack—is nodding.

"But what if there isn't no work?" A guy behind me says. And that's all it takes. The complaints start rumbling up and out like they've been bottled up too long. Even though I—probably all of us—have heard them lots of times before.

No work.

Plant layoffs.

Welfare. (I decide not to remind them how food stamps feed a lot of their families. How the government keeps their farms from flat-out failing.)

The war.

The bad guys. Foreigners. Mexicans. Blacks. (Not a black man for miles here in New Hope. Another thing I don't say.) Others.

Taking our jobs.

Time was, I could dispute that. Back when the best jobs still went to us. The shit jobs—pickers, diggers, cleaners—to the others. Now, though, there's Mexicans at the plant. Bert and Ernie, the Jewish twins who run the Ice Cream Shoppe. The Martinez family running the Stop & Go. A couple dozen decent jobs down. Not much in the grand scheme of things. But still. Citizens, though, I have to remind myself. Or legal residents, most of them. The plant is good at checking papers. The farms—well no one much cares who works the fields anymore. Mrs. Martinez and her husband Manuel are investors, and not only money and time. They're at the store just about twenty-four hours a day. And if they aren't, they have two local girls working the till. Job makers, the Martinezes. And then there was their son, Ramon. Ray, we called him. Can't forget him. Signed up as soon as he was old enough; didn't even wait for the draft. Ray had options, lots of them. Smart kid, good student. Hard working. Scholarships from all over, but like I said, he signed up. Killed his first month out. Like I said, too, the Martinezes invested.

I don't say that, though, at the meeting. I don't say anything.

James, I'll give him some credit, he tries. But he can't keep up. His Bible has all these pieces of ripped up notebook paper in the pages. He flips and flips, a verse for every complaint. Like he's heard them before. And like I said, probably has.

Commit your work to the Lord, and your plans will be established.

I was hungry and you gave me food.

I was a stranger and you welcomed me.

"That's just a book," the guy behind me says. His voice is familiar, but I don't want to turn around. No reason to make eye contact with a mad dog. A flash in my head: coming to the door of a tiny, well-kept house at the edge of town. Green pickup in the drive, front-left panel rusted clear through. Flowers up the walk. A man at the door. Sweating. Veins on his neck popping, pulsing. I smell bread, fresh baked. *What?* he says. This was the same voice. Behind him inside the house, everything's neat, tidy. There's a woman. His wife. Girlfriend maybe. Bruise blooming on her cheek. *You okay?* I say to her. *Yes,* she says. But she's not. *Fine,* she says. Me: *Your face? Fell,* she says. *Clumsy,* he says. And pulls her to him, hand on the back of her neck.

"This isn't no book," the guy says at the meeting. "This is real life."

And the lonely old guy next to me? The one with the sandwich and no one at home waiting for him? Says, "Amen to that."

The room is hot now, bodies and adrenaline and mad. The desk feels tight, the chair too small. I catch James looking at me. Pleading in his eyes. And I know now that this is why he'd invited me. "Friend," he'd said. But really, what he meant was, "Sheriff."

I feel like I did when I saw Edith putting that candy in her pocket. Like I did when I was at the door of that couple, when the wife pretended the bruises were her own fault. When she wouldn't speak up. When Nova gave me her mask face when I asked her about her brother and the fight. When Faith slammed the car door and Ellie got behind the wheel and they drove away. Fix things. Change things. And this is wrong, I know, but I blamed them some, too. That wife. Edith. Nova. Hell, even Mrs. Martinez. Like I blame Pastor James now at the Men's Group. You can stop this, I'm thinking. This is on you.

I get up from my little chair in the classroom. I walk down the little hall and out the door. It's near dark now, streaks of summer sunset traced over the trees, over the tops of the houses where families eat dinner, watch television, live together in goodness and bad. I want to call Ellie now. Want to talk to Faith. What would I say? *I miss you.* But Ellie knows that; we started missing each other long before she left. *Come home,* I could say. Like I didn't say when I saw her pull away. Like I never say when we talk now: it's just Faith, my job, Ellie's, the weather. Behind me, I hear through the wide open windows of the little church, the yelling of men, the fury and the fire.

At the edge of the parking lot, I don't know why I didn't see it before, the sign's been painted over.

Church of No Hope it says, the NO big and red. I climb in the cruiser, start it up, put it in gear.

The night before Ellie left, the three of us went out. Me trying. There we were coming back from burgers at the Inn after movies in the park. Me, Ellie, Faith. "Ice cream?" I said, thinking maybe we could make the night last, maybe things would go different. "It'll be closed," Ellie said. And Faith, I saw in the rearview mirror, sighed and pushed her bottom lip out. "It's too late," Ellie said, to our daughter maybe, to me for sure.

"We'll see," I said. I smiled at Faith in the mirror and pulled a u-ey on Main Street, heading for the Ice Cream Shoppe. This, I'm thinking. Just this.

The shop lights were off. All of a sudden, a bunch of kids running; we could hear them yelling and laughing and cans clattering.

"Are you fucking kidding me?" Ellie said when the headlights hit the storefront. There was red spray paint everywhere. Nasty stuff about Jews on the windows, swastikas with their arms crooked the wrong way. Ellie jumped out of the car before I even got it fully stopped. She ran in the wake of the kids, trying to chase them down. "Fuckers!" she yelled, and I wished I was in the cruiser so I could hit the cherries. "You little fuckers!" I looked back at Faith and she had something like that mask on, only scared. Shocked and shaking.

I pull away from the curb in front of the church, think about what I could say to Ellie if I call her. Once I get home, once I pour myself a shot, pop open a beer. Once I pull a pizza out of the freezer and stick it in the oven. She'd be done with dinner herself, by then, Faith helping carry the dishes to the sink, begging to watch one more show before bedtime.

Ellie, I'd say. I head toward the street and I see the rusty green pickup with its blinker on, making the turn into the lot. There's a woman at the wheel, she turns her face away from me.

The air shifts, goes cold like before a rain. I roll the windows up. There's lightning somewhere out there, and I'm waiting for the thunder.

Ellie... I'll say if she answers. On the other side of the line, I'll hear my Faith, close by and far away both, watching TV, laughing. I'll hear my wife breathing soft. Waiting for me to say something else. To do something more. I'll listen hard, wanting. But this is far as I get.

The Way it Really Went

One thing about cancer—and anyone who knows anyone who's had it knows this, too—it's the name of it that gets you sick. Here's what I mean:

A guy goes through his everyday life, not feeling bad or anything, not feeling anything different at all except one day feeling a little hard bubble of something under his skin. Say he's in the shower, soaping up all the parts he usually does, thinking about how he hates to have to ever get out from under the warm stream of water, hates to have to get a move on and put his uniform on and go sit on the little stool he sits on all day, doing the exact same job he's been doing for fifteen years, selling the same tickets to the same people for the same buses going to the same places. On automatic pilot, more or less, trying not to let it bother him, the monotony, the sameness, but knowing that it does. And then, all of a sudden, something is different, something has changed. And what it is, is this little raising of flesh here under his arm on his side. A pebble, it feels like. Tough under the fingertips, but it doesn't hurt. *Huh*, he says to himself and fingers it under the soapy slide of skin before he rinses off and shrugs it off and dries off and goes about his day. Only every once in a while, his fingers find their way back to that spot under his arm, play over the spot, pushing and wondering if the thing's bigger or smaller than it was the last time he messed with it an hour or so ago. When he gets home he pulls the tails of his shirt out of his pants and steps up close to the full-length mirror on the back of the bedroom door, studies the spot but doesn't see anything, not even the bump of it unless he uses two fingers of one hand on either side of it to stretch the skin back over the area—and then what he sees he can't tell if it's real or imagined it's such a small deviation from the flat, pale plane of his side. A cyst, maybe, he thinks, and tries to ignore it, doesn't tell anyone, not even his wife because she'd think he was whining and that makes her mad, and besides it's probably nothing. And the next day and the next when he takes a shower he presses on it, squeezes it, and gets to doing that so regularly that it becomes part of the routine, as mindless as the act of rinsing the shampoo out of his thick black hair. He still doesn't feel bad, not any more tired or achy than usual, just the pains of getting near forty and not doing enough besides sitting and watching TV and life from his couch at home, his stool at work.

But then one day it hurts. Really hurts. Like a stab of something when he presses on it, a sharpness that radiates up and down from his armpit to the lowest edge of his ribs. He remembers what it was like when he had that plantar wart once and it got so painful that he could hardly step on the ball of his right foot. And even though it hurts, this thing, maybe a wart, he still doesn't feel too bad, although he has been getting sort of tired lately. But he imagines that's because he doesn't sleep too well anymore. Dreams of dogs biting him and sinking their teeth in under his arm—shining slivers of enamel left in his skin when he finally pulls the beasts away—shake him up enough that he forces himself awake and keeps his eyes wide open and fixed on the ceiling until he's sure he won't fall back in with the dogs again.

So when it gets to hurting, the man makes an appointment with the doctor. And when the doctor asks, he realizes that he can't remember when he first noticed it, can't remember when it wasn't there, part of him. And after this test and that, the doctor tells him what he already knows, says the word in a stream of other possible words. And the man knows it's this one, recognizes the word that had been in his mind all the while, even though he'd never actually said it, even to himself. And the man's surprised that he isn't surprised by what the doctor tells him. Yet, familiar as the word is when he hears it, it still shakes him up, and he sits for a long while on the cold examining table, left alone in the room to dress. Only he can't move. Not voluntarily. He listens to his mind telling his legs to stand now, his hands to reach for his clothes; he even prods himself *Come on, get going* out loud, but it's like he's stuck there, trapped in the sterile white room by the word, trapped in this body which he thought he knew and trusted. Trapped in the body that had turned on him, and now turned on him again by not standing, not taking him out of there, but instead doing its own thing, shaking uncontrollably from toe to head, shivering and shuddering so hard that the paper of the examining robe rattles in the quiet.

And then, for the first time since he found that little bubble under his skin, for the first time ever, perhaps, he says the word himself. *Cancer*, he says, whispering the name as he shakes in the paper robe in the quiet, white room. And then, when the man names it, that's when he gets sick.

When Jim called before he left work at the station and said we needed to talk, I knew he didn't mean we'd have a real conversation where he says something, then I do. More than likely he wanted me to stay quiet while he talked. I knew something was up, I saw the signs. He'd drift away somewhere while we sat in front of the late news, his fingers strumming his ribs, his eyes blanking out. He wouldn't answer me when I'd say something then, not hearing. Ignoring, maybe. It doesn't matter which. The thing is, it was me who always did the talking anyway. But now I figured he probably wanted me to sit tight and listen while he said one of those three-word sentences most women live in dread of hearing: *This isn't working* or *I've met someone*. Like I said, there were signs.

The way I imagined it would go:

At Anchors Inn, the only rib joint in town and Jim's favorite restaurant (never mind that I'd given up red meat), he would be on his side of the table looking twitchy, the sweat shining in his thick black curls; I'd be on mine, dressed up for once, figuring what the hell, might as well step out of those old jeans and T-shirt I live in mostly and slip into the black mini-skirt pushed to the back of the closet. Heels, too. Figuring if it's going to be him leaving me, he better damn sure know what he's leaving behind.

I'd sit on my red vinyl bench across the red plaid tablecloth from my ten-year husband and listen to him hemming and hawing around those words— *This, er, I've, uh....* I imagined when he finally did say it—his brown eyes focused on a spot somewhere off to the side of my head, his Adam's apple bobbing— I'd just smile big and nod nicely, and stand up and lean over to kiss the top of his head. *Good luck*, I'd say, and leave him there, walk away and leave him getting an eyeful of my good side

The way it really went:

I sat in the flickering light of the fake lanterns tacked up on the rough-paneled walls and watched Jim squirm. He looked small in his white shirt and black tie, his bus ticket seller's uniform, and damn if it didn't look like he might cry. He kept blinking and clearing his throat, and I waited for him to say something, like it seemed I was always waiting for him. I used to finish his sentences for him; it was as if he just didn't have enough words in him to make it through a whole conversation sometimes. But I got tired of that, like I got tired of the other things: the way he pretended not to stare at every other woman in the neighborhood—from the high school girls working at the Stop & Go with their tight bodies and too-tight jeans, to the new moms pushing their buggies-full, their ripe boobs bouncing; the nights I went to bed hours ahead of him so he could watch the round-up shows after the games, and then the highlights on the late news, and then whatever sports they'd be playing in some other part of the world in the middle of the night that he could get on that damned cable; the pools of water on the bathroom floor that I'd slip in every morning when I went in after him to pick up his towels, put the seat down, wipe the toothpaste splatters off the mirror. Like a goddamn bad rerun our life was, and I couldn't even remember anymore when things weren't exactly the same.

But that night at the Inn, things seemed different somehow. And as I sat there waiting for Jim to talk, my heart pounded in me. A good pound. A life's-about-to-change-get-ready-it's-your-turn kind of pound. It nearly made me giddy. And, God help me, I felt like laughing. But of course I didn't.

"I..." Jim started finally, after our busboy came by to fill our water glasses and put our place settings down.

...*'m leaving*, I finished the sentence in my head for him. But I kept my lips pressed tight together. And Jim, after that first false start, closed his own mouth and pushed back into his seat, then opened his mouth long enough to gulp down some water, then closed it again, his eyes skittering around, touching everything but mine.

Maybe I should have left him. Not like the thought hadn't crossed my mind a million times over the last, oh, not ten years (because the first two were actually pretty good I think, I don't remember how or why, only I have this feeling that there was something more than just pleasant about them) but in the last eight years I'd often considered going. Still, there's a certain comfort in what's familiar, and Jim was definitely familiar. We'd known each other since the sixth grade. He was the first boy I let slide his hand into my shirt, under the bra, back in freshman year behind the rear door of the field house. I looked across the table at Jim's hands. At the half-moons under his nails, the ones that meant money or luck, I'd heard somewhere. At the long, sleek white digits fidgeting with the spoon, the knife. His hands were what made me fall for him for real in the first place. Even before that day when he slipped one inside the cool cotton of my bra and it felt so wonderfully warm and smooth, a press of palm so real and alive, like nothing I'd ever felt before. When he slid that palm over my nipple we both took in air at precisely the same moment, a gasp so quick and deep that he just about snatched his hand back, and would have if I hadn't hugged it to me, pushed my whole self up against it and him, wanting the feeling of his electric warmth to take me over entirely until we had to pull apart and run around to the front entrance and get to homeroom before the second bell rang.

His hands were clean, always, the fingers long and solid. They looked good holding things. In seventh grade he came over to our house with a big brown casserole of beans and ham from his mom, an offering of sympathy the morning after my dad died, and when I went to the door and found him there, shifting from foot to foot, his nose red and runny, maybe from the cold October mistiness, I couldn't look in his eyes when he said he was sorry, *You know, about your dad and all, I mean,* so instead I focused in on his hands, white and strong around the heavy brown dish; and they looked so perfect, the nail beds pink and long and healthy, my heart broke and filled in the same instant, and I couldn't help but break and sob, and he dropped that big old casserole, beans and ham all over our front stoop, and he put his hands on me, on my back, in my hair, on my face, and how could I help but love him then?

But all that was years before. Years before we went together, broke up, got back together, had a child, lost a child, and so on. It all somehow seemed like an inalterable progression. After Jim and I were married, we seemed to just keep going on with our lives, nothing changing, unless you count that day of the accident and how after that we clung to each other at first, tried to start over, to have another baby with not a bit of luck, then stopped talking nearly except when I nagged him, hissed at him, and then stopped sleeping together entirely, sharing a bed, but not bodies, and how I started stepping out, finding someone or other to hold me, someone or other to want me. So even though I didn't ever go anywhere, I guess I had been doing my own leaving for a while, and now I figured Jim could leave me and we could get on with things.

I watched our waitress at the next table pull a long pepper mill out of her red apron pocket in an elegant arc, and twist the big thing over the plate of a woman with hair so black it was blue. The woman lifted her hand in a small wave. "When," she said.

Jim picked up his menu, put the plastic wall of it up between us. "What're you gonna have?" he said. The first full sentence since we'd been there.

"I'm not too hungry," I said, not even bothering to open my menu. "I'll just go for the salad bar."

"Yeah," Jim said and put the menu down again. His lips pulled down at the corners and a line creased deeply across his forehead. "Maybe I will, too. Red meat's not too good for you."

Now here was something different. Jim was the kind of man who joked about not getting enough fat, not having a high enough cholesterol level. "More salt," he'd say at the movies when he ordered popcorn, "keep pouring, keep pouring! I can still see some yellow from the butter."

And it was at this moment that I got scared.

"Jim—?"

"I went to the doctor today," he said and turned his head toward the bar, away from me. He began to roll up his sleeve. There was a purple patch of skin spreading out from under a bandage in the crook of his elbow. The back of my neck got cold.

And then he said it. Three words, the number I knew there would be. But not the right three words.

"They found something."

An odd sensation seeped through me. I don't know what you'd call it, but I know I'd felt it twice before. That time when my mom came home and told me about my dad, the heart attack that took him down to the cement floor of the bays of the trucking company right before lunch time, made him dead before the first of the guys on the way back from the cafeteria found him down there, cold and totally empty of breath. That time, and the day of our daughter's accident.

My eyes burned, and I swallowed and swallowed, trying to get that thing out of my throat so that I could talk.

"It's just a lump," Jim said finally, reaching one of those perfect hands across the table to me. His fingertips touched the white knuckles of my own hand gripping the edge of the table. His voice was soft now. He sounded young. Scared, maybe.

"What the hell does that mean, Jim?" And here's the thing, I heard my own voice get too loud, raggedy. And the feeling that covered me a minute before was burning off into anger. Even I knew this wasn't right, this wasn't what Jim needed from me right then, to be pissed off at him. Pissed off *again*, for chrissakes. But I was. And maybe I was at least a little mad at myself then for not seeing this coming, for imagining something else, protecting myself from the wrong thing by imagining something entirely impossible, Jim having an affair—boring, settled Jim, as loyal and unambitious as a fat old house dog. Mostly, though, I was mad at him. "What's 'it's just a lump' supposed to fucking mean?"

Our waitress—Christy, her brass name pin said—was at our tableside then, her hand on her pepper mill, just doing her job but caught in our little moment and frozen there, it looked like. It was all I could do not to reach over and snatch the damn wooden pepper club from her and swing it around in an elegant arc over Jim's head. I'll give him a lump.

"Uh, I guess you need more time," Christy said when I turned my face to her. The fire I felt in my forehead must have shone in my eyes. She patted the table twice and smiled her good waitress smile and backed away.

I looked back at Jim, at his skinny neck in the wide starched white collar. His fingers had slipped from my knuckles but his hand stayed stretched across the wide table, the pink pillows of his palm up. He blinked and blinked, his deep brown eyes fogging and clearing; his lips worked like he was trying to say something but couldn't. The spot under the bandage on his outstretched arm looked colored on, a fake bruise.

"Ah, shit," I said, when the strangle hold of it all finally let go of my throat. I took his hand in my own, startled by how strange and how familiar the skin-to-skin warmth and smoothness of it felt. Jim tilted his head up and watched me stand. He looked so damn small there surrounded by red vinyl, a boy at the end of the marred arm. "Come on," I said and jiggled our hands held together like a double-sized fist. "Let's go home."

Back at the house, we let go of one another's hands just long enough to undress and—Jim in his T-shirt and boxers, me in my panties—we got into bed on our backs and on our own sides. Our hands found their way to one another across the span of cold sheet. Jim fell fast and hard into sleep. I lay still and silent, stared at the black flatness of the ceiling and wondered if something as routine as sleep would ever come to me again. And when it did, I didn't notice until I was pulled out of it, away from dreams with no movement, still pictures of people and objects vaguely familiar yet unrecognizable. Jim's crying woke me, but not him. He whimpered and shuddered, but didn't come to, so I slid over the mattress and into him, pressed myself against the back I'd gotten used to having turned to me at night. Each sob shook me, and I held on, clucked in a way that came natural to me, even though our bodies, pressed together, felt changed—my own softer and fleshier than whenever the last time we touched like this was, his thinner and somehow brittle. His shirt was soaked through, so I pulled it up his back and over his head, and in his sleep, he let me. The slick skin of him was hot and cold at the same time, but I stayed close until he felt just-right warm against me. The crying stopped and gave way to even breathing, heavy and thick with sleep, and when he's five minutes' calm, I run my hand up his side, smoothing his skin until I feel it. And it's true, there's not much there, a couple stitches over a pea of sickness, and I wish that I could bite it, take it between my teeth and pull back quick and hard until it's out of him and in my mouth and then I could spit it out. In the toilet, I think, and I'd flush it away and when Jim woke up it would be gone, and he'd be old Jim again, same old same old, and I'd be Annie, just like before—whatever, whoever, that was.

The surgery came four days later. In the recovery room everyone was smiling, Jim even, ready to believe that was that. *Optimistic* was the word the doctors used then. I wanted to believe, too, but the tightness I'd felt at the Inn had turned into a knot, a hard blister of dread. And then the day after surgery when they read his tests, the blood work and the lymph nodes, they found more.

They say what doesn't kill you will only make you stronger, but I'm not sure that goes for chemotherapy. Jim couldn't eat from the queasiness, and after his daily shots he'd vomit up all that nothing. From my cold plastic chair outside the treatment room, it was like I could hear his bones rattle with the dry heaves. When he'd come back though the doorway, gray and wobbly, I'd go to him and curl under his arm, make myself a crutch for the slow move down the long, bright hallway to the exit. It was like we used to walk, back in high school, wrapped into one another so tightly that if one tipped, both would.

At home one day I heard the shower running, but it sounded like it was falling straight down, like no one was moving under it. I put my ear against the door and listened hard. "Jim?" I whispered against the wood. And then I heard that sound of his crying, a soft whimpering, and the quiet distress of it ran through me like ice water. "Jim?" I said again, a little louder this time, and rattled the doorknob. He sniffed. "Yes," he said; I heard the shoring up under the word, the effort it took to keep it steady. I stepped inside the bathroom, waved my hand in front of my face to clear a path in the steam. "Honey?" I pulled back the shower curtain and found him sitting there on the floor of the tub, knees pulled up to his chest, arms wrapped tightly around them. "Go away," he said into the space between his knees, and from where I was I could see through his hair to the white of his scalp, something I'd never seen before. I stood there, my hand still holding back the curtain, not sure what to do next.

"I said go away." He didn't raise his voice, there was no edge in it. He said it like a plain and simple fact. But I wouldn't go.

"Jim," I said again, almost a whisper, running out of words myself this time. I put a hand on the back of his neck. He tilted his face up to me. His eyes were rimmed and red, his cheeks slick with steam and tears and snot.

"I can't even take a fucking shower anymore," he said softly, and his eyes began to fill. "I'm just so damn tired." He put his head back on his knees and his shoulders shook. So I climbed in there with him, right down on the porcelain next to him, jeans, T-shirt, socks, and all, pulled him into a circle I made with my legs, into the circle of my arms. We rocked there for a good long while, him crying and me thinking about crying but unable to. I hadn't shed a tear since the news first came. I wasn't trying to be strong—I knew that in some long-guarded, hard-sided spot near the blister-knot inside me, I wanted to sob. But I couldn't. We lay out long in the tub then, felt the water pour down over us, clutched together chest-to-chest, legs tucked up and around one another so we could fit in the small space. When the water ran cold, I reached up and turned it off, but we lay there still, who knows how long. And later, much later, we stood up together and I pulled off my own clothes and turned the water back on and held him with one arm and ran the soap over him with my free hand. Even in its whiteness and stick-thinness, his body felt familiar under my hands, and when I lowered to my knees and soaped his balls, his dick, the long, hard muscles of his thighs, I couldn't help but remember the times we'd done this for fun, lathered each other up and slipped our bodies against one another. And his dick remembered, too, because it stiffened some, but not much, and I kissed its little head for old time's sake before I stood up again and hugged Jim to me while I reached around him to scrub his back.

He sagged into me while I washed him, his arms resting over my shoulders and his legs shaking under his weight. But then I felt a gathering of energy in his body, and he pulled back from me just enough to look into my face.

"I'm really sorry, Annie," he said, his voice low and thick.

There were a lot of things I wanted him to be sorry for over the years. Sorry for not being able to keep a better hold on our daughter. Sorry for giving up on our having another kid without ever talking to me about it. Sorry for my feeling like I had to go out on him, look elsewhere for what I thought he should be giving me. Sorry for standing by while all we had that had been warm and familiar turned to cold, cold routine. Sorry for us. Sorry for me. But this? This was not his fault. There was nothing here for him to be sorry over.

The water poured down on us, cold again, and I moved in for some of Jim's warmth. When I did, I felt myself slip. Jim lifted a hand to me and I grabbed it, held onto it, and then slid it over my breast. I wished he could push his fingers under my skin and through the bones that cross over my heart and find that knot inside me. I wanted him to rub away its hardness. He cupped his other hand behind my neck, and we pressed together. "I'm sorry," he said again. I wanted to tell him it's okay, *Don't worry, it's okay.* But standing with his hands—those same old perfect hands—on me, holding me, keeping me steady, I couldn't say anything. So I nodded. That's all I was able to do. Just nod. I couldn't do anything more.

The Twin

Ernie heard the yelling first as he climbed out of the front seat of the old Toyota. "Buy American," some punk or other was always yelling at them, him and Bert, when they drove past the park or the high school. But that wasn't what he heard when he arrived at seven that morning to open up the ice cream parlor. From the parking lot, the yelling sounded like wailing. Or howling. A desperate, long, low-pitched sob.

Ernie thought maybe it came from the storefront meditation church, the Temple of Air. The ice cream parlor and temple shared a wall in the small strip shopping center. There was always singing or praying or some sort of joyful noise going on over there, sometimes yelling even, especially on a Saturday, their main day of worship. But this was a little too early for the temple, and the parking lot was empty. The white stripes between the spaces looked like they needed painting, which they did; they were much too ghostly and weak on the faded blacktop to keep the cars apart. On a busy temple morning, which this was sure to be when the sun moved up into a warm spot that would burn off the early mist, cars would be parked in nothing near order, spilling over the lines and squeezed in too tightly, or parked at odd angles meant to protect side panels and doors from bumps and dings. It about drove Ernie crazy.

But the yelling. The sobbing. Ernie stood beside the Toyota for a minute to try to hear where it was coming from. It sounded like it was in front of him in the shopping center somewhere, but also above him somehow. And then it stopped.

"Hmmph," he exhaled, and turned the key in the lock of the car door (a habit left over from the city) and then spun the big jangling ring of keys around until he found the one for the ice cream shop. He stepped up to the door and put the key in the lock, turned it, then pushed the door open so that the bell over it rang out prettily.

"Hey! Fuck! Hey!"

The yelling rose over the hum of the freezers and stopped Ernie still under the bell. "What the...?" he mumbled.

"Hey, help! Back here! Help!"

It wasn't Ernie's morning to open the shop; it was Bert's. Those weren't their real names, Bert and Ernie, but the ones they'd taken on when they took off from the city, from the Chicago Mercantile Exchange, where they'd shared the position of back office manager at Bronstein Financials for six years before they got the idea to slide a couple of winning trades into an account with their real names, Robert and Henry Saltzman, on it. Well, it started with a couple of trades—but then when no one noticed, and it seemed so effortless, so easy, unlike the rest of their days filled with brokers and clients bothering them all the time, all the time, calling on the phone and standing over their desks clearing their throats,

tapping their feet, yelling and bossing and whining—
they did it again. And again. A winner here, a winner
there, and suddenly they had something, some
money, a tidy little sum, a significant retirement
package, as they liked to call it. And still no one
noticed. Why would they? Robert and Henry handled
the statements, checked for errors and out-trades
and margin calls, and this would be the sort of thing
they would watch for in everyone else's accounts. But
then the Commodity Futures Trading Commission
showed up for a routine audit, and Robert and Henry
left the job at lunchtime, which was unusual since
they mostly ate lunch in the break room, sharing
sandwiches out of one bag, chips and sodas out of
another. It was hard to tell them apart sometimes;
they were fraternal twins who always wanted to be
identical. And even near thirty, they wore identical
glasses and dressed in look-alike suits and similar
ties made from the same polyester fabrics. So that
day when the CFTC came in, Robert excused himself
at lunch to go to the dentist, he said, and for fifteen
minutes Henry (dumb with nerves) sat in the break
room with two sandwiches and two RC Colas and a
baggie filled with greasy potato chips and then, as
Robert had instructed him to, got up and went into
the men's room in the hall, and then out to the
elevators and down to the lobby, and some of the
brokers said later that they thought they'd seen him
get in a cab, but maybe it was Robert, it was hard to
tell. And then they packed their bags, four identical
Samsonites with silver metal locks, and wedged them
into the Toyota and pulled out of the underground
garage of the apartment building with the parquet

floors and low ceilings and wide windows where they'd lived together since their sophomore year in college at Circle Campus where they'd enrolled to stay out of the draft, and they drove and drove until they got tired—which wasn't too far because neither of them liked to drive very much.

And they ended up here, New Hope.

So today it was Bert's turn to open up the ice cream parlor; they took turns on Saturdays coming in early. But Bert's allergies were acting up since things were starting to bloom, and this was one thing the men didn't share, allergies, so Ernie had offered to go in.

"Come on, man! Fuck!"

Ernie had never been partial to swearing. That had been a real liability working in the financial markets; the traders were all so rude.

"W-where are you?" Ernie called out into the dark. He still couldn't quite place the sound, but it might have been coming from the storage room. Or maybe the roof. He was aware then, like he always was, of the smell of the place. It surprised and delighted him, even now, after these years, the sweet scent of this place where he worked. Sugar and milk, the cookie smell of ice cream cones. So different from the Exchange where things always smelled like men's sweat and socks and stale cigarette smoke, burnt coffee. Today though, in the shop there was another odor that cut through the soft sugary scent; it smelled like copper a little, like wet pennies. Ernie sniffed and called again: "Where are you?"

"Here, man, here! In back." The last words sounded quieter than the others, deflated.

133

Ernie lightly stepped over the black-and-white tiles until he was behind the counter. He reached over the cash register to the light switches, and threw them all up. The place filled with the glare of fluorescence on shining steel and bright white walls.

"Fuck, man, shit! My eyes!"

And then there was no doubt. The voice was definitely coming from the storage and prep room, in the rear of the shop, near the big freezers. Ernie tiptoed back.

At first quick glance the room appeared empty except for all the normal stuff, the paper cups and boxes of spoons, plastic boats, sugar cones and safety cones. The metal racks of paper napkins and fresh dishcloths from the linen service; toilet paper and the toweling they put in those holders near the slop sink and in the bathrooms, big round rolls of it with a blue stripe down the center.

"Man, finally. Shit, finally."

Ernie looked up. A head poked out from the ceiling like a piñata. From the air duct, actually. A man's head, or a boy's maybe, with too much hair. It hung down from the top of the boy's upside down head, and Ernie's first thought was that he should be wearing a hairnet, the boy; it was unsanitary, all of that greasy hair hanging down over the paper cups and plastic spoons and sugar cones. He followed the line of it down and then saw on the floor beneath the hair a metal grating that was usually stuck in the ceiling where the air came through, and it looked as though it had been ripped from its place among the ceiling tiles, bits of the foam-like material still clinging to its edges. And on closer inspection, Ernie noticed the white dust everywhere. And the dark spots of something wet.

"Oh dear," he said, like he did when he got nervous or mad or sad or excited. "Oh dear."

"Fuckin' A" the boy said. His mouth was where his eyebrows should have been, since he was upside down, and it looked to Ernie like his forehead was talking.

"Language, please," Ernie said.

"What?" the boy's forehead said.

"Language. Please. Watch your language."

The boy shifted some above Ernie, tilted his head at an odd angle like he was trying to turn it over, trying to right himself, or maybe just his head, so that he could see Ernie better, right-side up at least.

"Ow, fuck," the boy said, and then, "Sorry. Man, sorry. Hey, help, can you?"

Ernie moved closer to the boy, and when he did, he recognized him. He wasn't a boy, really, but a young man who was just past his teens when Ernie first saw him a couple years before at the edge of the parking lot where those kids hang out late at night. His name was Eric or something. Jared. Ernie shook his head. That wasn't it. Derek! Yes, Derek. And his last name started with "J", Ernie was pretty certain. One of those Bohemian names they all had around town.

"What are you doing?" Ernie asked. It hurt to strain his neck back like he had to in order to talk with the man, so he dragged over a step stool, the one he used to get to the extra boxes of napkins he stored on the high shelves. He climbed until he was nearly face-to-face with the fellow. Forehead to chin at least.

The man's eyes were bloodshot and his face was very white. He was perspiring.

"I'm stuck," he said. His voice was quiet now that Ernie was so close. He, Derek, sounded spent. The wet penny smell wafted from him.

"Yes, I see," Ernie said, and he peered into the air duct above Derek and saw that one shoulder was wedged against the ceiling and an arm was bent funny with something, blood, Ernie could see now, tracing small lines down the fingers that looked like they were sticking out of the man's neck. "Very stuck, it looks like." He reached up to touch Derek's fingers and the man's eyes went wide as a frightened cat's. "Don't worry," Ernie said, even though he couldn't think of any reason at all why Derek wouldn't worry; this was a bad situation, a real jam, that's for sure. The tips of the fellow's fingers were clammy and cold. "Hmm," Ernie said, and pulled his hand back. And he couldn't help it, he smelled his own fingers, discreetly, and there was that sharp coppery smell. "Well," he said, and he backed down the rungs of the step stool. "We'll have to do something, won't we?"

Derek made a movement with his head that looked like a nod, only upside down and very, very small. He closed his eyes.

"Are you tired?" Ernie asked. It seemed like the right question, a polite inquiry.

"Yes," the man said. His breath smelled of beer and sick.

"Yes, of course," Ernie said. He couldn't help but think of himself as a host to this man stuck in his air duct. And even though he and his brother served ice cream to dozens of people every day, the way Ernie felt in relation to this fellow was not exactly the same thing. On hot, busy days, the ice cream parlor had a continuous stream of patrons, and the twins worked like a short, efficient assembly line: Ernie scooping and Bert taking the money and making change, and then Bert scooping and Ernie at the cash register. On those days there wasn't time for much small talk and pleasantries. On slower days, there was always something to do when they weren't dipping cones. "Got time to lean, got time to clean," Bert would say while he flipped through a fishing magazine at a table and Ernie busied himself with a towel, a mop, the push broom. Now, though, before the door was open and the customers lined up, before Bert came in and things shifted under the weight of their shared responsibilities, Ernie found himself considering Derek a guest—not a patron, but a visitor. And since Ernie and his brother Bert never had visitors (they were, after all, on the run) this feeling of playing host was not entirely familiar to Ernie. Surprisingly pleasant, though. Because if Ernie were to think about it at all, he would have to admit that this life he and his brother had designed for themselves, this life of work and not much else, of hiding from their past and keeping their present small, close, easy to share and to manage—Ernie would have to admit to himself (but never to Bert) that he was, in fact, lonely.

When Henry and Robert first arrived in New Hope those years ago, they stayed at the High Hope Motor Court located on the wooded slope of one of the hills at the edge of town. They'd paid for two weeks in advance, in cash, and Robert had signed them in under their real names, but scribbled their signatures so they were essentially illegible—a messiness he prided himself on because he thought it made his name look more important. At the trading firm he'd signed hundreds of checks and thousands of statements, sweeping the pen over the documents with a flourish and a sigh, fully aware that hundreds of thousands of dollars were accounted for or released under indecipherable squiggles and lines made by his own hand.

"What's that say?" The old lady at the desk lifted up her bifocals and leaned closer to the register. Henry could see her scalp where her dyed black hair parted, and the whispery lines of gray on either side of the pink line of flesh. Would they have to dye their own hair, Henry wondered. Clearly they had to become someone other than who they were now. New names, new jobs. New hair? New clothes? Maybe he'd go blond if Robert chose black; he'd take to wearing blue jeans and gym shoes.

The incredible possibility of becoming another person—not just Henry of Robert and Henry, not just one of "the twins" like everyone called them at work, at school, at their apartment in the city, like their parents had called them up until the day Mr. and Mrs. Saltzman loaded their moving van and left the cold winter suburbs for the sunshine of Florida and had skidded off the road in a freak ice storm in Tennessee, leaving behind a tangle of overdrafts and unpaid bills and two grown-up sons to take care of it all—the opportunity to start again as someone other than whom he had been all of his life was exhilarating to

Henry. And terrifying. In equal doses. The enormity of it left him without words, there in the tiny office cabin at High Hope Motor Court, fascinated now by the wiry black hairs at the edges of the old woman's upper lip. She looked from one twin to the other and back, blinking as though clearing sleep from her eyes.

"Hubert," Robert said. "Call me Bert."

Henry was amazed (even after all these years) at how quickly Robert had figured things out, developed a strategy, responded to a problem with a solution. Robert smiled broadly at the woman, all orthodontist-straightened teeth and pink lips and soft eyes. He was the handsome one.

She smiled back, the hairs twitching at the corners of her mouth.

"And this one?" She pointed to the other name. "I can't make it out at all."

"Ernie," Robert said. "Like those puppets on television, only we were Bert and Ernie first. Seagram. Like the whiskey."

Henry tried the new name out in his head, Ernie, Ernie, Ernie, and Seagram, Seagram, Seagram, and it was okay, close enough.

"That Jewish?" The old lady asked. Her eyes swept over Robert's close-cut auburn curls and landed on Henry's nose, which had a bump made by Robert's elbow, an accident during a foot race when they were kids.

"English," Robert said, still smiling, always smiling, but Henry saw the tightening of muscle in his temple. "Our grandfather was Jewish," Robert said, the story growing so easily that Henry thought for a moment that there might be some truth to it. "We're not religious, though." And they weren't really, although they'd celebrated their bar mitzvah together, like they did everything together, with family and a guest list of nearly one hundred people.

The woman made a noise in her throat, a grunt it sounded like, but then she handed Robert two key rings made from wooden triangles glued together to look like pine trees. And in another few minutes the twins were in their own mold-smelling cabin, one of a half-dozen of them painted Indian red and scattered over the hillside. Wasps buzzed outside the screen door, hovering around a nest in the corner of the awning that was the color of a Dreamsicle. Robert, then Henry, showered, and they unpacked and sat down at the small Formica table near the window (blinds drawn, warm Frescas and bags of crispy cheese puffs in front of them) and began to make a plan.

The fellow, Derek, moaned in a small, quiet way.

"Are you hungry?" Ernie asked.

Derek bobbed his head again. His hair slightly swung beneath him.

"Help me, please."

"Of course," Ernie said. "You must be starving." He spoke with an expanding sense of hospitality, as though the man had just arrived in the shop after a long and complicated journey. Ernie spun around in the back room, turning this way and that trying to solve the problem of his guest's hunger when he decided on the easiest solution. He skipped back out to the front of the shop and saw out the wide windows that a half dozen cars were now in the parking lot. A skinny woman dressed in sky blue climbed out of the driver's side of her Fairmont and waved to Ernie before she crossed the sidewalk to the door of the Temple of Air. Ernie waved back in order to not seem rude, then locked the front door.

He slid open the glass window of the ice cream cooler and looked over the selection of twenty-some flavors in big, round, cardboard tubs. The frozen air lifted from the cooler and fogged his glasses; Ernie removed them and decided on something simple. Orange sherbet. He dug out two scoops from the tub, rolling each into a perfect ball before plopping them into a cardboard cup. He grabbed a pink plastic spoon and went back into the storage room and climbed the step stool to Derek.

"Why are you here?" Ernie asked Derek. He dragged the spoon across a ball of sherbet before lifting it to the man's mouth. It was disconcerting, the way Derek's eyes followed his hand upward, and how his head dropped when he opened his mouth, how his tongue lapped at the spoon from above. Ernie fed him some more, two big spoonfuls, one after the other.

"Whoa," Derek said around a mouthful of orange. "Brain freeze." But the color in his face was pinker than it had been before. He sucked the ice cream and swallowed, his jaw working. "I was gonna rob you. The store, I mean."

Ernie was amazed at the confession, and the ease with which Derek gave it.

"What?"

"Hey, you must've figured by now. And no use pretending." Derek opened his mouth and made a small gesture with his head and the fingers at his neck. "More, please," he said. Ernie filled the spoon again. "I mean, I'm stuck, right? What could I possibly say to the sheriff besides the truth, right? I've been thinking about it for hours now—"

"Hours?" Ernie said, incredulous. The fellow had been here, upside down and alone and bleeding over the black-and-white tiled floor of the back room of the ice cream parlor for hours? Hours?

"Yeah. Pretty much since you guys closed up last night. What was that, eleven or so?"

"Eleven thirty." They were supposed to close at eleven, but a rush came in just before Ernie had a chance to twist the lock on the door, a swarm of folks from the drive-in movie theater close by.

"Plenty of time to try to think up some excuse, but, what excuse could there be, man. You know?" Derek had regained some of his strength from the orange sherbet; his words filled in the space of the storage room. Ernie remembered this about him. Derek was always the loudest in the bunch when he and his friends came in and sat at the small ice cream parlor tables. He was big, too, and he would make the dainty bentwood-backed chairs wheeze slightly under his heft—muscle, mostly. And he would sit with his long legs spread out in front of himself, taking up enough room for two or three people. And talk and talk. "So when the sheriff gets here, I'll just tell him the truth and suffer the consequences. How bad could it be? That's what I've been thinking all along. I mean, I didn't take anything, yet, right? How bad could it be?" Ernie tried to think of an answer, a response at least, but he was unaccustomed to so much conversation. He and Bert always communicated in that way of twins, never saying much but knowing everything, and as they grew older here in this tiny town, they spoke even less. "I'll just tell him everything," Derek said, and shifted in the ceiling and wiggled his fingers. Bits of dust fell into the cup of sherbet, and a small drop of blood.

The sheriff. Ernie looked down at the dust and blood in the paper cup, along with the last melted bit of sherbet. He shivered.

It hadn't occurred to Ernie to call the sheriff. He had thought of calling Bert, obviously, but he wanted to feed Derek something first, to maybe try to make him more comfortable for a little while before his brother got there and started figuring things out, started making a problem out of the visit. Of course they should call the sheriff, that would be the logical thing, wouldn't it? But Ernie knew, even before he went out to the front of the parlor to where the white phone hung on the wall in order to telephone Bert, that they would never call the law.

Certainly they'd had encounters with the police since they left their life in the city. In fact the afternoon they took off, they stopped at the bank in order to clear out their account—a substantial bit of cash that they had to carry in more than one bag—and on the way out an officer was on his way in, and they passed each other at the front door. The man was shiny and blue in his uniform, with a little gold pin fashioned to look like handcuffs holding his tie in place. When he saw first Robert and then Henry with their almost matching polyester sport coats and same haircut and glasses, the officer stumbled a bit, a snag in his shiny, perfect presence. And the twins were used to this reaction, they got it all the time. But then when the officer swept his eyes over the men and caught sight of the matching bags they carried, money bags, he stopped in his tracks and said, "What's this then, bank robbing twins?" And he looked serious, the officer, his face grim and stern and his hand on his gun in its holster, but then he broke the spell by snorting and laughing and holding the door open for Robert and for Henry in his wake. "Have a good day, gentlemen," he said, still laughing, and they nodded at the officer and walked—not too quickly—out to their Toyota and tossed the bags in the back and pulled carefully out of the parking lot.

Since then they always drove the speed limit and kept their license plates up to date and gave the local sheriff—a hometown boy with an associates' degree and friends on the council—free ice cream when he stopped by in uniform or brought his family in on a Saturday night.

Ernie let the phone ring eleven times like he always did, even though their rented house was tiny and it usually took no more than five rings to reach the phone in the kitchen, regardless of which room you were in. No answer, though, and he knew that Bert must be in the shower or way out back checking on his bonsai bushes, his nose full and his eyes streaming.

Ernie returned to the back room.

"You call the sheriff?" Derek asked, his eyes closed.

"Yes," Ernie lied. "There's some trouble out at Jack's Super, though." The fabrication grew easily. "Not sure what it is, maybe a real robbery. It's going to be a while." He picked up the grate from the floor and leaned it against the legs of the prep table and went about sweeping up the dust and bits of ceiling tile. It puffed up in little white clouds that made him sneeze.

"Bless you," Derek said, and opened his eyes. Ernie could feel him watching his movements. He used a dustpan to carry the debris to the big trashcan near the back door. Bert had left it unemptied the night before. Emptying the trash. That was one of Bert's jobs. Ernie shook off the twinge of irritation and turned back to his guest. Derek blinked upside down.

"You must be thirsty," Ernie said. Derek raised—or from this angle, lowered—his eyebrows. Ernie took it as a yes. Hours, he thought, the poor boy had been up there for hours, and now he just ate a couple of big scoops of ice cream which was filled with salt, everyone knew that, and of course he must be thirsty. Ernie was sorry he hadn't thought of it before.

He filled one of the large waxy paper cups with water from the prep sink and took a straw from a box. He climbed back up to Derek again, and lifted the straw past his eyes and nose to his mouth.

"Take it easy," Ernie said. "This could be tricky." But Derek, in that way that was becoming familiar to Ernie now, took too much of what was offered, gulped and choked and coughed, and Ernie had to duck his head to not get spit on. "What did I tell you?"

"Sorry, man. Sorry." Tears streamed down Derek's forehead into this hairline. His eyes were wet and wide and red. He coughed some more, craning his head away from Ernie's face. "Okay," Derek said finally, his voice quiet and rough. "Can we try that again?"

And so they did. And after some minutes of patience on the part of both men, the water was drunk and the cup set aside. Ernie got a soft terrycloth towel, one of those they used to wipe down the counter and tables, and pressed it gently against Derek's face, dabbing up the tears and water and snot left over from the coughing. The two men held eyes for what seemed like a full minute, and the gratitude that Ernie saw in Derek's gaze filled him like something warm. He folded the towel neatly before tossing it across the back room into the laundry bag next to the trash can, and stepped down from the stool.

Some time before Robert and Henry ran off, Henry had begun to see a girl. She was someone he had met in the laundry room of the apartment building, a chubby woman in her early twenties who had deep brown eyes and a soft smile. Weeks went by when the two of them always seemed to be there in the laundry room at the same time. No matter what day Henry did laundry (laundry was his job), the girl, Rachel, would show up in a matter of minutes after he did, carrying a white wicker basket of things, sometimes barely enough to make one load.

"Hello, stranger," she always said to Henry, even after the second time they'd bumped into one another, and she had reached out her hand and shook his with a remarkably firm grip and introduced herself. So they weren't really strangers, and yet Henry felt something like strange around her.

Whenever they met he got itchy and tight at the back of his neck, and tongue-tied and hot in the face. Rachel didn't seem to notice though, carrying on most of the conversation by herself, talking about her cat and her roommate and her mother's bad knees and her job managing the office of a chiropractor in the Loop. She had a way of tossing her hair back from her forehead, a slight lift of a hand and a flip of her head, even though she wore her hair in very short coils that only bounced in place when she did this. The gesture made Henry's stomach clench in a small, pleasant way. One day Henry watched as Rachel dropped two dishtowels, a washcloth, and one pillowcase into a machine.

"That all you got?" he said before he could think of any reason not to. "Barely worth the thirty cents, don't you think?"

Rachel blushed a pink that spread under the freckles on her round cheeks.

"Busted," she said and turned to face Henry. Her lips, he noticed, were the color of plums. "I'm not really here for the laundry," she said and tossed her head and made her curls quiver. And after what seemed to Henry like an agonizing few seconds of silence and staring at one another, Rachel spoke again. "I live on this floor," she said slowly and nodded at him. It was like she was helping him figure out the answer on a quiz. "I hear everyone when they come down to the laundry room." She paused again and shifted her feet; Henry noticed that they were very small and she was wearing bright white sneakers and no socks. Her ankles, peeking out from the bottoms of her blue jeans, were tan. And then Henry got it.

"Oh," he said, and he felt as though he'd just awakened from a confusing dream.

They'd dated for what seemed like a long while before Henry and Robert had to leave. Movies each time, and they sat in the balcony and made out like the teenagers around them. Rachel was Henry's first real girlfriend since college, since their parents died and Henry, in his grief and love and fear felt attached to Robert in a way that took most of his breath, a way that left him little room for anything else. But Robert, easy, handsome, confident Robert, had had plenty of women, short intense flings that Henry witnessed through the walls of their apartment. Now, though, he could not get enough of Rachel: her lips on his; her tongue, tasting of salt and butter and chocolate peanuts, in his mouth; her cushy flesh under his fingertips; her hand rubbing down the front of his pants; her hot breath on his face when they came up for air. He wanted to go all the way, but he didn't know quite how to do that, and now in his twenties he felt too old, too embarrassed to ask anyone, least of all Robert who already teased him horribly in incredibly juvenile ways. "Henry's got a girlfriend, Henry's got a girlfriend," whenever Henry dressed for a date. Henry ignored Robert except to see what he was wearing in order to put on something else—not the blue striped shirt like Robert had on, but the red plaid. Not the tan trousers, but the black ones. The oxblood loafers instead of the brown Hushpuppies. He never brought Rachel home; he never introduced her to his brother.

Henry suspected that Rachel would let him know when she was ready. That's how he thought of it, being ready, and he waited for clues in the things she did when they kissed at her front door. (What would it be, he wondered, a tug on his belt, a slight lifting of her skirt, an invitation inside for a nightcap like in the movies they only saw a few of the opening minutes of?) Only Rachel always said good night at the door, mumbled something about her roommate and Henry's brother and slipped into her own apartment and sent Henry home to more of Robert's teasing and a cold shower.

And then things came apart.

"Hey," Derek said, "Which one are you anyway?"

Ernie used to like it when folks couldn't tell him and his brother apart. After all, Bert was the good-looking one, taller and more at ease with things than he would ever be. Bert's eyes were hazel, and in certain lights almost golden, while Ernie's were plain old brown. Ernie had a chipped tooth in front, a childhood leftover from when Bert threw a snowball at his face once, a snowball packed hard as ice and hurled with significant force when Ernie thought they were just playing, just messing around, and had lobbed only handfuls of powdery snow toward his brother's back. But when Ernie started to bawl and threatened to tell their dad, a stern man who was always embarrassed by Ernie's weaknesses, his girlish hands and skinny chest and easy crying, Bert talked him out of it like he could talk him into or out of everything. Like he had talked him into stealing from the company's accounts.

"I'm Bert," Ernie said; he didn't know why. Bert would never have fed Derek; he would have taken care of everything right away. Ernie wasn't sure how he would have done that, but ran through a series of possibilities in his mind. Maybe he would have gone ahead and cut the hole in the ceiling even wider, allowing the boy to fall into a heap on the floor. Or perhaps he would have pulled Derek free, ignoring his howls of pain as he twisted and turned the intruder's body in the air duct, working it and working it like a loose tooth, wiggling it from the roots, ignoring the hurt and the blood. But then what? Would he let the intruder go? Make him promise not to say anything, and they wouldn't either, Bert and Ernie, they wouldn't press charges so long as Derek kept quiet about everything, too. But Ernie knew, and Bert would know, that Derek, loud, boastful Derek, would have to tell someone and who knows what sort of attention that would bring to the ice cream parlor, to the twins, to their made-up, entwined lives in New Hope.

"Bert," the fellow said. "Bert and Ernie. Those really your real names?" He squinted at Ernie, his cheeks pulling down toward his eyes.

"Yes, certainly," Ernie said. "Why wouldn't they be?" He turned from Derek's inspection and busied himself with the things he needed to do to open the shop. He was already behind schedule. He'd have to do something about the smell that came from the air duct, metal and something else now, like some small animal might have died up there. And the tables needed to be wiped down (Bert never did this at closing time) and the sidewalk in front swept clean of the night's debris—cigarette butts, candy wrappers, bits of leaves. Once he'd found a single baby shoe resting against the curb, scuffed and laced tightly. Another time he found a pair of panties, teenage girl-sized and yellow, with the word "Tuesday" written in red script under the waistband. That was on a Friday.

Ernie pulled a sheath of napkins from one of the boxes and put it on the prep table. He excused himself and went out front to gather the metal napkin holders from the front counter where Bert had lined them up—empty or near—the night before.

"You're not the mean one, are you?" Derek said when he returned. Ernie pushed a handful of napkins into a holder.

"Mean one?" He said over his shoulder. "One of us is mean?" He tried to sound light, like this was a surprise to him, this opinion, like he hadn't ever thought of it before.

"Yeah. You're the nice one. You always give away free stuff, samples and shit." Ernie flinched at the word and Derek noticed. "Sorry, I meant stuff." Derek's words were beginning to sound slurred, like maybe he'd had too much to drink. "Samples and stuff," Derek continued. "And say someone's on a date, you know, trying to impress or girl or something, you know, in order to get a little...you know what I mean. And so you take this girl to the ice cream parlor, only it's about closing time. You're the one who lets us in, who lets us hang out a little while, lets us prime the pump with some ice cream, if you know what I mean." Ernie faced Derek then and saw him smile and wink, only from where he stood next to the prep table it looked like it was Derek's bottom eyelid that closed. "You forget about the pennies if we don't have them, you scoop heavy."

In fact, it was Bert who did all of the things that Derek spoke about; Bert who gave away samples and kept the shop open late and waved off the pennies and scooped heavy. Ernie made rules and followed rules, but Bert did things his own way. For instance, it was Bert who got to go all the way with Rachel years ago—or Robert, rather, not Bert—and Henry who didn't. Henry, Ernie, didn't blame Robert for that, really; after all it was Rachel who came over to the apartment when Henry was at the grocery store. (Shopping was Henry's job.) She was drunk from a party at the office, a celebration of the chiropractor's impending nuptials. (Rachel had already invited Henry to come to the wedding as her date; he'd bought condoms just in case.) And how could Robert resist Rachel's mouth, her flesh, her tan ankles and warm, strong hands? It certainly wasn't Robert's fault that Rachel—at first—had mistaken him for his twin. Henry wondered when Rachel did catch on, did notice that Robert wasn't Henry at all but someone different, someone taller and handsomer and more experienced. When he got home with the bags of groceries and found Rachel crying on his couch, their (Robert's and Henry's) couch, and pulling the flaps of her cardigan around her body and Robert humming and scrambling eggs in the kitchen (cooking was Robert's job), he was certain that Rachel knew who was whom, which was which. And when she looked up at Henry standing near the open door with his arms full of groceries, he stared back at her, dumbfounded and aching and queasy, unable to move or speak when she stood up and picked up her sensible navy blue pumps and ran past him and out the door.

People always got them confused. But Robert, Bert, was the friendly one. Which meant, according to Derek's description, that Henry, Ernie, was the mean one. This rattled Ernie—even though he always secretly suspected it—that people thought of him as the mean one. He was only following the rules. Keeping a certain order. There was comfort in order. He'd always felt it. It was one of the reasons he'd gone into bookkeeping years ago. All those columns and tiny squares on the pages of the ledgers, all the contained figures in his handsome, neat script. Since he was a child, he'd spend hours practicing writing numbers and letters in blocks, working to get the tops and bottoms lined up, the width of the characters uniform. It satisfied him. While Bert's homework assignments were scribbled in uneven lines and turned in on ripped and wrinkled paper, Ernie's were even black marks on bright white sheets. Perfect.

And yet, Bert always got better grades. Things came so easily to him.

Ernie forced another batch of napkins into a holder.

"Ernie's not mean," he said to Derek, his voice tight. "He's just careful. Cautious."

"Sorry, man, you're right. It's not my place. That's your brother, man. I get that." He closed his eyes again, and Ernie saw that his face had gone pale once more, the color of buttermilk. The dead animal smell was stronger. Ernie ran cold water over another clean towel and touched Derek's temples with it, then the back of his neck. "That's good, man," Derek said, his eyes still closed. "I owe you," he said. Up close like this, Ernie saw that Derek's skin was smooth, absolutely without lines, as though he'd never had to worry about anything in his life, never had to hold a difficult thought. In the mirror each morning Ernie studied his own face and the crooked grid of lines that now passed over it, new ones, it seemed, etched there every day. He rinsed the towel and used it to cool Derek's forehead.

"I'm sorry about that Jew crap," Derek said then, and Ernie pulled the towel away.

"Excuse me," he said.

"You remember," Derek said and he opened his eyes again, looked at Ernie. "Years ago. When you first opened up. We were just kids then. Stupid. You know. We didn't mean anything."

Ernie's mind was blank for a few moments before it came back to him, that bright June morning when he and Bert arrived to open the shop together and found the windows painted with insults and threats and a backwards swastika. They were pretty sure it was the teenagers who did it, the boys who stood in line for ice cream and feigned big, loud sneezes into their fists: "Ah, ah, ah JEW!" and cracked up laughing. The twins had been in town for just months then, their bad deeds still fresh in the summer air around them. So when Robert said to get the bucket and the turpentine and forget about calling the sheriff, forget about what they saw and what they knew and what they imagined in the words on the glass, forget about everything, Henry agreed, pushed it out of his head, washed it away with a smelly rag and enough water to make it no longer visible, no longer there. This was something he could do, Henry, Ernie—he could make things neat. He could make it all clean.

"I don't remember," Ernie said.

"All right," Derek said. "I get that, too. But in case you do—remember I mean—remember that I'm sorry, okay?" Ernie went back to the sink and after a minute Derek said in a voice Ernie could barely hear over the water running, "What's up with the sheriff?"

"Yes," Ernie said. He poured bleach into the water and turned off the taps. "You're right. I'll go call again."

At the front of the shop, Ernie picked up the receiver and twirled the dial while holding down the metal cradle. He continued to hold it down while he spoke into the dead receiver: "Yes, this is Bert again, from the ice cream parlor. Yes. Yes, he's still here. Yes. Yes. Oh good. Thank you." And he noisily replaced the receiver in the cradle. "They're on their way," he called back toward the storage room. "Any time now. I'll be right back; I'm going outside for a minute." He listened for a response from Derek, but heard nothing. He pulled the push broom from its spot in a narrow cabinet next to the shake machine and unlocked the front door and stepped out into the spring warmth.

Close by, the door to the Temple of Air was propped open, and Ernie could hear the loud hum of voices spill out from it. He couldn't make out any specific words, but the sound reminded him of childhood and home, of Saturdays at the synagogue in the suburbs, a chorus of sounds aimed at something beyond knowing, at something greater than the everyday, something bigger and brighter and more beautiful than all that was visible. Ernie often stood silently outside the Temple of Air on a Saturday morning, listening and remembering and longing for something he could no longer name, something, he was certain, that was no longer available to him.

Once on a family vacation to visit their grand-parents in Florida, the Saltzmans had gone to a Mexican restaurant in the lobby of a nearby hotel. It was the first time any of them had eaten Mexican food, and Grandfather Saltzman complained through the entire meal about the spices, his gall bladder, his impending need for an Alka-Seltzer. The food was too exotic for Henry as well, only he would never say as much for fear of disappointing his father who sat across the table with his face pinched up against the complaints from the older man. Robert, however, loved the stuff, doused it with extra-hot salsa and washed it down with numerous Cokes. And after, the boys were allowed to join a dozen other kids on vacation in the tiled courtyard at the back of the restaurant, where they were blindfolded and given a stick to swing at a red, white, and green papier-mâché donkey until it busted wide open and spilled out squares of plastic-wrapped candy that tasted like cough drops and coconut.

The next morning Henry's grandmother wanted them all to go to synagogue together, but his father had made plans to go fishing instead. It hurt Henry to see Grandmother Saltzman's eyes moisten when they left the apartment in shorts and T-shirts, bound for the beach.

On the small motorboat (Henry had been expecting something else, a yacht maybe, like he'd seen in magazines at the dentist office) Robert began to feel ill, the night's overindulgence tumbling around inside of him as they bounced up and down on the waves. And Henry couldn't help it; when his father looked over at him, rolling his eyes in annoyance at Robert's moaning and heaving, Henry felt superior then, the stronger brother, the tougher, the better one. And when Henry caught his first-ever fish, a big thing, long and thick and silver-gilled and it flipped and slithered and thrashed at the bottom of the boat, Henry's father gave him a club, something that looked like a sawed-down baseball bat, and instructed him to hit the fish over the head, hard, and he did, tentatively at first, like he had the night before when he first swung at the piñata until he had slipped his blindfold up just a bit so he could see where to aim (he knew it was cheating, but no one noticed) and then swung harder. And the fish's head exploded, blood and scales everywhere, and Robert's face went absolutely white, except for where the bloody scales landed at the side of his nose and there wasn't even time for him, for Robert, to turn his head away, to vomit overboard into the sea. And Henry couldn't help it, he laughed at his brother covered in his own puke, and his father did, too. But then Henry helped Robert get cleaned up, throwing salty, cold water at him by the bucket, all the while picturing his grandmother later, home from synagogue and, once she saw this big, beautiful fish he'd killed for their dinner, willing to forgive him his truancy.

Ernie tested the weight of the push broom's handle as he swept the sidewalk. In another hour he'd have to open the shop. He wondered when Robert would arrive to work; he wondered if his brother felt better. On their childhood vacation, Robert had joined the family in eating Henry's fish; he had forgiven his brother for all those things he did and didn't do on the fishing trip. He knew that whatever happened, his brother meant him no harm. But life was complicated, and sometimes you did things in order to survive, and sometimes you did things just because you could. Sometimes you cheated and sometimes you stole. Sometimes you hurt people or insulted them for no apparent reason, and sometimes you were sorry, and sometimes you weren't. Sometimes you pretended to be who you really weren't, or finally became who you really were.

Robert understood Henry like no one else did or ever would. They were almost the same man. Ernie knew this. Maybe that's why he had told Derek that he was Bert. He was Bert. And Bert was Ernie. He pushed the pile of cigarette butts and bits into the sewer next to the curb and felt the sun on his shoulders as he went back into the ice cream shop. The bell rang and the freezers hummed, but even as he neared the back room, Ernie didn't hear a thing from Derek.

Good, he thought. Good. He was tired of Derek's talking. In fact, he was tired of Derek altogether. He had things to do. He smelled the sharpness of the bleach in the sink. It was time now— the twin knew as he hoisted the broom to his shoulder—it was time now to get things done.

This and Other Miracles

She was on the lookout for miracles. She'd seen one before. Two, really. That first one on the carnival ride and the little girl in the air. Maddie watched her pass by, her tiny hands reaching. *Oh*, Maddie thought. *Oh. Flight.* And the boy she was with, what was his name? She couldn't remember now, not so many years later. But he was cute, some, curly hair to his shoulders, a big nose that looked good on his broad face, over his sweet lips. She remembered that now, too, his lips, even if she couldn't remember his name.

But the little girl. The miracle. They were up there, she and the sweet-lipped boy, going round and round in that cage, high in the air when the girl fell. *Oh*, Maddie said out loud, maybe, because the little girl rolled a bit in her flight, and she looked at Maddie, smiling, giggling, and Maddie leaned forward, reached through the bars as the girl fell by and the boy said, *Careful, careful now, darlin'.* And another time Maddie would have thought that was the miracle, a sweet-lipped boy calling her "darlin'" like no one ever had, like no one, she thought, probably ever would again. But that wasn't it. There was more. The little girl rolling and tumbling and flying, and looking right into Maddie's eyes, reaching out, Maddie, too, but not close enough to touch, not close enough to catch. And then she was gone, the little girl. Or so Maddie thought.

There was a commotion above and below. And the ride stopped and then went, stopped and then went, one car and another emptying out on the midway, and even though they never said anything, Maddie and the boy, not the whole way down, not at the bottom where they got off the ride, they moved together like they had planned it, walking quickly away from the crowd gathering and gawking, from the parents of the girl, the sheriff quick to get there, the hubbub and the spot where the flying girl had landed. And past the rides and the games, away from the people running the other way, toward the girl, the boy (who Maddie didn't exactly know but had agreed to go on the ride with when he asked her while she stood in line by herself, alone and a little lonely) held Maddie's hand and led her to his friend's pickup truck and helped her into the flatbed of it and held her close and kissed and kissed and kissed her. She remembered that. How he breathed on her, and in her, like life-giving his breath was because she felt herself swell with it, go buoyant under the hot summer sun. They were doing it, then, it wasn't the first time, not for Maddie, and maybe not for him because he had a rubber and he stroked her first with a calloused hand and said, *This good? This good, darlin'?* And it was when he pushed inside of her and she caught her breath and looked past his shoulder that she saw the little girl again, her eyes bright and her hands reaching and smiling, she was smiling, and Maddie knew this was a miracle, the girl coming to her and the boy calling her darlin' and the rush of love and heat that lifted her up, up off the hard bed of the truck and so far out of her head that she couldn't remember her own name, much less his, the boy who called her darlin' and who after, when she passed him in the hallway at school, reached for her face with his calloused hand and walked on by, leaving his touch and something else on her. Like the little girl had left something on her when she fell, and then again when she appeared to her in the back of the truck.

A touch. A seeing. A sort of miracle.

The second one was when the tornado hit town and she ran outside into the mess of it. It was prom night, but Maddie was alone, no date, no dance for her. Her father forbade it and her mother said, *Listen to your father, dear.* And so she could not go to prom, and that was sad, and even sadder still, no one had asked her. Not the boy from the truck, and not the other boys who, at school, looked at her a little meanly, but showed up sometimes in her backyard and tapped on her window, told her to come out, just for a little while, come out and look at the moon, at the stars, and let them look at her, Maddie in the moonlight, and kiss her, touch her. And she would.

When the tornado hit town on prom night, the wind rattled her window and she thought, when she looked, that there was someone out there, a boy, a man, a shadow. Her mother and father were in the living room in the dark, drinking she knew, because they always were, fighting, she knew, because they always were. So Maddie opened her window like she had done so many times before and slipped out over the sill, felt the push of wind and rain against her face, her bare legs under the nightie she wore every night, even those nights when she met the boys outside to look at the moon. But it was good, this weather on her skin, and cool and thrilling. She ran toward the boy-shadow, but there was no one there, no one, nothing. Just empty lawn. Still, she loved being out there in the night, in the tornado. The *chugga chugga* of the wind made her vibrate; she tried to do cartwheels, but the wind blew her over. She laughed and laughed, her whole body wet now, her hair in strands, her teeth chattering. She stood up and tried to do a backflip, she was pretty good at gymnastics even though her parents didn't let her join the team, wouldn't let her try out for cheerleading. *Gotta keep your horizons small,* her dad said. She didn't know what that meant except that he never allowed her to do anything. One flip, not bad. A little low and wobbly on the landing, but she was getting there. Another, better still. She planted her feet and the wind came stronger and she counted under her breath, *one two three.* She sprung up into the air and reached with her hands over her head and felt her body lift. And lift. And lift.

Later, who knows how long, when her folks found her in a pile in the wet grass, her father lifted Maddie in his arms and carried her inside the house, and her mother patted her and patted her, her face, her hands, her clammy legs.

What, Maddie said, coming to, but she remembered what. The flip then the flying, the house and the world beneath her. She knew then, while she flew, what her father had meant, because she could see the horizon then, a long line of darkness and roiling clouds, but at the edge of it, where she knew the earth began its rounding, a glowing stripe that beckoned her. She tried to get there, pulled herself like swimming in the air, in her flight, but that is where her memory stopped. Then there was her father and her mother and her bedroom that smelled green and wet like the outdoors, like an open window, a way out. And she was sure her father would punish her like he did sometimes, a smack and a dark closet, but he didn't. He just leaned in close and looked into her eyes, kissed her forehead. His face looked soft like it never did, sad and tired, and he kissed her again. *Darlin'*, he said. *Oh my sweet darlin'*.

Another miracle.

And it had been a few years since the miracles, the first one, the second. Still, Maddie watched for them, wanted them. She even prayed for them, a little, at the Church of New Hope up the block from her house where Pastor James stood at the front and spoke quietly and without, Maddie thought, much conviction. He looked at her sometimes, the way those boys used to in high school. Like he could see right into her and what he saw there was not too pretty. She knew it was the residue from her miracles he could see; she felt it herself, a murky blackness like something untended and unwashed. Like the miracles came and left, and in their wake a thick, dark tangle.

Her parents had died one after the other, her father from a broken heart Maddie wanted to believe, just days after her mother went. The house was found to be filled with carbon monoxide, the windows nailed shut ever since she ran into the tornado, the furnace failing over a couple of months. But Maddie preferred her version of heartbreak and loss, even as she stopped feeling sick herself once the furnace was fixed, once the windows were opened wide and she came home from the hospital and was allowed back inside. At the Church of New Hope, Pastor James gave the sermon, quiet still, but kind. *Good people,* he said about her parents as though they might have been, *Good people and bad things.*

There weren't many people at the service, and even fewer came to the house afterward, afraid, maybe, of all that bad air. But Pastor James was there, and he sat with her after the last few left, and when she cried, he sat beside her and put his arm across her shoulder. When he followed her to the floor, to the old rug that smelled like tobacco and dust, Maddie wasn't surprised, not really. She knew this was what she did, lay down with boys and men; she—like everyone else in town—knew it was who she was.

Darlin' she said to him, whispered it into the spot where his neck met his shoulder. She hoped he would say it, too, but he didn't. He didn't say anything, only kept moving and moving; the rough noise from him reminded her of the tornado. She matched his rhythm and his breath, hanging on, hanging on. And Maddie looked up to the ceiling, to where the stains from her father's cigarettes made yellow clouds above her. And there, there, she saw something familiar. A little girl, maybe the little girl, the one who flew from the carnival ride all those years ago. She thought it was her, she hoped it was her. Because this was what she needed, she knew as she clung to Pastor James, as she felt her body lift up and up. This. Another miracle. This.

Deer Story

And when you see it there on the side of the road (above it, really) it's already too late. You know. "Don't," you say. Out loud maybe. But it doesn't matter what you want (or don't) it's too late already, and it's hitting the ground on all fours then up again and into the lights, into the way but in the air still, bounding, and for a second you hope—maybe believe—it will clear. It will beat you, you hope, over that spot in the road, or rise high enough so you might pass underneath. But no. Of course not. You clip it as it springs up, feel the impact of all four ankles at once hit the front of the car, watch—foot hard on the brake where it's been since this started—as it lifts and tumbles, sideways up and over, an antler taking a stab at the top of the windshield, a road map of cracks spreading out and down the shatterproof glass. And it's behind you now. It fills the mirror, big and brown and coming down like something stuffed and heavy. You squeeze your eyes closed to absorb its landing, and when you look again it's gone. And that's when you swerve—too late, but it couldn't have mattered any earlier. (You find out from the handsome neighbor with the scarred wife that it's a path they all follow in rut like they are, third killed in a week in a quarter mile. Killed by the rut.) But still, you swerve, and ahead, the man you thought you loved but know that you will leave—in his own car driving home in tandem from a bar in the city—sees your lights weave out of his rearview then in again and then out as you pull to the side of the road and sit there, shaking. And his taillights flash white and he's backed his way to you, jumps out of his car and in shirt sleeves, with his hands jammed down his pockets, he bobs foot to foot outside your window. "What," he says, and his breath is white shadow against black sky. He doesn't know. And you're mad that he hasn't noticed; it's just another thing he's missed. "A deer," you say when you open the window finally. "Stay there," he says then. (For the first time. But not the last.) And you do this time while he runs around in the cold in the weeds, to his car and back, in the weeds again. For the smallest moment you think maybe, just maybe, it wasn't hurt, just tripped more or less over the hood of the car. But then the man you know you will leave comes back, his eyes bright in the dark and his hands trembling, holding—of all things—an X-acto knife. "This won't do," he says, "it's not enough." And you know exactly what he means. Then he tells you to go on home, get the neighbor to bring a gun. (The neighbor's a hunter, you'd found out over burgers on the grill. They both— he and she—used to be. But his wife—nice woman, too bad about her face, one whole side scooped out from eye to chin—won't even eat meat now and hardly leaves the house.) So you do what you're told, drive on the last three miles alone, the windshield a kaleidoscope of darkness. You're crying now and it's hard to see, thank God it's a straight shot of highway.

And in the nice little subdivision, suburbs in the country, split-levels and townhomes where the man you are leaving built you a brand new house (like maybe that'd be enough), you pull into your drive and run to the neighbors' and when you pound, he's there in a flash. And you notice again how handsome he is. You remember how his back felt when you rubbed against him, his whole self a warm wall between you and the cold air of the open refrigerator, his hands choking the necks of the beers, and you reached around him for yours, flattened your breasts to him, wanted him. And the man you are leaving was out there, with the burgers and the wife, but you were inside with the neighbor who turned around and smiled so small it looked like it hurt. Then he circled one icy hand under your shirt and let it get warm on the low curve of your back. And outside there was small talk and quiet, and inside there was nothing but this. But tonight his wife's there, too, in shadow behind him. It's always dark in their house, you can't help but notice. And they listen while you tell and he's half out the door when you remember this: "Got a gun?" you say and he stops dead, one hand on the doorknob, his face draining, white. And his wife steps back and turns away. But it's just a quick moment, a small shift, before he says "I got something." And he spins off in his truck and you make your way across the lawns to your house and inside and crawl into bed, clothes and all; and under the warmth of the blankets you shake and you pray. You don't even know if you believe in God, but shouldn't you apologize to someone? You didn't mean to do it, but you did it, and you asked to be forgiven, it wasn't your fault, but you were sorry, so sorry, so very, very sorry. And when your head was packed tight from the praying and the crying, you rolled onto your back—still, finally—and stared at the ceiling. You waited in the wide bed you shared with the man you are leaving, watched for the white columns of his headlights to come through the window. And then out of a dream starting, you hear voices, and the neighbor says somewhere outside the window "accident" and "shotgun" and "face" and "fault." And you put it together in the dark, about the neighbor's wife. The part that seemed missing. And you get it now, you've figured it all out. He did it. He'd shot half her face off (an accident, what else could it be?) yet still there they were. Together. And you hear the man you used to think you loved outside the window, too. "Oh my" and "Christ man, I'm really sorry," and his voice sounds different than you're used to, sounds soft, liquid. But then they're laughing, the two of them, and the neighbor says, "We'd better gut this sucker," and you hear "Yeah, baby, fresh meat!" And whatever you'd started to think in that moment when his voice went soft, about changing your mind, about staying maybe, was gone. You hugged the blankets over your heart and turned your back to the window and knew in that way you knew when you'd hit the deer (there just isn't any other end to this story) it was already too late.

The Things That'll Keep You Alive

It was at moments like this one—naked and dripping from the shower, leaning over the bedside table, rifling through the drawer for a light—that I miss my breasts the most. That sounds odd, I know, but it's true. There's a definite body memory I have: the heavy swing of them, a slight tug from my shoulders all the way down to my rib cage. Only that's all it is, a memory. When I lean over now, the air is empty beneath me, and in some way that goes far beyond physical, I ache.

And maybe it's that ache that makes me stand back up again, and then not move even as I realize Alfred Huffner, Hoof, is there, right outside my window—checking some contracting matter, I suppose—and he sees me, exposed and scarred. He doesn't move, either, doesn't even flinch. His eyes travel down my neck to my belly button, travel side to side, following the scars. And it's like a whole day passes as we stand there, the warm breeze blowing in my window and bringing with it the sickeningly sweet smell from my mother's rose garden (neglected since her death), and the smell of earth and gasoline. Trucks pull up into my drive, I hear gravel spitting and men shouting, and still I stand. And still Hoof stands. He looks up into my face, and I look into his, and his eyes are sober and kind like they always are, like they have been on those mornings when we share a cup of coffee before his crew gets there and don't talk much, just sit in an easy kind of quiet. Then he shrugs a little and turns back to whatever it was he'd been doing before this moment. And though I don't want to (what I really want is to lean out the open window and feel the cool sill against my breasts) I pull the shade.

In the mirror I saw what he saw. The stick-straight posture passed down from my mother; hair like rusty coils, wild and full and thick in spite of everything; a slightly worn, but perhaps not unpleasant, over-thirty face; strong shoulders; hips without much curve; flat stomach (thanks to the chemo); and the empty plane of skin stretched tight and stitched across my breast plate, my ribs. I sucked on a cigarette to light it, watched the chest expand and lift. When I got my first glimpse after the surgery, I'd expected there to be nipples. I felt them still, phantom nipples, and even though they'd told me all that would be gone ("There won't be much," said a perky A-cupped attendant, "but there won't be the bad stuff either") I'd expected to find them. Sometimes it happens like that still when I look in the mirror: where'd they go? I'd had nipples long before I had breasts; you'd think I might have them after.

This is how the day would go. I'd dress in the dark and listen to my house. Someone would walk on the roof and it'd creak. I'd move from room to room, stay out of the way, and listen. This small creak, a quiet groan, an occasional slam. All the changes the house was going through, I kept hoping it might make more of a fuss. But through all its years of us as a family here together, then the three short ones when my dad was sick, the long seventeen my mom spent here alone, the single one of her dying, and now this one with me back and trying to make it all it's never been—bright, big, open—this old house took on its own stubborn silence. The noise came from the work and the men who did it.

In the evenings, when the house was empty and quiet, I would go down to the kitchen, pour myself a scotch, and take something to help me sleep. I knew this was no good for me, but it helped. It really did. Usually. Those times I felt sick, though, too much this, not enough that, I couldn't help but think about my friend Ariana who liked heroin "socially," she said, and how she said it made her sick each time she snorted it, but then she'd vomit and then she'd wait a minute, maybe two, and then, miraculously, she'd feel like she was pure and golden, like she was magic.

So I'd pour another drink, look out into the night through my big, new windows and wait (not always successfully) to feel like magic.

This time, it's bad. I'm going, going, going—all slipping down, down in the chair, down in my head, down deep and bad. I want to look out the windows, out into the cool black, but I can't keep my head up, it won't hold, and it falls back, rolls on my neck and it's the horrible bright white I see, the burning glow of the overhead fixture, big and smarting against my eyes. And I want to close them, close this out, this hot light, but I'm afraid, afraid if I do I'll go under, I've been there before, under the sickening spell of what's supposed to make me better. My stomach roils and my limbs loosen and I feel my forehead go slack and then my eyes roll back or close, I don't know which, but I'm not seeing my kitchen anymore, I'm in town, outside on the corner of something and Main, but I feel far, far away from everything, from everyone, and it's so dark now I can't see a damn thing, and the wind picks up, I can hear it, a great big whoosh like blood in my ears, and a tapping, and I can barely hold my ground, my arms are lifted from my sides and blow up and over my head like I'm flagging down a taxi with both hands high, but it's not me doing the lifting, it's the wind. And I know in a minute *I'm* going to lift off, to be blown away, up and over the houses I can't see but I know are there, out of the small town that for some reason I want more than ever to stay put in. And I feel a coldness creep up inside me, all the way from my feet up through my fingertips stretched and wiffling in the wind, and I'm afraid, terror-stricken and then, just like that, a hand is on my shoulder and it works its way up my arms and brings them back down and holds them, holds me. Not a hug, not that, just a hand on each wrist, and the dark starts to change, I can see things now, lights in windows and a shimmer of leaves on trees. And when I turn around, it's an old face I see, something familiar about it. *Don't I know you?* Maybe he can't hear me, the wind is so loud: whoosh, whoosh. He moves his head, a nod or a shake, I can't tell, and he says *You're okay, Sandy. You're all right.* And I shake my head hard, only I know I am barely moving and say *No* and I need to tell him that I am going to blow away. And he says it again, *You're all right,* and he's so close I can feel his breath on my skin, *You just need some grounding,* he says, and he lifts his hand up and holds out two fingers and wraps my hand around them and says *Squeeze.* And I do, but I can't even feel my own grip, much less his fingers, and I search his face. *Are you sure I don't know you?* And the houses around us go dim through their windows and he says again, louder, *Squeeze, Sandy, squeeze,* and I hear it sharp and clear through the whooshing, and I do and I mean it this time, I squeeze as hard as I can, and I feel it up my forearm and into my biceps and all the way across both shoulders and down to my feet, which I can tell are on solid ground. And the lights in the houses around me go bright again, and brighter still, so bright my eyes sting—but it's a good sting this time—and the whooshing slows and goes quiet, and in the bright silence I come to and there's Hoof, his face familiar and close and his fingers wrapped tightly in my fist.

"You didn't answer when I knocked," he said when I dropped his hand. He turned away from me while I used the napkin he handed me to wipe the tears from my eyes, the spit from chin. "I saw the light, and it's pretty hard not to see right in here with all the windows." He faced me again. "You didn't look too good."

I nodded. "Uh, thanks," I said, trying out my voice. It sounded rough and too loud. "I mean," I said more quietly, "I mean, thanks. Thanks."

Hoof waved a hand between us. "Sorry to come by so late, but I wanted to share something with you." He walked back to the kitchen door, and I couldn't help but wonder, like I always did, why he tilted like that, heavy and stiff on one leg, pushing off with the other. He opened the screen and picked up his briefcase from the stoop.

"Hoof—" I started. Even though the worst of things was over, I still felt shaky under the weight of the pills, the booze. I wasn't up to looking at blueprints or tile samples or paint swatches.

The briefcase seemed heavy as he hoisted it onto the table. "Hoof," I said again, but before I had a chance to go on, he popped both clasps and flipped back the lid. The case exploded open and full of red, and it took me a second to realize that what he had there were tomatoes. A dozen at least, maybe more, big, red, shining tomatoes. "Jesus," I said.

"Damn straight," he said. "Grew 'em myself." And he picked one up and lobbed it—a slow underhand arc—in my direction and I caught the cool ball of it sure and true and bounced it in my palm, admiring its heft.

"Lovely," I said.

"Tastes even better," he said, and he selected another from the case and wiped it against his sleeve like he was polishing an apple and bit from it in just the same way. Juice and seeds ran down his chin. He smiled through the scarlet and talked through the pulp. "Fruit of the goddamn earth. Here," and he pushed the glistening thing at me so quick and close that I didn't have time to think before I opened my mouth and took it in, glorious and wet and sweet.

"Mmm, mmm," I said like someone in a commercial, only I meant it. And then I realized that I hadn't eaten since midmorning, hadn't even recognized I'd been hungry, because I'm not much anymore. But I swallowed down the mush and its coolness calmed the hot roiling in my belly, so I took the tomato from Hoof and finished it off in a few huge bites. "More?" he asked and I nodded and he pointed to the one I still held in my hand and I laughed and got to work on that one while he brought down a plate from the cupboard and sliced another tomato and twisted a pepper mill over it and placed it between us. We ate, concentrating and slurping, and I felt myself fill up in a way that I hadn't felt in months—maybe years—and each bite made me want more and more until I was stuffed and sighing. We sat back and groaned and rubbed our bellies. I patted Hoof's hand. "You're a good man, Alfred Huffner," I said. And maybe it was just the crimson afterglow of tomatoes, but I could swear the man blushed.

"I'm an old man," he said.

"Yeah? How old?"

He used the edge of the table to push himself up, "Water?" I nodded. He pulled two glasses out of the cupboard that he designed and supervised the building of. "I used to say 'Guess', but somewhere along the line people started guessing older instead of younger. Sort of got to hurting my feelings." He handed me my drink. "Fifty-five," he said.

My dad was fifty-five when he died; the cancer and its treatment had wrinkled and shrunken him. I was barely nineteen and thought that was what fifty-five looked like: brittle and gray. But Hoof was tan and healthy, burly and white-haired. "I'd have pegged you for younger," I said.

"You're kind," he said. "It's the job."

"Really? Contracting? I'd think it would wear you out."

He must have seen my eyes slide over his legs because he slapped the bad one and said, "What, this? This damn war wound?"

"You were in the war? Vietnam?"

Hoof laughed. "Nah." He thumped his chest with his knuckles. "Asthma. But I've seen combat. Hell, anybody's been married has seen combat. You ever been?"

I shook my head. "No. I got kind of close once, but then—" I thumped my own chest. Then I said, "I guess I've always been partial to being alone."

"Being married is as alone as it gets." And he shrugged a little, like he had that morning at my window.

"Jesus, Hoof," I dipped my fingers in my glass and flicked water at him, "Lighten up, will ya?" But I thought I knew what he meant. My parents had been married twenty-five years before my dad died. Most of the time they were in the same house they'd be at opposite ends; or if they were in the same room, they could be sitting side-by-side on the couch, not touching, not speaking, each reading a book or a magazine or maybe watching TV and, the way they looked from the outside, single and separate—my mom and her perfect posture, my dad hunched and gathered into himself—they might as well have been strangers in a waiting room. And then, after Dad's death, whenever I came to see her, I couldn't help but think how Mom looked and moved exactly the same way she had before. She took up exactly the same amount of space she always had, sat on her side of the couch, slept on her side of the bed, set her place in the same spot on the dining room table even when she ate alone. I don't know what I was expecting. Maybe that she would spread out some, reclaim the house as entirely her own. Or, since she didn't do that, maybe I thought she should look un-whole in some way, like parts of her had died with Dad. Maybe I wanted her to walk like Hoof walked, listing to one side, her body yearning for a support that was no longer there. Phantom support. But her posture stayed perfect as always.

"How long were you married?"

"Eighteen years."

"What happened?"

"She left me."

"How come?" I don't know why I wanted to know this, or even if I did. But the thing is, I had been alone in this house for six months (except for the men working) and, while I liked the solitude, I missed real conversation. Most times I talked to the workmen about nothing—answered the questions I could, made small talk about the weather, the headlines. When Ariana called, we were always interrupted by her other line or her pager, and it was hard to navigate a dialogue through that chaos.

"I drank too much. She screwed around."

"Because you drank too much?"

"Maybe I drank too much because she screwed around. I'm not sure now. Sort of a chicken and egg thing, I guess. I don't really feel like talking about it, though." Hoof rubbed his forehead with his palm, worked his thumb and fingers into his temples.

"Uh, sure," I said. "None of my business, anyway." And I tried not to sound disappointed, but I was never very good at that. I got up and pulled a fresh pack of cigarettes from the freezer, lit one up, set an ashtray on the table next to the pill bottle. Hoof looked at me a good long time.

"All right, but just the short version." He took a deep breath, then: "Went out one afternoon with the guys after we completed a job way ahead of schedule. Got good and stiff. Now, I'm not too smart about what I can and can't do when I've been drinking, but I always knew not to drive. Paulie—you know Paulie? The good-looking young guy, my foreman—his first year on the crew, and he wasn't old enough to drink legally, even though we did slip him a couple of shots. Anyway, he's the most sober, so he gives me a lift, and I leave my truck at the bar. So now I'm home and watching TV and I hear this banging about on the roof. It's pretty windy that day, so I figure it must be some of those shingles I'd seen were starting to come a little loose. Anyway, drunk as I was—and I was drunk, let me make that clear—I climb up onto the roof and I'm not up there much time at all when Jess comes home and it's windy, like I said, right?" I thought he wanted me to say something here, but before I could, Hoof went on. Fast. "So when she steps out of her car she looks goddamn stunning, the wind blowing her long dark hair all around, she looks young and sexy and I'm thinking maybe I'll surprise her, you know, stand up and beat my chest like Tarzan up there on the roof, or maybe I'll do some flip off the gutter, land in front of her on the sidewalk, sweep her into my arms. You know, real hero stuff.

But then this other car pulls up and it's some guy I've never seen before and she stops on the walk and he gets out of his car, and my throat tightens up but I'm thinking, okay, all right, nothing out of line so far, and they can't see me because I'm on my belly on the roof, and there's no reason for them to be looking up anyway." Hoof stopped and took another swallow of air and then drank the rest of his water, picked up a tomato and rolled it between his hands. He met my eyes for a second and then looked over my shoulder and out through the windows into the night. "So they walk up the walk, her leading the way and he's pretty close on her heels, and then he reaches out, slick as shit, and slides his hand over her ass and then up the back of her little skirt. And she doesn't even tilt." I wanted to tell him he didn't have to finish, but I kept quiet and kept listening and he kept on talking, and it seemed like our only option. "And then they're getting so close to the house I'm starting to lose my view, so I scrabble over the roof toward the edge—and I'm still stiff, remember—and the next thing I know, I'm on my back on the front lawn and Jess and this asshole are looking down at me like I'm goddamn Dorothy waking up after Oz."

"Shit," I said.

"Yeah." Hoof blinked a few times and made a sound that could have been a laugh. "Good story, huh? Anyway, she came to the hospital later—that's how I banged up my hip, in case you didn't already figure—and I told her to leave. And by the time I got home a couple days later, she had."

"I'm sorry," I said, stupid as that sounded. Hoof waved it off.

"I'm not. I didn't want her around feeling guilty—or worse, pity. Didn't want her confusing that feeling with something else. It wasn't until just then that I realized that she always loved me best when I was hurt. Jesus, not like that's healthy or anything, right?" He looked at me like I should say something here, take his side, maybe. Only all I could think of right then was how when I came out of surgery and saw Ariana there and a couple of other people from work, smiling and crying at the same time, I felt my empty chest swell up and heard my own voice in my head, small, quiet, young as a girl's: *they love me*, it said, and I knew it was true, *they love me.*

Hoof went on. "So anyway, you'd think this would be the time for me to really go off, you know? Get drunk and stay that way. But the thing is, I didn't. Once Jess was gone, I didn't much want to drink anymore. I hadn't even realized until then how numb I'd been for so long. With her gone and the booze under control, I felt sort of alive again." Hoof picked up my glass of scotch, twirled it, put it down again. "Funny the things that'll keep you alive."

I stubbed out my cigarette, and without even thinking, lit up another.

"And those things will kill you."

"We're all dying, Hoof." I took a good long drag and blew the smoke in his direction.

"Now who should lighten up?" He said and swatted the smoke away, but then he added, "No offense."

"I'm thirty-seven," I said then, out of nowhere. Hoof nodded. I waited a minute before I said, "Okay. Now, you're supposed to say 'Thirty-seven? No way' or something here, Hoof." He nodded again and wiped his palms on the knees of his jeans and smiled that small smile, his eyes moved over my face.

"Looks like maybe you've seen some combat yourself," he said, almost a whisper. He took my hand and wrapped it around his fingers. "Even still, you're a beautiful woman."

And I tried to laugh, to lighten up, but instead what happened was I started to cry.

I'm not sure how it went then. Maybe he held me or maybe I held him. Maybe it was a kiss that started it all off, although who kissed whom is beyond me. But somehow it happened, and we ended up in my bedroom, my mom's room, really, on my big, soft, new bed and he's naked and I have my shorts off but my shirt on—I couldn't go that far yet and he didn't make me, this was as far as I'd been in almost a year and I kept thinking it should be more difficult than this, but it wasn't, it was easy—and he's on top of me and inside of me and his chest is fleshier than mine and hard, too. "What does it feel like, Hoof?" I can't help but ask.

"Warm, nice." He laughs a little. "Like I remember." And he pushes deeper into me.

"Not that," I say, and I put his hand up under my shirt on my flatness. "This."

He pulls back just far enough to look into my face. He runs his hand over my clavicle, my ribs, my scars. "Warm, nice," he says again.

"What else?" I take a deep breath and unbutton the shirt, slowly, slowly, watching his face all the while. He doesn't look away.

"Smooth, hard." He kisses that place where I remember the nipple, and, reflex I guess, I gasp and grind against him. He rubs his thick chest over mine. "Sort of like the first time." He moves with me.

"Like some flat-chested school girl?" I ask.

"No, not like that." He strokes my skin, traces the line of a scar with his fingers. "It's like how you imagine for a long time just what it will feel like, how wonderful and soft and electric, but still, that first time, it's not like anything you imagine." We rock together.

"Is that good?" The smell of my mother's rose garden mixes with the smell of his flesh, sunburn and Old Spice.

"Good, yes," he says.

I can barely hear him.

"So good," he says. Or maybe I do.

"So good. So, so, so good."

Ariana called from the trading floor, a slow day. "They miss you here," she said, and I knew it wasn't true, but I appreciated her saying it. "What's keeping you away from all this money?" She sounded giddy, her voice tight and high. I could tell she'd been winning.

"Come on out to the house," I said. "It's about done. The men will be around just a few more days."

"Men." And the way she said it, all thickness and breath, I couldn't help but remember the old days when after the markets closed we'd spend hours getting dressed up for the clubs, sucking in our cheeks and our stomachs in front of the mirror, making bets on who'd be wearing the same clothes to work the next day.

"Construction men," I clarified. I could hear the expanding sound of shouting on the floor. I looked at my watch. Twenty minutes to closing.

"Be out in the morning," Ariana said, and she hung up.

I knew better than to expect her in the morning; it was noon when the small, sleek BMW pulled in the drive. From the wide windows in the kitchen, I could see Hoof's crew rest their sandwiches in their laps and their sodas at their sides and it was like a moment of stopped time when the door opened and Ariana stepped out of the car onto the gravel drive in her three-inch platforms, second-skin black capris, and creamy white blouse. She tossed her short raven hair and smiled up the line of guys while she picked her way over the piles of lumber and scattered equipment that littered the path to my front door.

"Heaven, girl, it's like total heaven." And while she was looking around at the changes I'd made to the house—the new windows; the skylights; the bleached, highly glossed floors; the built-ins—I wondered if Ariana was talking about something else.

"Let's go out," I said, and I saw her face go dark, a quick pass, and then she grinned.

"Sure, sure," she said, "You're probably cooped up here most of the time, anyway, right? You change, and I'll wait outside." Before I could tell her I was already dressed, that shorts and one of my dad's old shirts I'd found in a trunk in the basement were pretty much standard uniform for me these days,

Ariana went back out on to the front porch, tossed her hair, and lit up a cigarette. I'd seen this opening act before, many, many times. So instead of sticking around for the rest of the show, I went to find something else to wear.

I dug around in a box to find my pencil-legged jeans, the ones I used to have to wriggle into and then lie flat on the bed to zip. They bagged now in the butt and at the knees, and I cinched them up with a wide black leather belt that I poked a new hole in with a corkscrew. My stomach I knew was my best feature now, so I found a cropped tee shirt with puffy shoulder pads (way out of fashion) and hoped that my bare midriff and broad shoulders would draw attention away from the empty chest.

Outside, Ariana was talking with Paulie and Hoof, and when she leaned in close as one of them spoke, when she threw back her head and laughed, eyes closed, I knew what was coming next. The men let their gaze move down her neck to her breasts and Ariana knew it, too, and she'd work the moment—like I used to—shoulders back, chest out. And it goddamn hurt me to watch.

"Let's go," I said, and took her arm.

"Where you women off to?" Hoof asked. It was good that he took his eyes off Ariana and put them on me then, on my face, on my belly, on my legs, on my face again. It was good that he kept them there.

"Get something to eat, maybe," I said. But I wasn't at all hungry.

"The Inn's got a good lunch special," Paulie said to Ariana, and I half expected him to ask to come along.

"Really?" And the way she said that one word, I knew she'd have left me to go with him, easy as that. It was an unwritten rule from the old days: better offer, no hard feelings. And for just a minute, I wished that it would happen. But then Hoof pulled Paulie back to work and Ariana pulled me into her little black car and we headed towards town.

When we got out at the municipal lot, I wished I'd worn my shorts. My legs felt weak beneath the heaviness of my jeans and my shirt clung to my back.

"We're here," I said and pulled open the heavy glass door to Anchors Inn. Ariana stepped past me and into the dark restaurant. I leaned back against the door and let its coolness work its way into my body. Slowly, my strength started to return.

"This place is famous for its ribs," I said as the hostess walked us to our table, "But it's got a pretty mean salad bar, too." Ariana looked around and I couldn't help but feel embarrassed by the tacky red-checked oilcloths on the table, by the fake, flickering, electric lanterns on the wall, by the red booths, their vinyl scarred with cigarette burns—and who knew what those yellowish stains were? "It's exactly the same as when I was a kid," I said. It sounded like an excuse.

Ariana smiled widely at me, "Very retro."

A couple was seated at the table next to our booth. They looked out of place, the man in fresh khakis and a forest-green Polo shirt, the woman in a linen summer shift, simply cut, the color of eggshells. Once the hostess moved away, the woman reached for the man's hand across the table.

"An affair," Ariana mouthed to me.

The two focused so intently on one another they were unaware of us studying them.

"Maybe," I said.

Ariana lit up a cigarette and slid the pack to me. "So? Who's the guy?" she asked through a mouthful of smoke.

"Don't ask me," I said, still watching the couple.

"Not that guy, dope." She threw her lighter at me. "Your guy."

"What guy?" I tried to stall, but we both knew it was no use. We had known each other since I'd moved to Chicago, a nineteen-year-old virgin. The morning after I'd had sex for the first time, Ariana bumped into me on the elevator at the Mercantile Exchange. "Your eyes," she'd said. "Yes?" I'd said. "You did it, didn't you? You can always tell from the eyes." And whether she knew from my eyes or from our big-mouthed desk clerk who had seen me the night before in the bar at Pago Pago with the man who would be my first, the bottom line was Ariana knew. Ariana always knew.

"It's one of those men hanging around your house, isn't it? Oh, see—you're blushing. I knew it—"

I dipped my head.

"Who? Wait, don't tell me, let's make it a game. I'll guess. If I get it, you buy."

And even before the game started I felt in my belly that it was a bad idea. But it was hard to deny Ariana her games.

"Good-looking?"

I nodded.

"Strong?"

I nodded again.

"Wait, what am I saying—they're construction workers for God's sake. They're all strong."

I could see her walking down the line of men in her mind's eye. She ticked them off with a click of her tongue. "The dark guy's kind of cute, but too ethnic for you." She made a small *X* in the air between us. "That boy, the young one?" She watched my eyes, I looked back at the couple. The woman was leaning forward now, speaking hard and quiet. The man leaned forward, too. "Nah, too much work with a young one like that. Not enough payoff—no matter what they say about recovery. A million quickies can't take the place of a good long screw, you ask me. So if it's not the young one—" I felt my shoulders tighten, my teeth clench. The man at the next table sat back now, crossed his arms over his chest, turned to look at something on the wall. The woman's hand stayed palm up on the table between them. "There is that old guy. Handsome, if you like that hard-ridden rugged look. But he's a bit damaged, isn't he?" Ariana went on talking, oblivious to what she had just said and to whom she had said it. I twisted my napkin in my lap. My head started to pound. "I mean, he's got that limp. Still, he is good-looking. But old." She dragged on her cigarette. "Nope. Not the old guy. Not like he wouldn't be grateful. They are, you know, those old guys. Grateful for what they can get." She twirled her cigarette in the ashtray, sharpened the ember. "That's sort of a cliché anyway, isn't it? I mean, any one of them would be a cliché, the construction worker and the lonely lady in the house." She laughed and glanced back at the couple, oblivious, still. I think maybe I hated her. "Not the old guy, that would be like fucking your father."

"You're running out of options," I said, grateful the waitress was there to take our order. We passed the couple on our way to the salad bar. The man was speaking now, "...bad timing...I'm less than...please." The woman looked to be in pain, her lips pressed tight, her eyes squeezed closed.

At the lettuce, Ariana looked back over her shoulder toward the couple and snorted. "Oh, please, it's all so dramatic." But for some reason, I felt the tiniest knot forming in my throat.

"I know," Ariana said when we were back at the table. She pierced a cherry tomato with her fork. "The tall one."

"Tall one?"

"You know, dreamy guy. Oh, it is, it is. I can just feel it." She grabbed my wrist. "Don't tease me, it's him isn't it? The one with the dark, curly hair. Nice ass. Come on, you know who I mean. Him."

I searched the crew in my head. "Paulie? You mean Paulie?"

"Paulie. Good name. Good solid, construction hunk name. And apparently he's not just a pretty face. I mean, you'd think he'd be sort of shallow, but—" and it was almost imperceptible when Ariana's gaze flicked down from my face to my T-shirt and back up. "Well, you know what I mean." Ariana lifted her white wine and looked at me over the glass. "Oh, you lucky, lucky girl," she said. I felt woozy.

Ariana started to work on her salad, satisfied with her choice. It didn't matter that I hadn't said yes or no. It was decided. The woman at the next table was talking again, only now she was crying, too, tears rolling down her face that she didn't even bother to wipe away. She sat back and tucked her chin into her chest. The man scooted his chair some, like he might move around the table to her, but instead he drank his water, spread butter on a roll. He started to speak, but then, he too started to cry. It hurt to watch, but I couldn't look away. And then they both just sat there, pulled apart from one another, quietly crying to themselves.

"Someone's getting dumped," Ariana said, and speared another tomato. And it was all I could do to not reach across the checkered tablecloth and slap her beautiful face.

By the time we got back it had clouded over and all but one of the trucks were gone. Paulie was there still, cleaning up scraps from the yard, covering materials with tarp. He told me that Hoof had gone into town for a bit, that he said he'd be back that evening.

"He left you here all by yourself, huh?" Ariana called through her window to Paulie. She put the car in reverse. "How convenient," she whispered to me and kissed the air next to my cheek. She revved her engine once, twice, and pulled off.

And then the rain came down fast and hard, and Paulie and I ran for cover. I left him on the porch while I checked the windows, grateful they were new so I could avoid my usual struggle with the one in my parents'—my—bedroom. I sat on the bed and watched the rain pummel the rose bushes outside the window. I thought about the last few weeks, about Hoof in this new bed with me. I considered what Ariana said. Hoof, a man as old as my father had been when he died. A kind man. An attractive man. An old man.

I thought of my parents in this room together, asleep with their backs turned against each other. I pictured my father in their bed alone, dying, and I recalled how my mother and I slept in one another's arms after the funeral, how I woke up in the middle of the night to my mom whimpering in her sleep, how I didn't know at first where I was, how I looked around the room until I recognized the paneled walls, the heavy oak furniture. I looked around again for my father, called out quietly, "Dad?" like I used to when I'd have a bad dream and he'd show up in my room and pat my head until I fell back asleep. Sometimes when I hurt myself, scraped a knee or banged my head, he'd just sit by me and hold my hand and tell me to breathe, "That's right," he'd say, "Breathe all the pain out." "Dad," I said again, lying there next to my mother that night, but then I remembered and filled up with such an ache, such a yearning, I had to lie flat on the floor and breathe the pain out of me. Or at least I had to try.

I followed Paulie into the bathroom because I figured if I was going to be a cliché, then this is the one I wanted to be.

"There's no leak—" he started to say, and turned around to where I was leaning back against the door, pushing it closed and tripping the lock without looking. "Ma'am" he said and I flinched at the old lady word, but in a second his face went from confusion to something else: understanding, maybe; desire, I hoped. And I turned off the light and we were there under the sealed-tight skylight and the rain thrummed the glass and the gray sky gave light, just enough. And the two steps across the big bathroom's floor were giant steps—like in Mother May I, I thought for some reason—and then I was there in front of him and sliding down him, unzipping and releasing on the way, and I could tell he was surprised, but pleased, too, judging from everything. And he grew bigger and harder under my breath, my tongue. And as I worked the magic there, he tangled his fists in my hair (thank God I had that) and spoke low like a moan or maybe a growl:

"Oh," he said. "Oh."

I was glad I was good at this, glad that I'd never been afraid like my mother had been. She'd told me toward the end of her life that she regretted that, never having tasted my father in that way, and after he died, never having another chance. "Things might have been different if..." she'd said. And her candidness surprised me and embarrassed me, and I changed the subject.

Paulie tastes good, salty and full and a little sweet, too, like I guess I knew he would, him being so young and all. Young and fresh. He smells of sawdust and hard work, and his smell warms me all the way through and then he says:

"What about you, baby? What about you?"

And with my mouth full like that, I can't answer, but what I'm thinking is how I got the only construction man in the world, probably, who wants to fuck when he can get sucked.

Then he says:

"I want you, baby. Let me feel you. Let me see you." And I'm grateful for that, so grateful: it's all I needed really, his desire. And he says it again, "Let me feel you." And it's like he means it even though his hands say what he really means, tangled up and pushing, holding me there, and for just an instant I consider pulling away and standing up and lifting my shirt and watching the complicated dark desire on his face fall away to something else like I'd seen before, that one time shortly after the surgery, before I moved back home, before I decided to be alone. "Take that," I'd say, "Take that." But he doesn't deserve that, being so nice to me like this, letting me have my way, so I just keep on and hang on his words—*I want you I want you I want you*. And for a little while, it's enough, this wanting, but he's a hard one and pretty soon my knees ache on the unforgiving tile and my jaw is dull with pain and I think, finish, damn you boy, finish. And then he does, a big, loud, juicy finish and I hold my place against his bucking and swallow it all, and when he stills, I rest on my heels and run the back of my hand across my mouth and look up through the mess of hair he made and smile.

"Oh my God," he says and he's beaming and hanging loose, the flat of his palms on the vanity behind him, the long muscles jumping and shaking in his arms. And he starts to laugh and reaches for me, but I tilt just out of his range and crawl to the shower—my knees screaming—and turn on the water. I push off the porcelain side of the tub and stand up slowly and say, "Undress." He's still willing, I can tell, his young cock already gathering strength again, and he pulls out of his T-shirt and kicks off his boots and in a moment of odd modesty folds his jockeys into the pocket of his jeans. He watches me the whole time. I pull back the shower door and wave him in and once he's closed in there I walk back across the bathroom (normal steps) and let myself out.

It was no surprise that Hoof was back when I came out of the bathroom, and even though I might have wanted it another way, I don't know, he just turned from me and went out to his truck and left me there and I stayed in my room until Paulie stopped knocking on my door, until he left me, too. I thought they might not come back, but they did, the next day and the next, courteous and cool, and they finished the job on time and finished it well. And Hoof mailed me the bill and I paid it in full, and it was months before I saw either of them again. I was working from home then, a computer in my kitchen so I could watch the market on the screen and the leaves go gold and red through all those big, new windows. Ariana came out for dinner and we went to Anchors Inn, and there leaning on his bum hip, one elbow on the bar, was Hoof. Paulie, too, and the rest of the crew. And I thought Hoof might be drinking again, like I thought—way back then—he might gather me up in his arms when he discovered what I'd done, like I thought he'd see that I was hurt, just hurt, and he'd forgive me and love me in spite of myself. But while the others held bottles of beer, he had a soda, and I'd be lying if I said I wasn't more than a little disappointed. He didn't see us and I haven't seen him since, and it was the last time, too, that I saw Ariana.

And now it's just me in the house, and it's bright and open like I wanted, but mostly it just feels big. I spend my days in the kitchen in my chair at the table, and my nights in the bedroom on my own side of the bed, and it's cool now so the windows stay closed and I can see the rose bushes shrinking and turning brittle.

Dripping from the shower, I stand at the mirror. My hair has grown some and my stomach is no longer flat. I light a cigarette and think again how I should quit smoking. Only I know I never will. Some days I still feel the phantom nipples, and some days (not many) it looks like the scars might be fading. I take in smoke and hold it, my lungs as full as my chest will ever be. Sometimes you don't have much, I'm thinking—I release the smoke and squint and there I am, fuzzy and blurred—and what you do have is bad for you. But the thing is—I lift the cigarette and fill my chest again—it's something. At the very least, it is something.

Gracias

The last time a man touched Edith was long before this occurrence at Jack's Super. Sky, maybe it was, right before he left home. This time, she wobbled near the avocados, her cane slipping on a smear of smashed grape and he was there then, not Sky, but the touching man, with his fingertips on her elbow, his hand on her waist. *Cuidado*, he said, *steady*. She looked up at him, his black hair silver at the temples, his brown eyes, kind. He was foreign, she knew that, the word cuidado, his dark skin, and he wore a name tag over his pocket. Manuel. She thought she might know him. She thought she might not. Manuel. A foreigner's name.

She, Edith, was not a foreigner. Her people had been here forever, generations buried on the hill up in the New Hope cemetery. Maybe before that, a century—more—ago, her folks were foreigners. Newcomers to the Middle West from Ireland, England. White people, like Edith, whose pink scalp burned under her transparent hair if she fell asleep on the kitchen chair in her backyard under the sun. The town, as she knew it always, was white, too. Until recently. Well, some years now, actually. Still, it seemed recent to Edith. Lots of things did. Workers first, coming in to farm for practically nothing, migrants who moved from town to town, from state to state. Following the seasons, the planting, and then the harvest. But it got so they stayed sometime along the line. Got so that Jack's had whole aisles of food for them—tortillas and salsa and beans in cans with Spanish on the labels. Candies like Edith had never seen before, sweets in colorfully tempting plastic packages with words she couldn't make sense of. She liked them, though, especially the ones that tasted like watermelon, only spicy.

Manuel's hand was on her waist still, right there over the spot of her back that always hurt so. Every morning, every evening. Every in between. Edith didn't always notice the pain anymore. But she noticed this: his touch. Gentle, warm. She wanted to sag into it, give in, but instead, she stood a little straighter.

"Thank you," she said. And she patted his hand on her arm, smiled up at him. It seemed like the right thing to do. "Gracias," for good measure. Edith didn't know Spanish, but she knew that.

"You're welcome," he said. He was good-looking, Edith couldn't help but see that. Like that man on the television show years ago, the one about an island. She didn't think much about good-looking men these days, except maybe when she saw one on TV. Otherwise, what was the point? She used to be a sucker for them, the good-lookers. Like her husband Henry, the bastard who left her when her daughter, Nova, was born perfect but for that hand thing. Left her and then came back and then left again. Good-looking, though, all along. Not like this guy, nothing foreign about her ex. Tall and blond. Like their son,

Sky, the boy he took with him the first time he took off, then left behind the second time. Sky, too. He was good-looking. Beautiful, in fact. Then. Still. She was pretty sure.

"May I help?" Manuel said, and Edith came back down. Coming back down: that's what she called it when she remembered where she was after spacing out. Spacing out. That was a Sky term. "Earth to Mom," he used to say, then: "Edith, come in for a landing."

She could still feel Manuel's touch on her waist, even though he stood with both hands in front of himself, turned up just a little, like he was holding the question in his palms. "Can I help?" He said it again, a little louder. Maybe he thought she didn't hear well.

She heard fine. Edith could hear the hum of the fluorescent lights above them, the quiet grind of the freezer motors one aisle over. She heard the music that crackled over the speakers, a song she used to know but that sounded different without words and only strings and piano. She remembered that Nova used to play this one on her little turntable in her bedroom after her father left, after Sky did. She used to play it and sing along. Nova had one of those voices that sounded good and sad at the same time. Like the girl who sang the song for real, the one who died. The one who didn't eat enough.

"You all right, Edith?" It was Jack, pink-faced and red-headed and carrying a box of tomatoes to add to the pile already there. Not Jack-Jack, the original Jack of Jack's Super. His son. Jack, Jr. The one who used to run around with Sky and those other boys. Troublemakers. Now it was Jack, Jr.'s store, and Sky was gone. Jack, Sr. was dead.

Manuel stepped back some, and Edith saw what he had. A frown on Jack, Jr.'s face, a dark question in his eyes.

"I'm fine, Jackie." She knew he hated that name. He always hated that name. Sky used to call him Jackie all the time. Edith reached for Manuel's arm. "This kind man is helping me," she said. She didn't need help. But she didn't need Jackie causing trouble either. Like he used to.

Jackie nodded, but he kept frowning.

"Okee dokee," he said. How could a man make *okee dokee* sound mean, Edith wondered. "Manuel," he said to the touching man. Mean-sounding, too.

"Jack."

Edith remembered now. Manuel. He used to own the Stop & Go over near the highway. Manuel... Martinez. Martinez, that's right. Edith looked up at the man whose arm she was holding. "Manuel Martinez," she said. "I know you."

"Yes, ma'am," he said and smiled down at her. His teeth were white and straight, but one of the front ones was broken. His pink tongue showed through the gap.

Manuel carried her groceries all the way to her door, all the way inside. He put the bags on the counter and turned toward her. Should she tip him? She wondered if she should tip him. On TV everybody tipped everybody. In New Hope, no one much tipped at all. She reached for her purse.

"Unless there is anything else," Manuel said, like he was in a hurry all of a sudden. They'd taken their time on the walk home, not intentionally, but because Edith could only take her time now. Her hips didn't work so well. Her feet hurt. Her back did. Still, they filled the walk with chit chat, small talk (*have you always lived here? ... In this house for just ten years, but in New Hope, yes. You? ... Oh no, my family is from Mexico. But I've been here years now, too. Years and years.* And even as they asked these things, it felt to Edith like they knew the answers already, didn't they?) and the walk didn't seem to take as long as it did when she walked alone.

Edith fiddled with the snap on her purse, and Manuel shook his head, a small, quick thing, and she knew he was trying to stop her before she did something that would embarrass them both. "I'll be on my way," he said. And he touched her shoulder and said goodbye.

This was the worst part. The back home all alone part. How long had it been since Sky left, since Nova did? Edith lost count of the days first, then the weeks and months. Now she couldn't count the years.

She tilted her cane against the side of the refrigerator, let it rest there. She put her hand on the back of a chair, then the table, then the counter, using the familiar things of her home to help her stay upright and navigate. She opened the cupboard and slid the box of oats in its place and the box of saltines next to it. She pushed the cans of tomato and cream of celery soup up onto the next shelf, standing on her tiptoes and reaching with her fingertips. Green beans, creamed corn, a small jar of peanut butter.

She put the loaf of bread into the tin breadbox that—despite her constant scrubbing—always smelled a little moldy, and she gripped the table again to ease her way around to the fridge. As she put her few things away, she named them: apple jelly, margarine, a quart of skim milk, a cannister of Hills Brothers. It helped with her remembering. It gave her something to do, it gave her something to say.

When had she begun to talk to herself? It felt like she always had, but maybe that was because she used to pray all of the time, day and night, night and day. *God, grant me... God, help me... God, please watch over me, Sky, Nova.* Asking, she was always asking God for something. That was what she had believed prayer was, a request, a plea. A sort of begging. And when she got so little in return (her husband left anyway, her bills too often went unpaid, she lost the family home out in the country, her children were gone too soon, she hurt, she got sick, she was alone) Edith finally let the whole prayer thing go. But the talking didn't stop, and the heavenly beseeching was replaced by something else, a constant muttering that gave her a little company even when no one else was there.

"Okee dokee," Edith said. She remembered how it sounded coming out of Jackie, Jr.'s mouth, mean, and she said it again, with a big smile on her face, trying to make it sound sweet the way she thought it should. The one time she took a class over at the community college (Oh, dear, how long ago was that? she tried to remember: before Henry, before the kids) it was in public speaking and her teacher (he was a good looking fellow, auburn hair that curled over his ears and his collar, hazel eyes) told them all that smiling while they spoke lifted the tone of their words, made them brighter. Edith smiled again as she settled onto the chair at the kitchen table. "Okee dokee," she said once more, and smoothed her skirt over her legs, patted her knees, and blinked her tired eyes.

The kitchen was full of shadows when Edith woke up. She was still sitting at the table. Her neck ached and there was a little drool down the front of her blouse and she was very, very hungry. She stood slowly, unraveling the kinks and sore spots out of her body a little at a time. She slipped a hand in the pocket of her skirt and felt the plastic, the lumps inside of it. She tugged the bag open with her teeth (they hurt, too) and pulled out two small sweet and spicy candies, unwrapped them and popped them, one, two, into her mouth. Just a little something to take the edge off. She reached over to the drawer beneath the junk drawer and tossed the bag of candies in with the others, all those strange Spanish words shining up at her like they did when she passed them in the candy aisle, beckoning Edith to pick the little packages up, to slide them into her pocket when no one was looking. Just a little something. Just a little something. No big deal.

By the time Edith had prepared a paper plate for herself—three saltines with margarine, a spoonful of creamed corn, two celery sticks and four spicy watermelon candies—the sun was fully set. She thought she should pull the shades down in the kitchen, the curtains closed in the little living room, but it was too much work, like washing dishes had become. She got exhausted when she looked at her cabinets full of plates and plates and plates, of cups and saucers, dessert and candy dishes, glasses and serving platters. Her grandmother's, her mother's, hers. She had one chipped mug with "World's Best Mom" in pink letters scrawled around its middle (she'd bought it for herself at the Dollar Shop, she thought it was funny, and it was on sale for 50 cents two weeks after Mother's Day, five months after the last of her two children had gone). She had a water glass made from an old jelly jar. A drawer full of plastic utensils she picked up from the deli counter at Jack's, the bins at the Subway. These things she kept close at hand and ready for everyday use, along with the paper plates stacked in a corner of the counter. The dish drainer never had more than a small saucepan and a glass or mug in it. She could handle that. Like she could handle sitting in the dim glow of the lamp beside the recliner, looking away from whatever was on the little television to the dark street while whoever was out there (Who would be out there?) looked at her inside the small house.

The phone rang like it hadn't in weeks. A sales call or maybe Nova, maybe Sky. But that was just wishful thinking, Edith knew, Nova or Sky calling. It wasn't Christmas, it wasn't Mother's Day, it wasn't Edith's birthday (in fact, neither Nova nor Sky called on Edith's birthday anymore). Edith set her paper plate on the table that Henry used to use for his ashtray, his pipe, his Bible, and pushed herself up from the recliner (also Henry's) and got to the phone on its seventh ring. She heard on the other end of the line someone murmuring, but she couldn't make out the words: *no S ta,* it sounded like, and a bunch of other things.

"Hello? Hello?" Edith called into the phone. "Hello?"

"Oh, oh, hello! Mrs. Edith, hello!" It didn't take any time at all for Edith to know it was Manuel, she heard his voice in her head from earlier, and if she thought about it, she knew that she'd been talking to him as much as to herself since she woke up in the kitchen chair. "Would you like some saltines, Manuel?" Edith had said. "No? Well, I am going to have some saltines. Candy? Here, I'll put four on the plate. Two for you, two for me. You can have them if you want them."

"Manuel," Edith said into the receiver. Outside her window she could see across the street to the house that had been for sale for almost two years. It was a funny place, old and new both, two stories of buttery bricks making the old part, tall windows, empty now, here and there a pane cracked or boarded over. The new part a squat, blocky addition with dark red vinyl siding, tiny windows framed with aluminum. She could no longer remember who used to live there.

"Mrs. Edith, I hope you don't mind my calling," Manuel said. There was a rustling coming over the wire, like maybe he was moving the phone from one hand to the other. She did the same, moved the receiver to her good (better) ear.

"No, of course not," Edith said. Something fluttered in her chest, lifted pleasantly into her throat. "I was just—" She didn't know what to say.

Gracias

She smiled so the words would sound bright. "I was just finishing cooking dinner," she said.

"Oh, that's nice," Manuel said.

"Yes," Edith answered. "Some nice porkchops and apple sauce."

"Mrs. Edith," Manuel said, getting to it, the purpose of his call. "I wanted to see if maybe you would like me to help you with your groceries."

"Oh, but you have, Manuel. You did help me." Edith was confused. She didn't like to be confused, but she was.

"No, I mean again. I mean every now and again. I can help you if you'd like." She listened to his breath over the line, she remembered the touch of his hand on her waist. He was very pleasant, that was for sure. And good-looking.

"Well, that would be very kind, Manuel." Edith stopped. "But really, there's no need." Edith said it, but she didn't mean it. Maybe there was no need for help, but another sort of need buzzed in her head. She was damn lonely.

"Oh," Manuel began, but Edith didn't want him to finish, she didn't want him to say goodbye, she didn't want him to hang up. She didn't want to turn away from the phone and the window looking over the wide, empty street, and back to her recliner that still smelled of pipe tobacco, years and years and years since anyone smoked a pipe in her house, pipe tobacco and something musty like unwashed feet; she didn't want to sit down with her saltines that weren't porkchops, with her watermelon candy that was not applesauce.

"But all right. Yes, yes. Thank you, Manuel. It would be so very lovely of you to help me now and again. Thank you," she said. "Gracias," she said.

Every Thursday then, Manuel came to call at 10 AM sharp. They usually walked, but sometimes, if the weather was not good, too cold or rainy, Manuel picked her up in a sedan that looked old-fashioned to Edith, something from decades ago, but that was shiny clean and smelled like the air freshener that wafted off the little pine tree hanging from the rearview mirror. Edith had taken to setting her hair on Wednesday nights; she took a bath first thing the next morning. She ironed her skirts, her dresses, her slacks. She even brushed her teeth. Before these shopping trips with Manuel, days passed between her toothbrushing.

Manuel was at least ten years younger than Edith, so she did not kid herself that he had romantic intentions. And besides, Manuel was a widower. One of those who never stopped being married, even after his wife died. He talked about his wife as often as she spoke about Nova, about Sky, which was very often: *Sarita and I fell in love in high school... Nova was valedictorian of her class... We married young and came here together, we worked in the fields first... Nova lives in California now, she is very busy. Sky moves around a lot; like his father used to... We only had the one child: Ramon. Our boy... Yes, I know. I remember.*

She didn't, though, remember much about Ramon. Only that he was about the same age as Sky. That he had enlisted to go over to Vietnam. That he hadn't come home. She wasn't sure why she remembered even that, except maybe he was the first in town who went over there, the first boy to never return. After that, there were a few others.

"I thought Sky might join up," Edith said. They had stopped at the diner on their way to Jack's. Manuel had let her buy the coffee. She sat across the table from him and leaned against the vinyl cushions, they squeaked in a funny way that made her blush. Edith lifted the coffee cup up and held it in front of her mouth while she spoke. She never liked her teeth—they were big and had gaps between them—and now there were even fewer than before. "But he said it wasn't for him, fighting."

Manuel snorted, but clapped a hand over the noise. His fingernails were clean and shiny. "Sorry," he said. "I'm sorry. It's just that that's not the way I remember him, Sky. He was—" and Manuel lifted his arm, made a muscle. "Un luchador. Fuerte. Strong," he said.

"You knew Sky?" Edith said.

"Oh yes," Manuel said. "Oh yes, I knew Sky." He blinked and Edith thought she saw something in his eyes, a light going dim. The waitress—what was her name? Edith couldn't remember even though the woman had worked there forever. Forever and ever—was at their table and Manuel turned toward her.

"Nada más, gracias, Maria," Manuel said. And Maria said, "Terminaste, entonces?" "Sí," Miguel answered. Edith looked away from the two of them; she felt too close, like she was eavesdropping on a private conversation. Behind the counter a photo of the president hung over the cash register. What was his name again? He was from Texas. That much she remembered. She thought. Manuel had turned toward her. "Yes, Edith?" He asked. "We are finished, yes?"

"Sí," Edith said, coming back down again. She nodded at Maria whom she had known, sort of, for years, but had only just realized was a foreigner, too. Like Manuel. Wasn't the world an interesting place? "Sí," she said again. They stood up, Manuel first and he held his hand out to Edith, who took it gently, felt the warmth of his palm, eased her way out of the booth and held back her usual groan. "Gracias," she said to Manuel first, then, "Gracias," to Maria. And Edith smiled around the word and let her teeth, the ones she had left, show.

When Sky called that evening, Edith answered on the second ring.

"Oh, Sky," she said, disappointed.

"Oh, Sky?" Her son repeated. "Well, that's a fine hello." He was right, of course. Edith hadn't spoken to him in months, she should be happy to hear from him. And she was, she was. It was just that—

"I was expecting someone else. I'm sorry, dear." Edith pulled the phone on its long cord to the table next to the recliner. She eased herself into the chair, a heavy sigh in her chest, and stretched her lips into a smile. She talked brightly into the receiver. "Sky, dear, how nice of you to call," she said. She meant that. She did.

"Who were you expecting?" Sky asked.

"Oh, no one. Pastor James, maybe," she said, though she hadn't been to church in years. She pretended, though, to Sky. He liked to believe she still had faith. "There's a bake sale coming up." Edith had always been a good liar. She knew that. She'd had plenty of practice. Like when she was still with Henry and she told him she wouldn't dream of taking that new birth control pill (after Nova, after Sky, when Henry had begun taking off on his "missions" he called them, and mothering got so hard). Like before that when she'd taken the class at the community college and she told the handsome speech teacher she was eighteen. When, a couple days later, Edith told her mother she hadn't come home because she'd spent the night at her best friend's house. Now she couldn't remember that girl's name, the one who'd gone to a real college in another state and never came back to New Hope. Lied like she did to the sheriff about not knowing where Sky was, and another time she told him the black eye was a silly accident, a left-open cupboard, her usual spacing out. Like she did every time she picked something up from the Spanish candy aisle and slid it in her pocket, telling herself *just this once*, and then *just this once more*.

"Earth to Mom," Sky was saying, and Edith knew she'd done it again, lifted off from where she sat in her living room, grounded.

"Yes, dear?" She said.

"Can you send me that check? I really need it."

He always needed it, Sky did. Checks. Cash. Edith tried to remember the last time he'd called, the last fifty she'd sent him. Fifty. A hundred. Once it was five hundred, and he promised he'd use most of it to come home for Christmas. She let the ham burn in the oven waiting for him. Sky hadn't been home in years. "I'm coming home, Ma. You'll see. I'll surprise you," he always said when he asked for money. Or something like that. Edith thought of Manuel on the other side of the booth that morning at the diner. Those words he called Sky: lucha-something. Fuerte. Strong. Was Sky strong? Edith couldn't remember. She remembered something, though, about the way he treated people. Nova used to call her brother a bully.

"Do you remember Ramon?" Edith said then. Where was she going with this? "Ramon Martinez?"

She heard Sky take a breath on the other side of the line. He was smoking again, she was certain. Even though he promised he wouldn't and it was the lung cancer that killed Henry. He drew air again. "Who?" Sky said, like he was holding his breath and only the word came out.

Sky was not a good liar. He never was. Oh, he lied plenty. All the time. But he was so blond and beautiful it was hard not to want to believe him. Edith didn't believe him this time, like she didn't believe him most times. This time, though, unlike most times, she didn't let it go. Edith said again: "Ramon Martinez." And she waited for him to say something, she listened to him smoking. Finally she said: "His parents used to own the gas station on the highway, the one with the convenience store. You remember. Sky?"

Edith looked at the dark window across the room. She hadn't even noticed that the sun had gone down. When was that? She'd probably fallen asleep at the kitchen table again after Manuel left, after she'd put away her groceries, after she'd had a candy, two. She'd probably be there still, asleep in her chair, if the phone hadn't rung. She could see her reflection now in the wide front window. Above her head was a white light, a kind of halo, she thought, and it took Edith a moment to understand that the light came from outside, from the streetlight near her front walk. A boy with dark curly hair walked under the light, and then, while Edith watched, two other boys, a blonde, a redhead, ran up behind him. She thought she heard something: *amigo* and *sister* and *hey.* The dark haired boy did not turn around, but the boy with the long blond hair grabbed him, he swung punches at his head. The redhead punched, too. The first boy fell forward, his knees hit the cement, then his face. Edith couldn't see it, but she knew his nose broke open. She knew there was blood.

Edith stood up and pressed the receiver close to her best ear. "Sky," she said. "Sky." But Sky had hung up already; the phone clicked and then buzzed. No one was there. She stepped to the window, something quick in her chest. The sidewalk was empty, no one was there, either. No boys. No blood. Still, Edith knew it happened. It happened.

At Jack's Super, Edith stood in front of the rows of Mexican candy. It made her feel buoyant when she stole something. It always had. There was so much to bring a person down, she thought whenever she tossed the colorful bags into the drawer under her kitchen counter. She watched her stash grow and grow and it made her lightheaded. (She would never be able to eat it all, the sweet things, the sour things, the spicy things.) She remembered how she used to lift a lipstick from the pharmacy every now and again when she was a teenager. How she used to palm a shiny barrette from the Ben Franklin's long before it closed down. She knew she had stolen from Manuel's gas station, but never much: Good & Plenty, Lifesavers. Back when the kids were still home. Never when Manuel was working, though, Edith was pretty sure of that. When his wife was. When Ramon did.

She spun away from the shelves of candy, twirling on her heel with her cane to give her a little push and there was Manuel, right behind her. Good thing, too, because Edith lost her balance, and he reached out, *Cuidado,* he said. Just like that first time. Still, she stumbled, and pulled her hand out of her pocket, and the candy, too. Manuel saw, she knew it. He saw.

"Oh dear, oh, dear," Edith said, and she dropped the little bag to the floor between them, put her hand on her forehead, peeked at Manuel from under her fingers. "Dizzy," she said, and for good measure, swooned, just a little. Manuel held her waist tighter, stepped closer, kicking the candy under the shelves.

"Edith," Jack, Jr. called out from the deli counter up the aisle. He wiped his hands (Was that beef blood? Tomato juice?) on a grimy white towel tossed over his shoulder. From where she and Manuel stood, he looked like he had as a boy: messy red hair, acne spotted face, round shoulders. "Edith?" Something sparked in her, a flash of a different time when Jackie and Sky sat at her kitchen table in the old house, eating the macaroni and cheese and franks she'd made for dinner, laughing and swigging down cold Cokes. She used to love feeding Sky. Nova never ate much, but Sky always ate like it was what he was put on God's good earth to do. And so there he was with his ugly friend (she'd always thought that about Jackie, she thought it still) at the table (Where was Nova? Edith couldn't remember) and then the sheriff was there at the back door, pounding and pounding, calling, "Edith? Sky? Jackie?" And, "Edith, let me in. You gotta open the door, you gotta let me in." Edith peered out at the uniformed man in the dusk, at the moths swirling around his head under the bright back porch light, at the cruiser in the drive, at the other man standing next to it, in a uniform, too, but different, gray, and with a name patch over his breast pocket. She could see that. He looked mad, some, but sad, more. And, Edith saw this now as she watched the memory play in her head, that man was Manuel.

"I'm sorry," Edith said in the candy aisle, and she reached for Manuel's face, his handsome, handsome face, just before everything went dark (for real) and she slid to the cold, cold linoleum floor.

Was that what he wanted, Manuel asked himself. Was that why he had started all of this, the helping, the groceries, the small talk, the coffee? He wandered Edith's rooms, muttering. He could hear the quiet purr of her snore when he passed her bedroom doorway. She'd been asleep since he'd brought her home after she fainted. "No, no," she'd said when Jack, Jr. wanted to call the clinic, was about to call the sheriff. "I'm fine, really." She'd pushed herself up and sat on the floor between the candy shelves and the chips and pretzels. "Dehydrated, that's all," she said to Jack, Jr., and grabbed his arm to help her stand. "Happens more than I'd like to admit. Don't make a fuss." Manuel could see her gathering her wits, the way her eyes cleared and focused as she made her excuses. He remembered this look from the time he saw her at the gas station putting candy bars in her purse without paying for them, when he asked her about them. The look from when he and the sheriff came to her old house at the edge of town looking for Sky.

"Manuel will take me home," Edith said to Jack, Jr., and Manuel took her arm and walked her out of the grocery store and settled her into the front seat of his old Ford Fairmont. They drove to her small house in silence, mostly, except for when she turned to him once, twice, three times. "I'm sorry," she said at each turn.

Was that what he wanted? Edith to apologize?

In the hallway outside her bedroom, Manuel looked at the photos on the wall. Little kids, probably Nova and Sky, but the pictures were old and faded, the faces of the children blurred in front of a once-bright, pink sunset. A man who looked like an older version of Sky (as much as Manuel could remember him), blond and broad-shouldered, standing next to a car on a country lane, trees turning orange behind him. And Nova in a cap and gown, head tilted, and her hands clasped in front of her, the good one wrapped around the other one.

Nova. Just as Manuel remembered her: what she looked like coming out of Ramon's bedroom that one early morning, happy. Was that the same day that, later, Ramon had come home bloody, weeping? Was that the day the phone rang, over and over, when

Nova, on the other end of the line whispered: "Ramon. Ramon, por favor. Necesito Ramon." Even after Manuel had told her no, Ramon would not come to the phone, he did not want to talk to her. "Nunca," Manuel said, because Ramon told him to. "Nunca." And was that the day that Sarita refused to leave their bedroom, the first day of many, and when Ramon, face washed but still swollen, decided to enlist?

"I'm sorry," Edith said. But did it matter? Now? All these years later, all these people gone? The gas station sold to a corporation well below market value, because, well, what did that matter without Ramon, without Sarita—dead so long ago from the cancer, the doctor told him. From her broken heart, Manuel knew.

He looked in on Edith. She slept on her back under an orange and green afghan, her mouth open and eyelids fluttering. The room smelled of urine slightly, and of dust, of mildew. He could kill her, Manuel knew, he could lift the pillow from under her head and hold it over her face while she struggled to breathe, while she kicked her crooked little feet, banged on his arms with her fists, all knuckle and papery, spotted skin. But Manuel did not want Edith to die—although there was a time when he did. He remembered the burning fuel of his sorrow, of his hatred.

And now?

He blinked back the watery blur of his tears and saw that Edith was awake; she was looking at him.

"Manuel?" She said, and he heard it again, the regret, the apology. It was all right there, between them.

"Sí, amiga mia," Manuel said. He stepped across the room and sat beside her on the bed. He patted her hand, he touched her face. "I'm here, friend. Estoy aqui."

And later, when Edith was able to stand up again, when she was able to walk from her bedroom to the kitchen, while he sat—as told—in the big recliner that faced the window and the town going dark beyond it, Manuel would accept the small, pretty porcelain dish of candies she handed him, the wrappers and flavors he remembered from when he was a boy, from when Ramon was. He would pluck a sweet from the dish and ignore the sugar ants that crawled in the creases of the colorful wrapping—because really, what did such small things matter? "Gracias," he'd say.

And he would savor the goodness.

The Temple of Air

When I saw Mom sneak a pack of HiDeeHo cupcakes out from the bottom of the pan cupboard and slip them in the pocket of her sky-blue bathrobe, naturally I thought they were for me. It was my birthday after all, we were supposed to do that kind of thing for each other, right? Kind of like how I'd get up every morning and start the kettle for her hot water and lemon. Like how I'd turn the shower on for her fifteen minutes before I'd shake her awake so's the whole bathroom would be steamy hot for her. Little things like that. You know. Like a candle in a cupcake. No big deal. Just enough to show she cared.

I gave her time to get it together down the hall in her room, sat on the old blue couch and pretended to read one of the newspapers I'd swiped from school. (Mom didn't believe in reading anymore, it weighed her down.) But when nothing happened—I mean nothing, no singing, no yelling, "Surprise!" or any of that—I decided to go see what was what. And when I got to Mom's room she was already dressed, her hair still wet and streaming water down the back of her blue cotton turtleneck, and there were no cupcakes to be seen anywhere. Not on her dresser, on her night table, in her hand, or anywhere.

"Morning, Mom," I said, quiet like she likes me to be in the morning (she's not too good at waking up). "Nice day." I stood with my back to the doorjamb, hands deep in my pockets. I tried to slide down and shrink up some because Mom was so teeny she always made me feel like a horse or something. Not like I was all that big. Just five-four and a bit over 110, pretty much average for fourteen (just turned). But Mom was one of those bitty ladies, under five feet and featherweight, doll-sized, more or less.

"Hi, Baby," she said, still looking at her own self in the mirror on the back of her closet door, working a big, fat-toothed comb through the tangles in her blond hair. Mine's dark. Like Dad's. "Water ready, Rennie?" she said like she always did.

"Yeah." Like it ever wasn't.

"Put me some lemon in it, 'kay?" Like it was a special request.

But I didn't smart off or anything, I never did. I was about as good a kid as you could imagine. It was just easier that way. And I strolled down the hall like everything was normal to the kitchen and poured water into her blue cup with the shining gold letters "T-o-A" on it and tried not to let the lump in my throat that swelled around my wanting to hear something like "Happy birthday, Baby"—or whatever—hurt me. And then it came to me while I was pouring. She probably was setting me up. Right that minute she was probably putting that candle in that silly little cake and maybe even pulling my present out of someplace at the back of her closet or the bottom of her drawer or wherever she hid things. So I took my time, squeezed an extra slice of lemon in the mug, and I pushed another down onto the cup's rim like they do in restaurants. I put it all on a plate with a spoon, stomped around extra loud on my way back to her room, gave her time and notice enough to keep the surprise a surprise.

"I'm back," I said, just before I turned into her room, but she was right where I'd left her, on that metal folding chair that was covered with a couple of pillow cases sewn together to look like some sort of slipcovers (which of course they didn't) in front of her mirror, still combing and combing through her stupid tangly hair.

"Took you a while," she said in that way she talked mostly now, sort of dreamy and soft. Like everything that took her attention only took it part way, like something else was going on in her head that didn't really have anything to do with what she was talking about. You know. Like when you're talking to someone and they're eavesdropping on a conversation behind you? They might be answering you, keeping up their part of the conversation and all, but what's going on between you is not what's uppermost on their list at that moment.

When I stepped over to the dresser to set the mug down, I guess you'd have to say I still had my hopes up. But next to the dresser there was Mom's little trash basket she'd got at the Temple, the one the same sky blue as her mug (and chair covers and sheets and blankets and throw rugs and lampshades and pajamas and our couch and and and) and with the same gold "T-o-A" stenciled on its side and inside the thing was some Kleenex and stuff, and underneath that, I could see, was the empty cupcake holder. Pushed down under the other junk, hidden away. Like Mom does when she's been eating stuff she's not supposed to—hiding the evidence. And when I looked at Mom in the mirror, I could see the slightest trace of crumbs on her shirt, that shiny chocolate stuff that crumbles from the HiDeeHos no matter how careful you are to try to keep them from falling apart. And at that moment I was so ticked off and hot it was like steam filled my head. "You got crumbs," I said and pointed, and she said "What? What?" all shrill like she does whenever you say something like that, something about eating. It's the only time she ever seems to pay attention to the conversation, and that's just because she has to be on her guard to get her story straight, that story about not eating anything, nothing, surviving on air—Air Only—like they tell you you can at the Temple. But only if you are worthy, truly worthy, like the floaters and the High One himself, Sky (I kid you not, that's his name, Sky. The High One, Sky.) So most times Mom's pretending to survive just on air, and it's clear that she is doing that a good bit of the time as skinny as she is and spacey, but then there's those times she cheats, or Sins as they call it at the Temple. "Forgive us our Sins," they say, but usually they're just talking about eating, if you could imagine. Like feeding yourself, taking nourishment could ever, *ever,* be called a sin.

And then "I'm late!" she says, still shrill and jumps up and brushes a hand over her chest that used to have boobs, not big ones, but something more than that flat plane she's got now, and grabs her purse up (sky-blue vinyl, like some old-lady Easter purse) and pushes past me and down the hall. And before I have time to say "Goodbye" or "Sorry" or "Hey, haven't you forgotten something—like the day I was born, maybe?" she's at the door and yelling back "Your father's here!" And I'm fighting not to cry, it's just a birthday, for God's sake, baby birthday shit, and hoping that maybe Dad's remembered, but knowing that will never happen, it's like some miracle he's remembered it's Saturday, our day, and that he's remembered his deal with the judge to do something with me, his only kid, his flesh and blood, one day a week, that he's remembered to come here at all. And I'm hoping as I tie the laces on my Nike Airs that maybe if he doesn't remember it's my birthday, I'll be able to forget too. And maybe then it won't hurt so bad.

"Where's your mom off to?" Dad asked when I stepped up into the cab of his jacked-high pickup.

"Church," I said, mostly because I was still mad and Mom hates it when I call it that. It's Temple or Service or even Worship.

"Again?" Dad said, and when I looked over in his direction I could see he hadn't shaved for a few days and his black hair wasn't combed and judging from his wrinkled up T-shirt and sweats he might have just rolled out of bed and jumped into the truck and come right over out of a dream. He smelled like beer.

We drove for a time, neither us saying anything. It dawned on me that I was singing in my head: "Happy birthday to me, happy birthday to me...." Then Dad said something, but I couldn't hear.

"What?"

"Fucking church shit!" He said and spit out the window. "Your fucking mom and that fucking church shit!"

Well it's probably clear to you by now that that pretty much sums up how I was feeling right then, too, but you know how it goes. You can say whatever you want to about your family to whoever you want to—you know, like "My sister is such a bitch," or "My grandfather is a perv," or "My dad is nothing but a drunk," and whoever you are talking to can even nod a little along with you as long as they don't actually say anything out loud. But no one else, no one else, can talk trash about your mother. Not even your own father.

"Shut up," I said without thinking. It just slipped out while I was still singing "Happy Birthday" in my head. I suppose I thought that I'd said it in my head, too, but I didn't. And as soon as they hit the air in front of me, those words, I imagined myself saying them into a big balloon like they do in comics and imagined myself reaching these hands up from out of my throat (heart hands, maybe, or soul hands) and pulling the string of the balloon back inside, the whole thing deflating its way back into me, and me swallowing it all down to my gut. And that entire little scene had to play out in just a millisecond because in the next moment Dad's hand was where the balloon had been in front of my mouth, and was closing in fast and smacking me—hard—across the teeth.

"Shut you up," he hissed, and that worked, because that's just what I did, I shut up and slid tight against the door and blinked and blinked and blinked the tears back (Baby, Big Birthday Baby) and decided right then I was not going to say another word to anyone all damn day. I ran my tongue over my smarting gums. Shut me up.

Of course, Dad hated that. See, he had that quick temper, but he also had that quick remorse some guys do, you know, a spanking followed by a hug. He needed you to tell him it's okay, you understood. So he was all soft-spoken then as we drove on down the highway past the old logging road that lead to the lake, past County Road G and GG.

"It's just that—" he started and put a hand out to my shoulder and I had to hold on tight to the handle of the door to keep from shrugging out from under him, "Your mother gets so confused. Well, you know that. And she is so gullible." And then he chuckled a bit, quiet, like he was remembering some little gullibility of Mom's from the past.

I didn't say a word.

"Like remember how she started selling that NewTriVision junk?" And he chuckled again, no doubt thinking about when I was around five and we were still all together in that little house in town (the brown one, all earth tones inside) and Mom had the whole front room stacked with boxes of NewTriVision powdered shakes and NewTriVision lo-cal cookies and NewTriVision tuna foodstuff or whatever it was in those little cans (the three—Tri—staples of the NewTriVision plan). And every night Dad would come home wanting dinner and every night Mom would try to serve him up one of those "NewTri-cious and Delicious Complete Meal Replacement Drinks." I could still remember how he laughed the first time she tried that, dressed herself up in some white short-shorts and tank top and that white NewTriVision apron with the yellow triangles on it (the one all the Tri-ologists got just for signing up) and sat on Dad's lap on the brand new brown plaid couch and put the frosty mug of the stuff to his lips. And I can still remember how he pulled his head back, but not until his mustache was frothy with what was supposed to be vanilla shake but looked as fakey yellow as banana bubblegum and, well, not at all appetizing. And when Dad said, "What's this?" and licked the goop from his mustache and made a horrible tight face but kept his hands on Mom's tiny little waist and she said "Dinner," he threw back his head and howled. And it was clear from where I was— at their feet on the braid rug tracing the yellow letters on the NewTriVision boxes over with a magenta crayon—that Mom didn't like that Dad was laughing at her, and she put her head down and her lip out but Dad kissed her neck and pulled her close and said "Sorry, Baby. I'm sorry—it's just that that's no meal for a working man is all." And she tried to tell him it was, "What with all the vitamins and minerals in it that fulfilled a hearty part of one's suggested daily requirements as determined by highly-trained New-tritionists." But Dad just laughed low while he went into the kitchen and pulled a Swanson's from the freezer and cooked it up for himself. And as the days went on like that, and the boxes stayed in the front room and Mom spent more and more time on the phone "recruiting," she called it, and Dad started working less and less with the weather turning cold and construction jobs finishing up, and dinner never getting made unless you were willing to try one of those fishy canned things or a shake (personally, I sort of went for the chocolate ones) well, Dad wasn't laughing so much anymore. And I can still remember when the fights started in the middle of the night, Dad talking low at first and Mom's voice starting out bright and tight and cheery like it was when she recruited. And then Dad would get mad and loud and yell about money and real work and Mom would babble about the miracle of success and the slow climb up the ladder and Dad would say "Ladder? What fucking ladder? It's a pyramid, Maddie, can't you see? It's a pyramid game—only they're illegal so they're doing this—" (and here I'd hear him slap or kick one of the dusty old boxes) "—instead!"

"But I'm on top, Ray, don't you get it?" Mom would say, her voice excited and filled with what I guess now I might call hope. But Dad would come right back with "On top? On *top*! There's only a top when there's a bottom. You got nothing, Maddie. Nothing. It's just you. Good old bottomless Maddie." And sometimes in my bed in my room listening, I'd giggle at that, because Mom was getting so skinny it meant something different to me than what Dad said. "But my prospects, Ray. My prospects," and usually about this time Mom's voice would crack a little and go soft and that always quieted Dad down, too, and this quiet talk hurt me more than all the rest of it because it seemed so thick with a sadness even then I guess I knew I'd get to feel soon enough. I was just a kid then, you've got to remember. And at this point in the arguments I'd squeeze my whole self into a little ball under my covers and stick my thumb in my mouth and rub my forefinger up and down, up and down the slope of my nose until it went numb. It wasn't long after that I'd be asleep.

We were getting close to town now, me and Dad, and my mouth didn't hurt anymore but I still hadn't said anything since he slapped me, and I could tell from the way he was squinting and working a hand over the leg of his jeans that he was getting sore.

"Remember?" he said again and of course I did, you know, but I wasn't talking. I rolled down my window. It was one of those summer-warm days, and the sky had that gold in it that it gets come fall. At the edge of town, the dry, stripped cornfields turned to trees with patches of red and yellow in the leaves. "And remember that—what was it?—Glamorous Miss crap that came next? 'Ray,' she'd say. 'You were right about that other stuff,'" and here he was making his voice all high and sing-songy like guys do when they pretend to talk like girls. I hate that voice.

But Dad was right. I even remember Mom saying that, "You were right about that other stuff," only not in the voice he was faking, but in her bright, tight, hope-filled voice. "*This* is it, Ray," she'd say. "*This* is it, Rennie," she'd say to me, too. And then she'd practice her pitch on the both of us, sell her way through the Miss Miracle Line. I'd bet she'd've been glad to sign us up, me even, a little kid who didn't have any money but what she gave me, and who was too young to wear the goo Glamorous Miss had her pushing. "Maddie, don't you see?" Dad would say when she'd start to draw her business plan on the big pad and easel Glam Miss gave to all its Glamourists— a triangular stack of empty squares where she'd fill in the names of her "downline" as she "engaged" them. "Look, Maddie," Dad would say and push back his dining room chair knocking over a stack of crates marked *GLASS FRAGILE,* and Mom would gasp and put a hand over her mouth when Dad grabbed from her the complimentary pointer stick (silvery pink Glamorous Miss in cursive up its shaft) and traced the shape of her plan. "Pyramid, Maddie. PYR—" he ran the pink rubber tip up one side "—A—" then down the other "—*MID!*" he'd swipe the stick across the bottom of the page, ripping it. And there was no telling who would storm out of there first, but soon it would be eight-year-old me by myself at the table wondering if there might still be some of that ice cream Mom had stuffed away in the back of the freezer behind the ice pack and freezer-burned rock-solid roaster chicken. Mom had never gone back to real eating after NewTriVision introduced her to her New Thin Self, so there usually wasn't much in the house besides that. That and Dad's beer.

Dad was stepping on the brakes now that we'd passed the town limits sign (*NEWO HOPE*) and the *SLOW 35 MPH* posting. And as we cruised the avenue past the park, I could see the slumped shoulders of the usual kids, and Lucia's dyed orange head, I was pretty sure, and maybe Paco's army jacket. But I couldn't have done anything with them anyway when I was with my dad, birthday or no. And then we were easing across the intersection of Main and Edison where the Temple was—just a storefront in a half-block long strip with Ernie and Bert's Ice Cream Shoppe and a dentist office and a daycare—and we couldn't help but see Mom's car out front. The big old

Ford Fairmont boxy and much too blue to go unnoticed next to the dusty pickups and wagons and compacts.

"So now it's church, huh?" Dad said sort of loud and narrowed his eyes before he pushed hard on the gas so his tires squealed. And he looked at me, raised his eyebrows up like "Well, got some insight here, smart girl?" But like I said, I wasn't talking. Only now it wasn't just out of principle, out of sticking to my secret pledge to shut me up. Now it also had to do with what I knew about the Temple of Air—Mom's church—and how it would really tick Dad off to know that this wasn't at all a different thing from those others (NewTriVision, Glamorous Miss, and the two or three more things Mom tried after he left) but instead it was painfully, horribly, exactly the same.

Like how you had to sell stuff to achieve a Higher Level. And while there was the usual junk—coffee mugs and T-shirts and bumper stickers (*Air Head*—I swear to God—*Aboard*) all sky blue and marked with the gold "T-o-A"—the High One, Sky, wanted more. He had bigger ideas. He figured they could sell everything that had anything even remotely to do with air. So as you'd expect, there was air freshener and balloons and kites and wind chimes and air socks and fans—even some old-fashioned gliders made out of that wood that's lighter than a popsicle stick. And then there was the other stuff: blow-dryers, vacuum cleaner bags and, no kidding, whoopie cushions. Now to me those last things were a stretch—and (maybe it's just me) sort of, well, disrespectful.

"I hear rumors those people are supposed to be able to fly," Dad said. We were pulling into Jack's Super, so I knew he was going for beer and cigarettes, which meant we'd probably go back to his place where he'd smoke and drink and jump from channel to channel with his universal remote control. Some birthday.

I looked at him.

"Hear me?" Dad asked. "I said, I hear rumors they're supposed to be flying in there."

Floating, I wanted to tell him, they call it floating. But now I was too deep into this shut-me-up stuff, so I kept it zipped.

"What, you believe this shit?" Of course I didn't. What'd he think I was, some goof? But I wasn't talking. And even if I was, I wasn't sure I'd tell him what I knew. How each member starts on the ground—earthbound, they call it. And how by selling all that junk and bringing in new members and not eating and probably some other weird this and that, you got a little higher and higher off the ground. Mostly it's figurative, this off-the-ground thing, but supposedly, those who are truly worthy—well, like Dad said, there are rumors. But he wasn't going to hear it from me.

Dad put the truck in Park and faced me. I stared at him. "Do you believe this shit? This flying shit?" He waited for me to answer, which, you already know, I wasn't doing. "Huh? Huh?"

Now I'm not a fool, I knew what was coming. But even if I started talking now, it wouldn't have made any difference. You know. So why bother? I just grabbed hold of the door handle like I did when he took me four-wheeling and I held on for the ride. "You believe this shit?" And then it was like an explosion, the cab of the truck filled with his hollering. "Fine! You believe it! You just fucking believe it!" And he balled up his fists on his thighs. "You and your mom. Exactly the same! Fine. How about it? Would you rather be with her right now? Want to be with her at that—that—church?" He started to sputter, and I just kept my grip on the handle and watched his whole body shake. "You want to go with her? Fly around? Do you? Do you?" His face was close to mine now, and the beer smell was right there on his skin, like he was sweating the stuff. His eyes, right up in front of my own, looked electric and shut off at the same time. How did he do that? And then he reached behind me for the handle, slapped my hands off it and pulled it up. "Go. Get the fuck out of here. You want to fly? You fly! Fly away, chicky!" I nearly fell out of the big old truck, but I got a foot down first to right myself. I sure didn't want anyone to see me on my ass on the cracked cement of the Super lot. On my ass on my birthday. And then Dad was squealing tires out of the place, the door hanging open and flapping on the side of the cab until the truck turned hard back onto Main and it slammed itself closed.

Fine.

He'd be back. I wasn't worried. He always came back. But this time, I'd be gone.

I somehow ended up at the little brown house. A big hand-lettered sign stuck in the patchy front yard read *FOR RENT*, and underneath in smaller letters, *furnished*, and, *like new*. Around back was an alley I used to ride my bike up and down. The earth-colored couch, the one Mom and Dad and I used to sit on to watch "Family Ties" together stood upended against the garage. The cushions, worn through so the stuffing popped out of their centers, were stacked in a sad little pile. And seeing it all there, our house empty and our furniture garbage (sure it had been three years since we lived there, and we were just renters, but still) well, it was more than I could take. I put my butt down on that little pile of pillows, sunk close to the ground, and thought about crying. Big Birthday Baby.

Well, you know how it goes. Crying and feeling sorry for yourself only works for a little while, and once I'd had enough of it, I had to figure out the trick of getting home. No way was I going to Dad's. I liked the idea of him rolling back into Jack's—all slow and sorry—and not finding me there. Maybe going in and asking at the counter, maybe knocking on the Ladies' Room door. And then cruising the avenue, under the speed limit and watchful. Getting scared maybe. Especially when he'd pull into the park—sure that he'd find me there—and no one would've seen me. That'd teach him.

I decided to go to the Temple and wait Mom out in the parking lot. It was just a couple of blocks, but I kept to the alleys and side streets so there'd be no chance of running into Dad.

"Can you see anything?"

The voice, out of the clear blue like that, made me jump. I whirled around from where I was trying to see through the Temple's front window.

"Are they flying?"

He was less than a foot from me. I don't know how he got there without my hearing, but there he was. I knew this guy. Everyone in town did. Well, knew of him, I mean. He was the homeless guy. That's what we called him. No one I knew knew his real name, and he was the only person who was homeless in town. The Homeless Guy. Only, up close, he didn't look how you'd expect a homeless guy to look. Sure his hair was long and he had a raggedy beard and jeans and a shirt all worn through in those spots that go first—knees, elbows, butt—but from where I stood he looked clean and, well, as far as I could tell, sane. Like he stood up tall and wasn't talking to himself and wasn't scratching or squinting or whatever you might expect some crazy homeless guy to be doing.

"Michael," he said and held out a hand to me. A surprisingly clean hand.

The way I saw it, I had a couple of options here. I could keep on not talking, ignore the guy. But that would be rude, and my mom didn't raise me to be rude. And I wasn't mad at this guy—heck, since I'd sat down and had that cry, I wasn't really mad much at all anymore. So it didn't seem quite right to take things out on this Michael. So, "Hi," I said, taking the second option, the talking one, "I'm Rennie." But I kept my hands to myself. I figured I was just fourteen; it was okay if I wasn't into shaking hands.

"Did you see them fly?" Michael stepped in front of me and put his eye up against the window where I'd been looking through. There was a little space between the blue curtain and the wall inside, but the angle wasn't right. All you could see was the edge of a blackboard or something. "There's a better place to watch from," he said, his head still pressed up against the glass. His words made a circle of steam on it. "Wanna see?"

I really just wanted to go home. But I was pretty much stuck. I wasn't allowed in the Temple, Mom had made that clear the last time I went with her a couple of months ago and made the mistake of asking if it would be all right to have one of the candy bars she always kept in her purse. You'd think I'd asked for a joint or a gun or something the way the whole "congregation" gasped and tsked. Mom got so red I thought she'd pop. And so here I was stuck outside waiting for her and the Temple was open for another hour. And Mom never, ever left Temple early.

"Sure," I said to the guy and shrugged just enough to show him how much I didn't really care. "Let's see."

And then the thing is, I was following this guy who didn't really look crazy like I said, but who I had pretty much come to believe was crazy ever since I first saw him right here, in front of the Temple, sleeping in the doorway some months ago. And even though he didn't look like what I expected (damn TV shows, give you all sorts of wrong ideas) he still wasn't anyone I knew or should trust. And at first I had all those thoughts you get, you know—he's gonna kill me, or he's gonna rape me, or he's gonna mug me—and in that order, starting with the worst and then getting less and less serious. But there was something about this guy. Something quiet. Quiet, but intense. It might have been scary, this way he was, like if you met him in some back alley or someplace dark and deserted maybe. But as we went around the side of the building, past the daycare and behind the place, in all this broad daylight, I wasn't scared at all after a while. We climbed up onto a crate, then up onto the top of a dumpster, then he reached high and grabbed hold of the wall that edged the roof and used a doorframe to step up and over. He held a hand down to me and finally I got the doorframe under my foot and was up and over and onto the roof next to him. Then he turned his back on me and started fast across the roof, the tails of his shirt flapping behind him. I followed, slower though, my hands deep in my pockets.

And you know what? Up high like that, I have to admit, things looked pretty good. The tops of the trees were bright with those leaves turning red, turning yellow and orange. You could see all the way down Main Street to where the highway came in, and the fields beyond town tilted up with the rise of the land. Shimmering, it looked like from up there.

"Here," Michael said waving me in. He fell to his knees and pushed his face against the roof. I kneeled next to him. He smelled like the woods around the lake. Like fresh air and damp earth. "Yup," he said and moved a little to the side so I could get a look. "There's old Sky himself." I was surprised that he knew the High One's name, but I guess it's sort of like how I knew he was The Homeless Guy. In a town this small, everyone knew everyone who wasn't one of the regulars.

I looked through the crack, just a small opening, but big enough to see through with one eye.

And the place was exactly as I remembered it, pale blue and empty pretty much, except for a couple of bulletin boards and blue blackboards and the display case where they kept the smaller things they sold. The only thing different was that the chairs were out of the way, folded up and pushed off to the sides, and the floor was covered with mats. Big, lumpy mats, like they had in the wrestling room at school. Blue mats.

I saw my mom. I recognized the top of her head, although I'm not entirely sure how since I don't know that I ever looked at it before—but I did. She sat in the middle of the mat, her legs crossed over in that way people do—swamis and stuff—the feet on top of the knees. I didn't know she could do that. And there was Sky, skinny as a reed, in front of her on the mat, sitting the same way. Even from up here I could see how tan he was, especially in his blue robey thing, and I thought like I did whenever I saw him that it was funny how he always looked sort of windswept. His bright blond hair flew back away from his face—from using the official Temple blow-dryers, no doubt. They were knees-to-knees, Mom and Sky, no one else was there. They sat absolutely still.

"Are they flying?" Michael asked. If someone else asked me this question, I'd pretty much have to think they were joking. Flying. Right. But Michael sounded really sincere. Not like he was making fun or anything. Like he really wanted to know. Like it could ever be possible.

"No," I said, keeping watch. The two beneath me didn't move. I tilted my head a little so I could use the other eye for a while. But nothing happened. They sat and I sat watching.

I don't know how long I had my eye pressed against that crack waiting for something to happen (which never did) but when I sat back up, rolled the kinks out of my neck and looked around, Michael was gone.

Back on solid ground again I went into Ernie and Bert's. The place was empty except for one of the old twins, Ernie, I think, or maybe Bert. And in that place that never changed (tinny door chimes, eight-panel menu board, white plastic tables and chairs, red trim at the tops and bottoms of the bright white walls) I couldn't help but remember when I was five, the first time we came here, Mom, Dad and me, on my birthday—back when Mom would still eat in public. "Whatever you want," Dad had said as he lifted me up so I could see into the big tubs. Twenty-three regular flavors and four monthly specials. Millions of possible combinations. "Whatever I want," I said to myself after I let go of the memory, and ordered the biggest thing they had: triple banana split, whipped cream, nuts and cherries. Why shouldn't I?

At the front table by the window, I dug in. When I stopped eating long enough to get a breath, I looked up and there was Michael—outside looking in. I waved to him, and I guess he took that to mean come on in, because that's what he did. The chimes banged on the door as he passed through, then he came over and plopped into the little white plastic chair across from me.

"Looks good," he said, "Special treat?"

"Yeah," I said. I was half-way through the middle scoop (rocky road) and working my way toward the rainbow sherbet. "It's my birthday," I said. And it was sort of like letting loose a secret you've been dying to tell. Once I said it I was glad I'd said it, but a little—oh, I don't know—ashamed, I guess.

"Yeah, well, happy birthday," Michael said.

"Thanks," I said, and looked at him. He had an okay face. One of those smooth ones that makes it hard to tell how old a person is, but I figured him for thirty or so. Maybe forty. He had bright blue eyes, kind of gold, too, like the autumn sky. Or maybe it was just a reflection. He stared at my banana split, followed the spoon from the banana boat to my mouth and back with those eyes. It got to be kind of hard to keep eating, him watching me like that, so I put the spoon down and tried to come up with something to say. I looked out the window at Mom's big blue car, then over at the plate glass front of the Temple.

"You know Sky?" I asked.

"Used to," Michael said. He kept his eyes on the ice cream.

"When was that?"

"Back as kids. Long time ago. But we parted ways." He scratched a spot on his nose and looked up. "You, uh, gonna finish that?"

Well, I wanted to. Bad. But it didn't seem quite right then, so I shook my head and pushed the banana boat across the tabletop toward him. He reached for my spoon and scooped up a mound of the stuff. I watched him for a bit. It was like there was barely time for one spoonful to melt in his mouth before he shoved another one in there.

"Parted ways how?" I asked when he stopped long enough to wipe his mouth with the back of his hand. "I mean, besides the obvious."

"Obvious?"

"Yeah, you know. The eating. You guys clearly have different ideas about eating."

"That so?" He closed his mouth around a spoon of rainbow. He went back to work on the banana split without answering my question. I tried again.

"Were you ever a member of the Temple?"

Michael just snorted. Green and pink sherbet spotted the edges of his mustache.

"But you know about the floating."

Michael shrugged and picked up the boat with both hands and licked the inside clean. Then he slid it aside, tilted his head slightly. Behind him I could see Ernie working a towel over the counter, cleaning like he always did.

I didn't say anything for a bit, and neither did Michael. I don't think he intended to do much talking. So I went on. "Do you know how that floating stuff goes?" Michael shook his head.

"I do. I've seen it."

"Yeah?"

"Yeah. Supposedly Sky is the one who can really float. You know, truly worthy and all. And a couple of the others sort of can." I figured he must know this, but he let me keep talking. "It's not floating, though" I said. "It's jumping." Michael leaned across the table, watched my mouth as I spoke. I couldn't help but lean back a bit. "Seriously. They sit like we just saw them sitting," I pointed my thumb out toward the parking lot, "and then they gather up all this energy, and jump. They keep their legs crossed, so it doesn't quite look like jumping. But that's what they're doing. Only they're so full of themselves and so dizzy from not eating they think they're levitating. A few inches off the ground and a couple feet covered. Big whip. You ask me, that's not floating."

"What about Sky?" Michael says in a polite way, like he's taking part in the conversation just to be nice, like maybe I'm not telling him anything he doesn't already know.

"Same thing. Only he's really good at it. He rises up pretty high and goes a pretty long way. To me it's like he's the champion of the cross-legged long jump. And whenever he does it—and he rarely does, you know, to keep the mystery going—everyone starts sighing and gets all quiet. Like they've just witnessed the Second Coming or whatever. Like it's a goddamn miracle."

Michael's staring hard at me now, his sky eyes locked with mine. I've got to look away. "No such thing as a miracle," I say.

And that's when I hear the squeal of tires in the parking lot behind us, and I know even before I look that it's my dad. And when I do look, there's Mom, too, coming out of the Temple doorway. She sees Dad's truck first, and I can't help but notice how she reaches a hand up to her hair and smooths it down, how she puts her shoulders back and holds her head high—like she used to when she heard him come into the door of the little brown house: "Honey? I'm home!" And I notice, too, through the dusty windshield of his truck, how Dad smiles first when he sees Mom, and then how he runs a hand over his face and pulls the smile off. And how when Mom sees him do this, she frowns, too. And I know I've got to get out there before it really hits the fan, and I jump up quick and hold out a hand to Michael which he shakes.

"See ya," I say.

"Yup," he says.

I dash to the door and pull it open, and here's where things get weird. The chimes that have been ringing in that place for as long as I can remember sound different then. Brighter and, well, sort of magical.

"Rennie," Michael says, and I turn to see him stand. Funny thing is, he's much taller than I remember, his head rising closer and closer to the ceiling. And then his feet are hovering over the tabletop, and I follow the line of his legs up past the holes in the knees of his jeans, let my eyes make their way to his.

"Happy birthday to you, Rennie," he says. And I quick look around to see if Ernie's seeing this, too, but his head is down in the freezer case, attending to some cleaning matter. And I look back toward the parking lot to see if maybe Mom and Dad—but they're standing face to face and talking, not yelling or anything, just talking. And I look again and Michael's still up there, floating and floating and floating. He smiles at me, and nods. "There you go," he says, and then I nod, because the way I see it, that's pretty much all there is for me to do.

And so I step out onto the sidewalk and start to cross the parking lot toward Mom and Dad and they turn and see me, and they both get that look of relief only parents can have at those times when they know their kid is safe from whatever. And I'm thinking maybe my folks will remember now, maybe we'll go out and celebrate or something, I mean it is still my birthday, right? But then the look starts to turn a little gray on each of their faces, and I know what to expect next. I glance back over my shoulder and into Ernie and Bert's, and it's just Ernie in there now, clearing the table, throwing away my empty. And then up ahead I see Dad reaching for his belt and Mom's eyes go blank and spacey.

So that's when I do it. Float, I mean. I just swallow and swallow and fill up with air and close my eyes and rise. I rise up and out of this here, up and out of this now. I lift and lift, higher and higher, over the tops of their heads, over the tops of the trees starting to die, over the top of the goddamn Temple of Air. Over and over and over it all. I'm floating, damnit. I'm floating.

Interview with the Author

If you've finished the last page of this magnificent collection, you might now be experiencing that hollowness, that book hangover as some people refer to it, when you feel a little blue. Rereading a book is different than experiencing it for the first time but I'm feeling that sadness.

But the reboot by Tortoise Books of *The Temple of Air*, originally published in 2011, provides the hair of the dog to cure the ache. I hope that what follows cures your ache too.

This revised collection offers everything I loved about the original edition—characters whose loss and grief and deep heartache are starkly told but tenderly rendered—plus three new stories. And upon my second reading of *The Temple of Air*, different themes took my attention.

Whether you've read the collection before or are reading it for the first time, we might agree on a few things. One: in the world of this collection, the girls and women struggle to understand the world of men, do what is expected, get by. Two: the men are often arrogant and unperceptive, wielding absolute power but ruling cruelly.

No?

Let me try again.

If you've reread the collection or are reading it for the first time, we might agree that, in this world, girls and women hold enormous power; we might also agree that the men muddle through a world ruled by women.

No?

Do the adults hold power while the kids wrench it away?

Throughout the collection, power dynamics shift and morph. At one moment, one character is up and, just like that, she's down.

At least we can agree on that? What else? Tragedy. It touches every character, leaves them confused and vulnerable and then, for better or worse, binds them together.

McNair and I caught up to discuss power dynamics, well-drawn characters, how a collection takes shape, stories that make me weep, and (lucky for us) the re-publication of her glorious collection, *The Temple of Air*.

CMR: Rereading the collection and experiencing the three new stories for the first time, I kept thinking about your deft use of power dynamics. In the new story, "This and Other Miracles," you fully explore one of the original characters, Maddie (the mother in the titular story "The Temple of Air") as a teenager. You also flesh out the town Sheriff, Manuel, and Edith. These characters react out of their vulnerability in the face of power.

What drew you to those characters? To their stories?

PMc: I am taken with this idea of power dynamics shifting, Chris. When I first started writing, I am not certain I understood that characters I wanted to make real on the page had to be able to shift in their positions much. As a reader, though, I have always admired the nuances of well-drawn characters. How did Ann Petry make me ache for her character Johnson in "Like a Winding Sheet," and then make me hate him, and then make me ache some more? How did Dostoevsky get me to almost understand and empathize with the very flawed thinking of Raskolnikov as he plans to murder his landlady in *Crime And Punishment*? It must have been the humanity these writers found in their characters, the ever-shifting good and bad we all carry with us, whether we want to admit it or not. And as our characters shift in their goodness, their badness, the way others react to them must evolve, too, the dynamics of their relationships teeter and totter.

The main characters in the new stories were very small characters in the original collection; I didn't even name some of them. Maybe that's why I gave them space in these stories, allowed them their take on things. I don't think I would be far off if I said that in the original stories, they were types more than people. I wanted them to be people, humans. And so I looked for their humanity and tried to plumb that. If they were ineffective in certain situations, how might that affect the story? If they were in control of things, what then? What more did these characters want, and how would getting it (or not) tilt the scales of their relationships? These kinds of questions and trying to answer them on the page through characters, their internal points of view, and their interactions with other characters excited me when I thought about writing new stories. And it excited me to ask these questions of characters I may have shortchanged in the first edition of *The Temple of Air*.

CMR: In his memoirs, Sherwood Anderson wrote:

> *The stories belonged together. I felt that, taken together, they made something like a novel, a complete story... I have even sometimes thought that the novel form does not fit an American writer... What is wanted is a new looseness; and in Winesburg I had made it my own form. There were individual tales but all about lives in some way connected... Life is a loose, flowing thing.*

I love that line: "Life is a loose, flowing thing." There are many parallels between this collection's overall structure and *Winesburg, Ohio*. Can you talk about the way the stories originally came together in this collection and how the three new stories emerged and fit in?

PMc: It sometimes surprises me how few stories I ended up with in the original publication; I'd written a number of others that didn't make it in the cut because they were not successful stories on their own; they didn't stand up.

Why is that? Perhaps because the stories that did survive—for the most part—were written as stories first, collected later. And when I initially put a bunch of them together, I tried to write the missing parts, too, tried to be very chronological about it, tried to answer whatever questions folks might have from one story to the next.

I wasn't up to that task, though. This isn't a novel, not even a novel in stories. It is a collection of linked stories. Moments highlighted from a number of lives connected by place, mostly, but also by circumstance and history. What Sherwood Anderson says about life—calling it a "loose, flowing thing"—helps me understand more about this book. These are the moments that take my attention—you know this principle, Chris, from our teaching together in Story Workshop classes; we always coach our students to look for what is taking their attention most strongly.

And still, I think I needed to write the other stories to know more about the ones that survived, to know more about the collection as a whole. Like starting with a huge block of granite and chipping away until the real thing, the thing I am trying to make, (or maybe more accurately, the thing it wanted to be) appears.

When I gathered the stories together, though, I still had to make choices and changes. Most of the stories were published previously, but in the book they might have changed point-of-view or character names here and there. I wanted to get a sense of a broad range of ways of telling, and I wanted to pull some threads through from one story to the next. That was a lot of putting it all in one place, looking at the book as a single thing instead of as a bunch of parts, and working toward a certain unity of purpose.

And I had some rules for the new stories. They had to do all of those things above. I suppose I wanted them to work apart from the others, and as a part of the others. I also knew I wanted to make more use of male characters, and not just as seen through the lens of my female characters. That's where Sheriff comes in, where Manuel does. And I looked for ways to fill in the timeline of things. Not as a way of supporting a chronology, but as a way to look at how a place can change (or not) over time, and how people's lives and attitudes there can as well. I hope these new stories tell more about this place New Hope, and about the way things have evolved over time. And in doing so, shine new light on the stories and characters I published originally.

CMR: Anderson also said, "There are no plot stories in life." With linked-story collections, like *The Temple of Air*, the "loose and flowing" narrative is, for me, wonderful to experience. As I reread each story (and read the new stories), I asked myself: Where have I met this character before? And then I would page through the book to figure it out. It was like fitting together a wonderful puzzle.

PMc: I have never really considered plot very much, and for a long time had some disdain for the idea of it. So it surprised me when Donna Seaman, in a review of the book in *Booklist*, said that the collection was "strongly plotted."

The contemporary novel has become so many different things, and some of the old rules about plot and structure are being challenged. That is very exciting to me. Still, in my mind what makes a book successful in its creation is when it finds a certain wholeness. Sometimes that comes from plot. Sometimes that comes from a different sort of knowledge, like in *Winesburg, Ohio*. Life is plot-less even as it has structure: you know, beginning, middle and end. But plot or no plot, traditional structure or something experimental, books should bring the reader to a deeper awareness of what it is to be human, to be lonely, to grow, to despair, to exist. In thoughtful books, in well-written stories, there are questions raised and one thing causes something else to happen. Is that plot? Perhaps somewhat. At the very least, these things—the questions posed, the stakes, the physics of events and actions tumbling into one another—lure the reader along from page to page.

CMR: When I first read the collection, back in 2011, I remember mourning when I'd finished the last page. I felt that hollowness I get after closing a book I thoroughly enjoyed. The stories are crafted so beautifully.

For the original collection, the writing took over a decade. Can you talk about that process? And how did it feel to let go of characters you'd held on to for that length of time?

PMc: I think one reason why these stories took so long was because I kept revisiting the characters: Nova and Sky, Michael and Annie, Hoof, Christie, and some of the others. Once they appeared in a couple of the stories, I wanted to learn more about them, write them out. In some cases the stories weren't originally meant to be recurring characters, but it started to become clear to me that they had to be—the man in "Running" was too similar to the man in "The Things That'll Keep You Alive" not to be the same guy. They even looked the same to me when I imagined them. The same with Sky. I kept creating this type of character, a sort of dangerously charming, long-haired blond guy with green-blue eyes that my girl and women characters were attracted to. So of course he had to be just one guy: Sky.

But you asked something else—about how it felt to let go of the characters. Frankly, I haven't entirely. That's why I was so pleased when Tortoise Books wanted to reissue the collection. It gave me the opportunity to revisit some of the characters again. Not just in rereading and preparing the manuscript for publication, but by writing some brand new stories with some of that recurring cast. One thing that is interesting to me about the new stories is how my focus has shifted in the years since the original publication. I always thought I would tell more about the young characters—particularly about the teen-aged girl characters. (I love that time of life—we are young enough to not know everything, yet guileless enough to think we might.) But as new stories opened up for me, it was the older characters who wanted my attention. Perhaps that has something to do with my own advancing age.

Also, I had been working on a novel set in New Hope, the same fictional small town, and despite not being able to get the novel quite right, I found myself exploring some of those "old" characters' lives once again, particularly as they rubbed up against new ones. I mined that material some for the new content of this edition. There are small-town issues I grappled with in the failed novel that weren't in the original stories. Migrant workers and bigotry for example. Even though I was willing to let the novel go (for now? forever?) I wasn't willing to let go of those topics. The new stories let me dig in again.

CMR: These stories never turn away from the moment of dramatic tension—no matter how difficult. No cliché endings here. Were you ever tempted to let your characters off the hook?

PMc: I am not sure I could do that even if I wanted to. Why is that, do you suppose? I am not an unkind person; I like folks to be happy. But I am drawn to stories that are bittersweet at best, or the ones that make you ache. I remember reading Raymond Carver's *What We Talk About When We Talk About Love* when I was an undergraduate, and it blew my mind. Not so much the minimalism—exaggerated by his editor at the time—but by the fact these stories did not end happily. I don't think I fully understood that was possible before that. And while I have had a happy, lucky life for the most part, the moments that probably shape me most as a writer are the small heartbreaks: my brother's face when we were told my dad died; being picked on by the neighborhood bully; being lonely in a relationship. And I don't know if this is going to make any sense, but when I remember those experiences I feel honored to have witnessed them. As a reader, I feel some of the same privilege to be trusted with these moments and to be able to read them on the page.

All of that said, I was eager to find moments of hope in the town called New Hope. I hope I've done that.

CMR: In the opening story, a baby falls out of a carnival ride. It's a wrenching event that touches the entire town of New Hope. Here's our first taste of tragedy—not buildings blowing up or car chases ending in mangled steel. The tragedies aren't only in the physical world. Tragedy scrambles your characters' internal worlds too.

PMc: While I was pulled to an event that the whole town would be able to witness and be stunned by as my opening, it was important to me to make that thing (and some of the other tragedies) horrifying, yet believable. Dare I say familiar? Or at least not too far out of the scope of everyday, ordinary life. But the worst of what folks experienced had to be internal, you know? Like loneliness and crises of faith and culpability and grief. To me, those personal devastations and quiet desperations are more interesting than the fictionalizing of blowing up buildings. I wanted the feeling a reader might carry away from my stories—the loss she might feel from what happens in the first story; the sadness instilled on a small town in a time of war; the disappointment a teenager feels when betrayed by the adults around her; those sorts of things—I wanted those emotions to stick with a reader. Not the manufactured pyrotechnics of destruction.

CMR: Your writing is lush. Can I use that word?

PMc: Lush is a good word if you mean lush like thick and fertile and dense and green. If you mean drunken, well...but maybe that's okay, too. Sort of swirling and rambling. I think the writing swirls and rambles, too. But—I hope—in a good way.

CMR: In a very good way. Even "dickhead" and "motherfucker" sound amazing wrapped in your prose. It all seems to work together. How is that possible?

PMc: Wow. That's about the nicest thing anyone has ever said about my writing. I'm going to take this question seriously, because I think you mean it seriously. Those places where words like "dickhead" and "motherfucker" hit the page are entirely in a character's voice, and I like to think that maybe readers have developed some sort of affinity for the character, even if she or he isn't all that likable at first. So if there's compassion, there can be acceptance—or tolerance, at least. Beyond that, though, I am really interested in the rhythms of language, and I think that helps those words fit, too. Are you a fan at all of David Mamet's plays? I am, and I think his dialogue is very poetic. Complete with all the bad language. It's a rhythm thing there, too, partly. Some anti-swearing folks think that "creative cursing"—you know, highly euphemistic, indirect, and highly elevated language—is more cerebral, more artful than plain cuss words. Not me. And I love to let sentences wind out and out; love to catch the precise metaphors, too. So maybe that is part of what you are referring to when you say such nice things about the language.

CMR: There are a few motifs running through the book: hands, air, faith. Those things that can slip and morph. How do those connect the stories?

PMc: Some of those motifs are part of my own everyday makeup. For some reason I am fascinated by hands. I still remember what my dad's hands looked like, what they felt like. He had these sort of paws. He patted us like we were his cubs. My mom was a fidgeter. Her hands were like mine. Sort of bony and veiny and always moving. We had a baby-sitter when I was a little girl who had the softest hands in the world. I can still feel her fingers on the back of my neck when she put my hair in a ponytail. So hands are a detail I notice, make note of, often put in my writing. In this case, they became even more important, what we hold onto, what we drop, etc.

Faith—the religious kind—is the same for me. I don't understand it in any way. I come from a very non-faith-based upbringing, despite my parents having been the children of churchgoers, my mom a missionaries' kid. So why we believe what we believe or don't is fascinating to me. It all became a big puzzle for me when I was the age of some of my characters and when my father—an atheist—died.

Air turned out to be a good connection to faith for me here. What we need, what moves things, what we can't see around us, what howls, what caresses.

This answer so far makes my choices sound far more deliberate than they actually were. I think the writer's mind does a lot of this work on its own, in the subconscious. And eventually, if we work at it enough, listen to what the story is saying, what the words might mean, we can start to see the connections, the repetitions, the patterns of meaning and motif and discovery. I wrote some stories that had similar things I attended to—hands, air, faith, my own current concerns and obsessions—and the patterns presented themselves after a while, and then I pushed the patterns.

If I had started to push before the patterns revealed themselves, if I'd had a plan for the connections I wanted to exploit, it would have been a disaster. So intentional. So manipulated. I am not smart or talented enough to execute such a deliberate plan.

CMR: "The Way It Really Went" made me weep. It reminded me how we think we know what's going on with another person but, most of the time, we're just completely off and how people grow distant right under the same roof. And forgiveness. It's mostly first-person from the wife but, for some reason, I think of the narrative coming right from Jim. How did you get that sense of Jim so strongly on the page in a first-person telling from Annie's POV?

PMc: Thanks for crying, Chris. My goal is to make everyone cry at some point. It is a very cathartic thing, crying. (I might be kidding here. Might be.)

But your question is about point of view. The story began as Jim's story in early drafts. I spent most of my time close to him. It wasn't until I wanted to see what Annie had to say for herself that it switched to first person. So maybe that is part of why Jim still seems present even when he isn't telling the whole story.

That said, the opening is in second person, a thinly veiled first person POV of Jim. We start the story nearest to his perspective, are lured in by his dawning awareness that his life is not what it seems, that he may be in some real trouble health-wise. And then we find out from Annie how the rest of his life has become something other than great.

If you read the book in order, starting with the first story and moving forward, you also get to know Jim's despair in "Something Like Faith." He is actively involved in the events of the book from the beginning, so I hope readers will come to care for him, understand him, recognize him in the stories that follow. (And an aside: you don't have to read the book in order...I mean for the stories to stand alone, too.)

CMR: I have one more question: Two of the new stories investigate original characters as older adults. In "Gracias," for example, we see Edith as an elderly woman, a woman struggling to navigate the world in a body she barely recognizes, a woman coming to terms with the harsh realities of her life, memories she can't quite square. Why did Edith take your attention on the page?

PMc: Edith is the mother of two of my younger characters, Nova and Sky. When I first wrote her, she was absolutely in service to them, to their stories. Frankly, she was a little flat. She was unquestioningly religious, abandoned (but uncomplainingly) by her children's father. Nova, the character who holds the first story's point of view, would say Edith was small-minded. Perhaps because she could not see the full complexity of Edith, her mother. Perhaps she wasn't looking for it.

I, however, found myself looking for it. She was religious, but what if she were an obvious sinner? Edith is a shoplifter. A liar. She holds her son Sky on a pedestal, ignores his solipsism, his dishonesty, his acts of violence. This imagined son helps her fill the holes in her soul.

An aunt of mine was a very faithful person for most of her life. However, in her last decades, her faith was challenged by everyday things—loss, loneliness, disappointment—and so she gave up on God. What if this were Edith's story, too?

I also wanted to explore how people might come to recognize someone different from them, someone they might perceive as threatening, as a stereotype, as a human worthy of friendship, consideration, and care. The connection in "Gracias" between Edith and Manuel helped me to do that, from—as the current cliché goes—both sides.

Finally, the aging Edith was interesting to me because I am aging. The creaks and pains in her body, the slippery memory, the need for company and kindness, these concerns (my concerns) have made her real to me. And I hope they make her real to the readers of this new edition of *The Temple of Air*.

Acknowledgements

Much gratitude to the editors, journals and anthologies that published versions of a number of these stories along the way: *American Fiction 10: Best Unpublished Stories by Emerging Writers*; *Coe Review*; *Criminal Class Review*; *Dogwood*; *Dunes Review*; *F Magazine*; *Great Lakes Review*; *Other Voices*; *Superstition Review*; *The Thing About Hope Is...*; *The Thing About Second Chances Is...*

Much gratitude, too, to the institutions and organizations that provided financial and moral support, as well as gifts of space, time, grants and awards: The Illinois Arts Council; Vermont Studio Center; Glen Arbor Arts Association; Ragdale Foundation; Interlochen College of Creative Arts; Bath Spa University; my writing pals, The Wild Herons; and the much-missed community of students and faculty of the Fiction Writing Department of Columbia College Chicago.

Thank you, Christine Maul Rice, for your help and support always. Gerald Brennan, you made it all a bit better. And Jotham Burrello, my original publisher at Elephant Rock Books, well, you did this, man.

About Us

Patricia Ann McNair has lived 95 percent of her life in the Midwest. She's managed a gas station, served as a medical volunteer in Honduras, sold pots and pans door to door, tended bar and breaded mushrooms, worked on the trading floor of the Chicago Mercantile Exchange and taught aerobics. McNair's work has appeared in various anthologies, magazines, and journals including *American Fiction: Best Unpublished Short Stories by Emerging Writers*, *The Rumpus*, *Barrelhouse*, *The Nervous Breakdown*, *Superstition Review*, *LitHub*, *Hypertext*, *River Teeth*, *Fourth Genre*, *Brevity*, *Creative Nonfiction*, and others. She's received numerous Illinois Arts Council Awards, the Chicago Writers Association's Book of the Year, the Devil's Kitchen Reading Award, and a Finalist Award for Prose from the Society of Midland Authors. An Associate Professor Emerita of Creative Writing at Columbia College Chicago, McNair facilitates adult writing workshops and is the Artistic Director of Interlochen College of Creative Arts' Writers Retreat. She lives in Tucson with her husband, visual artist Philip Hartigan, and a yard visited by feral cats.

Christine Maul Rice's award-winning novel, *Swarm Theory*, was called "a gripping work of Midwest Gothic" by Michigan Public Radio and earned an Independent Publisher Book Award, a National Indie Excellence Award, was a Chicago Writers Association Book of the Year award finalist, and was included in *PANK*'s Best Books of 2016 and Powell's Books Midyear Roundup: The Best Books of 2016 So Far. In 2019, Christine was included in *NewCity*'s Lit 50:

Who Really Books in Chicago and named One of 30 Writers to Watch by Chicago's Guild Complex. Most recently, her short stories, essays, and interviews have appeared in *Allium, 2020: The Year of the Asterisk*, Make Literary Magazine, The Rumpus, McSweeney's Internet Tendency, The Millions, Roanoke Review* and *The Literary Review,* among others. Christine is the founder and editor of the literary nonprofit Hypertext Magazine & Studio and is an Assistant Professor of English at Valparaiso University.

Slow and steady wins in the end, even in publishing. **Tortoise Books** is dedicated to finding and promoting quality authors who haven't yet found a niche in the marketplace—writers producing memorable and engaging works that will stand the test of time.

Learn more at www.tortoisebooks.com or follow us on the website formerly known as Twitter (assuming it still exists when you're reading this) @TortoiseBooks.

Printed in the USA
CPSIA information can be obtained
at www.ICGtesting.com
JSHW020240060424
60652JS00002B/27